THE MAN WHO KILLED

K LL

fraser nixon

THE
MAN
WHO
ED

DOUGLAS & MCINTYRE
D&M PUBLISHERS INC.
Vancouver/Toronto/Berkeley

Douglas & McIntyre
An imprint of D&M Publishers Inc.
2323 Quebec Street, Suite 201
Vancouver BC Canada V5T 4S7
www.douglas-mcintyre.com

Cataloguing data available from Library and Archives Canada
ISBN 978-1-55365-569-5 (pbk.) · ISBN 978-1-55365-788-0 (ebook)

Editing by John Burns
Cover and interior design by Peter Cocking
Cover photograph by John Sherlock
Printed and bound in Canada by Friesens
Text printed on acid-free, 100% post-consumer paper
Distributed in the U.S. by Publishers Group West

We gratefully acknowledge the financial support of the
Canada Council for the Arts, the British Columbia Arts Council,
the Province of British Columbia through the Book Publishing
Tax Credit and the Government of Canada through the Canada
Book Fund for our publishing activities.

PROLOGUE

COMING ATTRACTIONS

. . . .

T HE ASSERTION IS made that since Noah came out of the Ark, never have so many new and mysterious things been presented in a single evening's performance as Houdini, the world famous magician and mystifyer will offer when he appears at the Princess Theatre for his engagement of one week beginning Monday evening. There will not be a dull moment in the whole entertainment, it is promised, and the mysteries will not only astonish and bewilder but they will enthuse as well, for the charm of newness applies to the entire programme.

Houdini's production for his evening's entertainment is something so new, so big, so compelling that one cannot possibly conceive in advance. It can truthfully be said that it is the most novel and wonderful entertainment ever presented within the realm of the theatre. It will sweep you off your feet and transport you to a land you never knew existed.

Montreal *Herald*, October 15, 1926

FRIDAY

OCTOBER 15, 1926

JACK WAS LATE. The silver hunter my father had given me was gone, pawned for fifty dollars a fortnight past, but the clock by the river read half past six. I fished into an inside coat pocket for my cigaret case, the next to go for the needful. Inside were three Forest and Streams. With a sparked vesta I lit one, smoked, waited, cursed Jack and his ways. A rat slouched along the stone walls by the pier. Porters sweated by. Stevedores pulled barrels down from loading cranes and trundled them about. River gulls circled and screamed over the septic stink. Ranked grain elevators nearly hid the tower clock; five more minutes passed. Five more after that'd be forty minutes I'd waited. Goddammit. With an invisible .22 I drew a bead on the rat's head. Vermin were loaded with bacilli. No clean things around the harbour. My fingers dropped the smouldering fag end, adding it to the general filth. To my left a long freight train ground by, vomiting black coalsmoke from a bent funnel, the engine's whistle howling agony. Automobiles in low gear whined and sounded their horns at slow horses straining at harness, dragging wagonloads uphill over cobblestones. Second-to-last cigaret. Let the matchwood burn to the quick and crush the charcoal under my boot. This is who I am. The sole still figure in the moil.

Jack had somehow found me at my digs. He'd left a telephone
message with my bitch of a landlady. Whilst forking it over she'd
given me the fish eye. I'd been skipping her revolting meals and
walking the streets all hours, boring myself to death in the reading room of the Mechanics' library, sneaking in after curfew only
to slip back out before dawn. I was two weeks late on rent. Grudg-
ingly she'd handed me Jack's imperative only after I parted with
my last ten dollars. She smelled money in his command, and the
old baggage was probably correct. Jack always had the stuff or the
wherewithal to get more. I counted on him.

Eastwards and directly towards me a steamer bore down,
passing between the high cement uprights of the harbour bridge
being built there by ants. Looked like an Empress, first link in
the All-Red Route, Southampton–Montreal. Filled, no doubt,
with brainless debutantes returning from the season in London
and presentation at court. Lucky girls were rogered by dukes in
leafy bowers on spreading estates, the unfortunate given pitying
notices in the society pages of the *Star* and wed off to dull bank-
ers with patent-leather hair parted down the middle. The whole
class was in thrall to our ostensible betters, the English. British
garrisons had marched nearby on the Champ-de-Mars under the
banner of St. George in golden days of yore. Even now the Union
Jack did wave above us. Jack, damnation. Where the hell could
he be? A Red Ensign flew at the ship's stern as she loomed closer.
The *Empress of Scotland*, red chequerboard flag of the Canadian Pacific at her bridge. She drew alongside an enormous cold
storage warehouse, a building filled with thousands of frozen
carcasses of good Canadian meat ready to be shipped south and
butchered in New York City, say, chewed over at Delmonico's or
some lousy speakeasy, mixed with rotgut and shat out through
pipes into the Hudson, or the East. I toed a coil of ship's rope
and set flies buzzing. The sun was near gone now. Soon I'd turn

around and return to the heart of the city I'd grown to hate worse than poison. As a rat slid into the river I picked it off between dead eyes. Had never shot a Siwash or a Hun. Draw the bolt and eject the spent cartridge. Smell burnt gunpowder.

And there: Jack. He was talking to a monkey in a gold-frogged velvet uniform down the end of the quay. Jack looked spruce as hell and wore a grey topcoat over a pearl-grey suit, hat pushed to the back of his head, hands in pockets, and an odd white stick in the crook of his arm. He said something and the monkey laughed. The pair looked up as the massive Empress drew by. Final rays of the setting sun shone off her spanking brasswork. Happy sailors waved to lubbers ashore. It seemed as though a horla looked at me from the crowd as the ship's whistle sang out. I spied Jack handing the monkey something as they parted ways. He turned to see me standing in the corner underneath a rusted green plaque. Jack sauntered over, smiling. Inwise I seethed. He raised his chin and spoke.

"*Nei hao ma*, Mick."

"*Geih ho.*"

"You done look tore up now, lad."

"I give a damn."

"Faith be, son."

There was that look in his eye I'd seen so often. A sort of secret amusement. I did as I always do: played mute and waited. All the something in the world.

"I owe you a drink," he said.

"If you say."

"And a square meal. Care for a stroll?"

"On the level?"

"Patience," Jack said.

We crossed the train tracks and climbed up into the Old Town, turning left towards the market square. The last carts from the south side of the river were packing up for their slow Friday night return. The farmers' beasts champed, flicking their tails at bluebottles swarming around slick cobbles. Pigeons strutted through horseshit. Vendors hawked their wares in rotten country French. I saw October pumpkins, apples, squashes. It was end of season. What wasn't sold would be fed to the pigs. Jack selected an apple from a cart and dropped a sou into a habitant's outstretched hand.

We kept walking and came to the pillar topped by its statue standing across from the Hôtel de Ville, Nelson with his back turned to the river. Two old ladies in black stood at the column's base under the stone crocodile of the Nile, gumming at dark round fruits they pulled from a waxpaper bag.

"Like in that book," Jack said. "Ever read it? What'd they call Nelson? 'The one-handed adulterer,' I think. Have to love the Limeys' gall, sticking the man smack plumb in the bosom of his foes. Come to it, this lot here're all Bourbons at heart and never fell in with the Revolution and Boney. Still, I'm surprised they haven't stuck a bomb beneath Lord him, send him kingdom come."

"Here or in Dublin."

Jack eyed me slantwise. We carried on along Notre-Dame. He tapped his stick upon the stones as I matched his pace. Jack paused at a corner. "Listen, I have a rendezvous."

"Congratulations."

"Not like that. Something else, something delicate. I dug you up because you've always been game, man. Might need your help. Your eyes and your hands. Are you in?"

He waited, gauging the effect of his words.

Let the traffic signal change before you answer. Stop. Go. And so I did. Betimes I reached into my pocket for my case, opened it, and offered Jack my last smoke. Our eyes met and Jack laughed aloud. We shook hands, like back when we were boys. Some caper, this. He pulled out his own rectangle of metal and showed me a row of clean white machine-rolleds.

"Gaspers?" I asked.

"No, Turk."

"Thanks," I said, selecting one.

Jack set fire to the cigaret with what I took to be a platinum lighter and I inhaled a grateful lungful deeply.

"So what is it?" I asked.

"A very small fry, but one liable to scoot. Want you to bottle up his retreat if he does. Should be quiet."

He shrugged and raised his stick to rest on his shoulder. Dug me up was right. Some dirty work, with the chance of trouble. What was in it for me? My stomach made the decision. Jack would stand drinks and a meal. In my present state that was enough. I nodded assent and together we went along St. James between its gauntlet of grey banks, closed and frowning down at us, hoarding the Dominion's wealth. Here were the temples of our race: the Royal, the Imperial, the Dominion, the Bank of Montreal. Before us sat Molson's Bank, where one could with-draw ale scrip from the wicket and spend it on the selfsame bloody beer in a tavern down the street. We passed beneath their dour allegorical finery: gold-trimmed coats of arms, an engraved caduceus of Mercury the patron of thieves, granite Indians. Jack slowed and motioned to an alley.

"Our man's down there," he said.

I spied a dark shape waiting.

"I'll circle 'round. Wait here and watch. If there's a rumble back me up. Worse comes to worst, take a hike. You know the drill."

"Fallback?" I asked.

"The Ritz," he said, disappearing in the gloom.

Couldn't tell if he was joking or no. I peered about. The street was quiet, suppertime for most. My eyes adjusted. I made out the figure of the stranger as it resolved in low light. He was a small slim man with a spare moustache, nervous-seeming. He wore a bowler, a bowtie, and clutched a furled umbrella though it hadn't rained in a week. Cocking my ears for any footfall I heard metal tapping, and then Jack's voice.

"Brown."

There Jack was, legs akimbo, hands on his stick planted between the bricks.

"Aye," said the man.

"No one's very happy with you. My lords and masters least of all. You know to do as you're told." Spoken calmly, the faintest mocking lilt to his voice.

Brown spluttered to life. "Now look here ye manky bastard, you canna talk to me like that."

"Your slip's showing."

"You've no bloody right to speak to me like this way."

"We own you Brown, and no mistake."

"You own me? Is that so? I'm an agent of the Crown, ye bloody weskit."

"Aye, but ye take the King's coin, ye soldier for tha' King."

"Pah. You canna make me do a Goddamned thing, you Goddamned guttersnipe."

Here Jack's stick flashed an arc up and Brown went down, clutching at his face, letting out a shriek. Jack pushed him from the alley wall to the ground and onto his back. He put his foot on Brown's chest and placed the tip of his stick near the man's aorta. Anatomy, simple.

"Listen close," he said. "Chicago bought you and your waistcoat, and you'll do as you're told. Happily. Tonight. In for a penny, in for a fucking pound."

Jack stepped off Brown and pulled out a wad of banknotes. He peeled off and dropped a flutter of bills over the now silent, cringing form. The little man was frozen, his hands protecting his phiz.

"My advice, Brown? Keep that dirty trap of yours shut, respect your elders in the kirk, and tie your bootlaces."

This was not an especially encouraging turn of events. My hackles rose and I looked around for an eyewitness. No one. Brown keened in his pain. Ugly. Watch your step, boyo. My mouth spat aluminum-tasting saliva out onto the alley wall.

Jack came to me where I waited at the entry. He took a handkerchief from his sleeve and carefully wiped blood off the shaft of his stick. Done, he dropped the rag on the sidewalk. Was I terribly shocked by what had happened? Life had thus far shown me much worse. Together we went west.

"Let's grab a 'cab," he said.

St. James opened up at Victoria Square and at the foot of Beaver Hall Hill Jack whistled a motor-taxi over. We climbed in and Jack directed the driver to wheel us to the Derby. He whistled an old-fashioned tune as we rode, "The Man Who Broke the Bank at Monte Carlo."

"Who was he?" I asked.

"A useful useless man," said Jack. "He's been trying to spit out his hook."

"Scotch," I said.

"No kidding."

"No, here."

My very last chattel. From its secret place I took out a flask of blood-warmed liquor and offered it to Jack. He took a pull and made a face.

"Christ in heaven. You must be broke."

"And how. One question."

"Shoot, lad."

"What's that, your stick?"

"Ah."

His eyes lit as he stroked it.

"Shark's spine."

AT THE RESTAURANT Jack paid the 'cabman and we got out. For a moment I worried about my mien. My suit was starting to shine at knee and elbow. I'd left my overcoat at my digs as a sort of hostage. Quickly I checked my fingernails and brushed my front, then tightened my necktie. To hell with it. Set your hat straight and march on in. Do as Jack does. At the door they straightaway took our toppers and Jack's damned stick. The maître d' led us to a lowlit booth of deep brown leather. We sank in.

"Peckish?" asked Jack.

My salivary glands winced at the aroma of good food.

"Like that Russian's dog," I said, and let out a strange unbidden laugh.

Jack gave me the once-over.

"Here."

He offered me his fancy case. I read Rameses II in blue ink on the oval cigaret I removed. Jack lit his own in the heat of a little oil lamp on the table. Convection. He hated wasting a match, I knew. The drinks steward came 'round.

"Claret," said Jack.

We settled in and smoked and looked at what was offered in the table d'hôte. A waiter minced by.

"Oysters," Jack said, looking at me. "For starters."

I shrugged.

"A clear soup, some cucumber, the roast beef with new potatoes, a celery, then the cheese and the rest. Sound good?"

I nodded. Wine soon appeared. The steward poured and Jack raised his glass. I looked through the ruby fluid to the flame.

"Your wealth and hell-being."

We drank. A cart rolled by bearing a silver salver. I caught my distorted reflection in the metal, dark and sour. Compare and contrast with Jack. He was hale, full of vim and vigour. Jack ran a large hand over his carefully combed red hair. My next question formed itself.

"How'd you find me?"

Smiling, Jack exhaled plumes of smoke out his nose thirls. The answer poured over me like cold water. Only one person on this earth.

"Laura," I breathed.

Jack raised his eyebrows. The oysters were set down.

"A good thing it was too," went Jack. "You're off the reservation. Tried the school, Smiler and the rest. Thought you might've skipped town."

"I'm out."

"How long?"

"Since the end of last term."

"Smiler suspected as much," Jack said. "What's this place you're staying now?"

"Rooming house. What is it Leacock says? 'All rooming houses are the same rooming house.' He's right, as always."

"Ran into him on campus as well," said Jack. "You tell your old man yet?"

"No point."

"And Laura?"

"Don't ask. Where'd you see her?"

"Dance out at Victoria Hall. Pure chance. She was being squired about by some local likely. Stole her and took her for a spin or two myself."

This wasn't news I liked the sound of. Jack's manner was bland and still. I knew better than to ask him anything, mostly because I didn't want to know. Ever thus he played the amused monarch, nature's aristocrat. As evidenced by the beaten man he'd left behind, power over others was Jack's meat. Try not to let suspicion eat at you. Say something.

"Doesn't matter now. She won't have a thing to do with me."

Jack smiled again, but did I detect contempt in his eyes? I toyed with a glass.

"So why'd you stay in town?" he asked. "Hike down to Hogtown or head back home. I would."

"To face down the Pater? No thank you. Besides, I'm skint. And there's something else."

"You're hung up on her. I understand. But where in the hell've you been since April? Could have used you before now."

"It's a fine question and I'll ask you the same."

"Ah," Jack said. "There you go."

A pause while we drank. Funny how quickly we returned to the shorthand of youth, a Pitman's of our upbringing. At length I said: "I went to ground. Her people summer down in New England somewhere so I got a shack at Memphremagog and sweated it out."

"Did the school push you or did you jump?" asked Jack.

"Both."

"What was it?

Here I took a drink and lit another of Jack's cigarets. He watched me. My hand remained steady. I breathed out slowly and told some of the truth. I'd been stealing morphine, mostly, from the hospital dispensary. They were never able to nab me outright but had come close. It was that and my grades. In the end I'd held a trump card and between the board of governors and myself was forged an understanding. I'd ducked a censure or quodding, but there'd be no medical degree for myself from McGill, and that was a fact everlasting.

There, I'd said it. It'd been bottled up long enough, and the confession was a relief, in its way. I drank more wine.

"How much did you pocket?" asked Jack after a spell.

"More than enough for me and to sell. You'd be tickled to hear my clientele. A few real hyas muckamucks. Some Chinamen from time to time. When I lost my entree I had to shift gears. It was none for them, then after awhile none for me. I had enough saved up for the shack by the lake. Read my Tacitus and had my fishing rod and thought I'd wait for her to come back in September to try again."

"She'll never marry you," Jack said.

"I know."

To counter the rising bile I swallowed more wine. Rancour. Jack squeezed lemon juice over wet bivalves. It was far better not to speculate on what you cannot control. That woman, the ache of my heart. Instead observe your present surroundings. Looming above were dark heavy beams bisecting white plaster. It was all cod-Tudor and pretense at the Derby, Old Blighty transplanted to the colonies. Best roast beef to be had, however.

"Look at this place," I said. "Do you know what it reminds me of?"

Jack tipped an oyster into his mouth.

"Remember the Royal Ensign? Seventeen Mile House on the Island?" I asked.

Jack peered about.

"You're right," he said. "When was that now?"

"Boat race weekend it must have been. Why else would we have gone over? Six, seven years ago. Swiftsure."

"We had bathtub gin with those two doozies, what were their names..."

"Elizabeth and Rebecca," I said.

"Then borrowed Billy's Ford and the keys to his pa's cabin."

"That cabin. *Quel bordel*," I said.

"They got sick on the booze. You broke the gramophone."

"You chopped down a totem pole in Sooke Harbour," I countered.

Jack put his hand to his face in mock shame. "Ye gods."

"Timber!"

My elbow was on the spread cloth and I let my forearm fall. When my hand hit the tabletop it rattled the oyster shells on the plate. Heads turned: old buffers with mottled faces. I chewed over a bland smile. Seventeen Mile House was far out on the road to Sooke, western Vancouver Island. The shores of the Pacific, our home at the edge of the world. They'd been good times together, years ago now, fresh back from the war.

"Liz and Becky. You burned their knickers in the stove, didn't you? Wonder where they are now," I said.

"Probably knitting booties," said Jack.

"Those were the days."

"And look at us now," he went.

We were back in the past for just a moment, until the soup came. We spooned it up. More wine. At last the meat arrived, good and rare and red. Spuds, celery as requested, squab and cress. Warmth coursed through me. A plate cleaned in steady, animal hunger, at last I leaned back, replete, and listened to other diners chewing. Heavy sterling fork tines squeaked on china. Gustatory grunts, a cork popping, a woman's laughter, the human hum of conversation and pleasure eased by money. Dark-suited men and gowned ladies gestured as waiters passed to and fro. Jack pushed his plate away and lit another cigaret. He demanded coffee of a flunky. As an aside to me he said: "Pass me your flask when it comes. For the *trou normand*. Bloody law, wine but no spirits."

"Break it then," I said.

Jack shot me a look.

"Knew that you were my man. If only you'd been around for the election last spring. That would've been something."

"So what is it now?"

"Guess."

"You said Chicago."

"You heard right."

"And Brown, who's he when he's at home?" I asked.

"Brown is a wee man who needed the fear of God put back in him. He's the worst kind of Caledonian, stubborn as a mule, but amenable to our ends."

"And those are?"

"I'll respect your intelligence and assume you've figured it out."

"Booze."

"On the money."

"The monkey at the quay," I said.

Jack laid out the rudiments. Rich wets down south don't like to drink piss. Leave the furniture polish for the punters. They wanted the real McCoy. The good stuff was supercargo shipped straight out of Glasgow or Liverpool as ballast or coal or what-have-you into Montreal, port of call. The monkey took care of the crew when they made land, and Jack indemnified the harbourmaster when the ship came in, as it did today. Brown was paid to look away and not make a peep.

"He's Customs?" I asked.

"Correct. We've exploited his vice, but a little reminder is always in order for that type. He's a weakling and a physical coward. In any event, tonight's the night, hence your presence."

"What are you, exactly?" I asked.

"You could say I'm an intermediary and guide over international frontiers. I truly could use your help. I want you to have a piece, for old times' sake. This is the real work."

"Repayment for your largesse?" I asked, gesturing to the dirty plates.

"No, not a favour. A job."

He reached into his billfold and took out five twenties.

"For your time and trouble. There'll be more tomorrow, on the other side."

Jack placed the money on the table and covered it with a serviette. I had perhaps a buck fifty in change in my trouser pocket.
These days it was two bits for twenty-five cigarets. I now had a
full stomach and a head of wine and no other prospects on the
good green earth. Here was something. Crime.

One of Jack's salient qualities was his ability to make things
happen. His talent was luck. My strengths, if any, were far different. This was the world, here, now. Living wasn't to be found in
the past with a woman who didn't love me, a lost profession, the
calumny of enemies. I'd tried to be respectable, to be righteous.
Jack had taken another path and seemed to have thrived. I asked
myself, having come this far, and with my back to the wall, what
had I to lose? Jack held my gaze as I took the money, then poured
hooch from my flask into his java. I tucked the notes away.

"Tonight," I repeated.

"Finish your coffee."

I did. The bill came and Jack paid up. We rose and while
exiting were smiled at by the pretty coat-check girl. Jack winked,
tipped her two dollars. Her eyes to him and then to me, a shadow
from his lustre. Back out on the street it was now cold, autumn-
grim, and I eyed Jack's warm topcoat enviously.

"Where to?" I asked.

"Griffintown."

A WIND WAS rising as we picked our way through the slum, a
maze of dirty brick tenements filled with quarrelling Hibernians
and their squalling brats, as per the Pope's orders. Go forth and
multiply, ye sons of Erin. Factories crowded by millworks and
stables. There hung throughout a pall of brown coalsmoke and
river stink, worse than St. Lawrence Main to the east. In Griffintown you had your shanty Irish landed from Cork and environs;
the Main, by comparison, swarmed with Chosen from their own

Pale of Settlement on the Ural Steppes. Both peoples crossed the water by way of an exodus, running either from the Famine and Major Boycott or the Tsar and his Cossacks to be jammed hugger-mugger in warrens and fresh misery. Micks and Kikes a pair of lost tribes here in the New World, same as the old one. Meanwhile stray cats loped down alleyways and skinny vicious curs growled at silent rats.

Corner hawks loitered and sized up we two strolling push-overs. Jack's easy carriage, boxer's build, and damn-your-eyes air bought us a pass, despite his Beau Brummell attire. I balled fists in my pockets and thought of my fresh hundred-dollar stake. They'd roll you for a piece of string down this way. Jack whistled a song I couldn't place. We were now near Wellington. A pair of drunks on a stoop fought over a bottle. Dark figures in recessed doorways grunted, copulating. I shuddered as dwarf streetlamps sputtered. Jack pushed open a door into a tavern. Smoke hung from the ceiling down to my celluloid collar. We were steadily watched by whiskered, simian faces as Jack made his way to a table near a smeared, greasy window. He jerked his head past the topers, their paws curled around quart bottles, and I went to the bar for two of Black Horse, two dimes all told, thank you very much. Back at the table Jack sat and watched an entranceway across the street.

"Looks clean," he said. "Shall we?"

We took our untouched, corked bottles with us out again and across the road to a beat-up pile of dreary lodgings. Indoors was the smell of wet woollens left too long on the stove, stewed cabbage, damp, mould, cruelty, and mice. Jack led up three flights of stairs. I heard muffled curses behind one door, someone sobbing piteously behind another.

On the topmost landing Jack took out an almost comically oversized key, like something out of a Vaudeville sketch, and used it to open a giant padlock on a numberless door. The security seemed needless. There was no electricity in the room, which was lit only by the pale glow from without. It was furnished with a chair, a basin on a dresser, an iron bedframe with sagging mattress, an ancient wardrobe, and a view out the window to the tavern we'd just been in. Jack took a long suspicious gander at the street below. Satisfied, he drew the curtain, lit a candle, and set it on the floor behind an accordion shade.

"Never too careful."

I took the chair. Jack removed his coat despite the cold. I put my hat on my knee. Jack passed me a corkscrew to open the bottles. We hoisted silently and drank. There was a framed picture on the wall depicting a saint. Jack took it down and laid it on the dresser face-up. Then he pulled a small glass vial from his pocket and yanked a rubber stopper from its neck with his teeth. From it Jack poured white powder onto the glass, over a print of St. Veronica with her mouchoir. I got that old anxious feeling, a roiling loosening of my bowels. Cocaine was near enough morphine in the pharmacopoeia to evoke a buried desire.

"We've a long night ahead of us," Jack said. "Need some pep. How's that sound?"

"Nerve food, sure."

"Chock full of vitamins."

He used a short tube to sniff some of the cocaine and passed the whole works to me. I took a noseful, tasted metal at the back of my throat, and touched the source of the flavour with my tongue. I drank some beer to wash it away. Jack offered a cigaret and we smoked.

"It's like this," he said. "Three trucks along the canal at midnight. Three drivers. I'm riding with the first, you with the last. Had another chap lined up but he's out sick, or so he says. Yankee I know. So it's just the two of us. Should be three at least but there's nothing I can do. We drive to a safe crossing near Indian land. You and I stick with the trucks all the way to just outside Plattsburgh. It's a long way 'round and not normally how things are done but everyone's shorthanded so this is how it has to be. I've got us a room at the Republic. Tomorrow we come back on the noon train. Do you have papers?"

"Militia. My library card."

Jack laughed. "Good."

He got up and went to the wardrobe, opened it and took out a hatbox.

"Artillery," he said.

He put the box on the bed and lifted out two revolvers and a case of shells. Now I saw why the ridiculous lock was on the door. Jack handed over a Webley Mark IV. It'd been awhile since I'd handled one. I hefted it, broke it open, spun the cylinder, and looked down the barrel.

"Where's the head?"

"Down the hall," Jack said. "I'm going to change."

He took a dark coat out of the wardrobe. With composure, I retreated and groped along an unlit passageway to the w.c. with knees no worse from quaking. Firearms. Revolvers are tools built for use. Pick one up and carry it around and you will pull its trigger, sure as shooting.

Carefully I micturated in the filthy lavatory without touching the surroundings. My fastidious medical training had augmented and grounded an abhorrence of uncleanliness; my sterile urine was probably the cleanest substance in the room.

I returned to find Jack knotting a new tie. While he whistled I loaded the Webley and sat down. We drank more ale, smoked tobacco, and let the world burn itself out. My mind sharpened to a whetted blade with clarity and insight. Previously unrecognized associations aligned themselves into an organized pattern. The potential danger ahead was evaluated and rationalized. I felt excitement at action after such sloth. The empty summer gone, autumn quickening. I wasn't going to leave on a train, not yet. This city, this city which had harried me from den to den, scoured by hounds, this city would see me turn and rue its hunt. I'd show my teeth. Money would lend an ease, command. Laura. I will have her, or no one will. I picked up the weapon while Jack hummed that tune and loaded his. What was the song? He checked his wristwatch and snapped his fingers.

"Time."

WE PREPARED OURSELVES. Another sniff of the powder. My gun in my belt for now, under my suitcoat. Out and downstairs, back on the pavement, and over to the canal.

"If we're separated," Jack said, "try the bar at the Dominion quarter past nine every night for a week. I'll either be there or I'll leave you a message. I'm Pete, you're Sam. No soap after a week, well..."

"Nothing to fear. This is good. Thanks, Jack."

I meant it. Once again he'd dropped out of the sky and got me moving.

"You bet. Here they come."

Jack shone an electric torch on and off thrice. Headlamps coming towards us along the slough dipped the same number of times. Our convoy. The lead truck slowed. Jack motioned me to the tail. We shook hands.

"See you at the Hotel Republic." he said.

"Live free or die," I went.

I climbed into the cab of the third truck. The driver was a big brute, unwashed and unshaven.

"Evening."

He grunted.

A freight pulled by as we set off. One of the boxcars had Santa Fe–Pacific stencilled on its side, a long way from home. I cracked my knuckles, a bad habit ill-befitting any prospective surgeon. Number it amongst the traits ensuring my unsuitability for a reputable profession. Our truck pulled ahead of the engine and we parallelled it on Commissioners. The driver shifted up, accelerated, shifted again, braked a little. The truck swayed. We turned away from the westbound train.

Later, crossing the river, I saw the village of St. Lambert lit up on the left. After it, heading south, darkness grew, with fewer lights, then none. One or two hardy motorists shared the road at this quiet hour. The convoy had scattered. Half an hour or so passed, then more. I saw an empty police 'car at a crossroads in the middle of nowhere with its headlamps on and doors open. I exchanged looks with the driver and unbuttoned my coat to reveal the gun handle.

Too late I realized I had nothing to smoke and gritted my teeth. The drug had me fast and slow. We drove. Eventually I crossed my arms and closed my eyes. Over the motor I imagined hearing bottles chiming together back and forth in the payload. Glasses clinked. There was the pop of a cork from a bottle of Champagne. A band played "The Japanese Sandman." Laura toyed with white pearls around her milk-white throat. She was ginger-haired like Jack, but green-eyed to his blue. Redheads have a natural antipathy; you never see them together at the altar. Isn't that so? Laura's gloved hands, her black gown, her emerald eyes in candlelight, auburn hair piled up in rings. She laughed at some stupid witticism of mine. The dancers turned on the parquet slowly, underwater. A drumbeat. The truck hit a pothole and jolted me out of my reverie. Some time had passed; it was difficult to reckon how much and no sign of the moon.

We were driving along a dirt side road and spotted our two trucks waiting ahead. They started up and turned right onto a rutted track leading into the woods. The driver pulled out a cigaret packet and passed one to me in either the Christian spirit or one of criminal solidarity. The brand was Taxi: "Smoked in Drawing Rooms and Clubs," yes, and in bootleggers' trucks. The tires rolled along the grooves in the dry ground, no lamps shining. Our train moved along in the dark by feel. My eyes were staring wide but all I saw were orange coals reflected in the windscreen. I opened my window and chucked the stub out. There was the smell of slack water, pine, night. We inched along in low gear. My hand moved to the revolver handle and I gripped it, palm slick with sweat.

The driver muttered: "*Contresaintciboire.*" Three blind mice. See how we run. A firecracker went off, a sudden stark light. We slammed into the truck ahead of us. More firecrackers. No. Shots. Headlamps from the woods ahead, beside, behind us. Ambush. Shouts. My hand pulled at the door release. The gun stuck in my belt. The driver tried to reverse. A crack. The windscreen shattered. Another retort, then it was Chinese New Year. My door opened and I fell out of the cab as the driver's head exploded red in the alien light. I landed and rolled into a ditch, frantically pulling the weapon free. More shouting in English and French. I crawled away into bracken through dead leaves and a dry gulch, away, away from the light and the noise. Light swung my way and there was a loud percussion as a tree trunk splintered near my head. Stray bullet, or was I in someone's sights? Move, move. Get up. Run. With leaden legs I lurched to my feet, crouching and shambling away, my collar sprung, now hatless. Boughs slashed at my face. Faster, faster. Deeper into the woods, into the night. I stumbled over fallen trunks, blood roaring in my ears. My knees collapsed as I blundered down a bank into a creek bed, then back up and deeper into the bush. Was it the cops? All sense of direction lost. It's dangerous to carry on. You'll trip a cordon, stumble into a trap. Go to ground, find some deep hole and crawl into it. Instinct of the hunted animal. Hide, rest, wait for dawn. I reached out to a tree. From pillar to post I snuck along until I found a windfall. I crawled under it, my hand a claw gripping the Webley, lungs gulping for air, my heart hammering, body now wracked and shivering in shock, ears pricked for any footfall. Dig deeper, deeper, wait for whatever comes and shoot it down. This is it. You're in it now.

SATURDAY

N|O NEED FOR nightmares: the night itself was enough. After a fitful, frightened sleep I woke to dull grey light. Wind in the trees, the shifting of leaves. A raven croaking an unreadable augury. Blackbirds shackled with silver manacles in the Tower of London kept God's anointed on the throne of Britain. My fatigue had overcome the cocaine and terror to leave me still and dead underground. The gun was fused to my hand by pinesap, my arms and legs cold and cramped.

I crawled out of my hole. The wind had obscured my path through the forest with anonymous leaves. The sky overhead was a ceiling of cloud the colour of oyster shell. And here I'd slurped them down only yesterday at the Derby. Now where was I? The light was too diffuse to make out east and the rising sun. Must orient myself. Be careful. Don't walk into a tracking party. They could've found my hat and counted heads. Or had Jack fought them back? Jesus, Jack. He was in the first truck when the firing started. Who was it? American Treasury agents or local law? Customs, Mounties, provincial police? No dogs, as yet. My fear was a living thing and got me ticking. If it wasn't police it might be much worse. A rival crew. They'd leave my body for the wolves. Bad, very bad.

Jack had said the crossing into New York State was near to Indian land. I might've already slipped over the border in my flight. Who knows, I could even run into a Vermont sheriff in these woods. There were also the natives themselves, an unhappy bunch. It wasn't too late in the history of this continent to be scalped.

I checked my Webley, my money, and my papers. All sound. Try not to make one. Unbuttoned trousers and emptied bladder. Twisting and sliding tendons across vertebrae cracked my neck. Roughly I welshcombed my hair and picked up a stone to suck on and stimulate saliva, combatting thirst. My flask was gone. Finger marks on the pewter could be dusted by police and used to tie me to last night's slaughter. It was impossible to doubt but that it'd been an all-out disaster. Goddammit. Yesterday morning I'd cursed the rotten bed at my rooming house and now I was worse than an animal in the wild. Now would be a grand time for a drink of that terrible Scotch. Might've been useful to trade firewater with local tribesmen for a canoe out. Back in the old days Jacques Cartier had beaten the bush in this neck of the woods, brewing spruce beer as an antiscorbutic to keep his teeth. He'd made it home and so would I. As the day's light grew brighter I walked the direction I best believed was north. To cheer myself I sang very quietly, whatever came into my head: "Three, three the rivals, two, two the lily-white boys, dressed all in green-o, but one is one and all alone and ever more shall be so."

Through stands of maples shedding rusty leaves, slender pines, and clean white birches I stole my careful way. My gun was in my hand and I halted at every birdcall. Presently I came to a creek, perhaps the one I'd splashed through during my flight. With dark mud I washed my hands of the sticky pitch and after spitting out the stone drank clear cold water. When I cleaned my face specks of the truck driver's blood washed downstream.

Following the creek led nowhere; it twisted on itself and petered out into a rank fen. Choosing an easy way I crept along through the undergrowth. Daylight grew stronger. In this manner I continued another hour or so until I smelled faint woodsmoke and heard metal on wood. With care I moved to the edge of a clearing.

A cabin sat alone with smoke trickling out a tin chimney. It was a ramshackle affair of unpainted boards, tarpaper, and crooked grey shingles. Staying upwind as best I might so as not to alert any possible dogs I slowly quit the tree cover, the gun now back in my belt under a buttoned coat but ready. Ready.

From the corner of the shack I spied on an old man with wedge and axe working away at a chunk of maple. Behind him a truck: my ticket out. No wires strung away from the shack and that meant no telephone, no chance for anyone to alert authorities. Play it easy with this rustic. Just a ride to the nearest town. As I watched the old man he took out a rag and wiped his leathery face. Gently and so as not to startle him I came out into the open and spoke: "Hey there."

He turned to look at me but said nothing.

"*Bonjour,*" I said.

Naught. He balled the rag up and stuffed it in his overall pouch.

"*Je cherche la route à la ville.* Looking for the road to town. Savvy?"

He moved with his axe but only to lean it against the chopping block.

"Lost," he said.

"That's right. You mind pointing out the road to town?"

From the sole word he probably wasn't French. A Yankee perhaps, or an Indian. There was a slight slur in his speech. For myself, I'd be damned nonplussed to see a stranger in a ruined suit walk out of the bush. This ancient in front of me was pretty nonchalant. It gave me a notion. If he was inured to wanderers in these woods it was because he'd seen them before. Ours wasn't the first convoy that'd headed south on this route. The Chevrolet parked out back looked new and the man hadn't paid for it splitting timber. Motioning towards the truck I said: "Maybe you give me a lift, eh? And something to eat. Go on in. I'll chop that wood. Got any grub?"

"Flapjacks."

"Good deal. I finish here, we go for a ride."

And with that I casually unbuttoned my coat, revealing the weapon. He kept his eyes on mine and I saw a faint flicker. The oldtimer knew. This was an act of will on my part. Had no mind to hurt or kill him, but would do what was needed in order to get out of here, even if it meant manual labour. At last he broke away and moved to the screen door. I followed to verify that he had no shotgun; I didn't care for the prospect of buckshot in my back. He shuffled through the door to a potbellied stove and started mixing flour, buttermilk, and an egg while I watched. As the man poured out circles of batter on the skillet I went and made short work of the wood and came back with an armful for the grate. The geezer flipped the cakes. I sat at an oilcloth-covered table. He brought me a plate and a cup of coffee and sat down.

"You hear any fireworks last night?" I asked.

"Nope."

"*Ayah*. You have any syrup?"

The old man reached for a can of molasses and I almost laughed. Here we were in the heart of sugar maple country and all he had was black glue from Jamaica. As I chewed, my backcountry chef sat mute, his black eyes downcast, a beat-down broken figure. I was thoroughly exhausted and didn't like him nearby while I ate. Strange sensation, cowing someone, making them fear you. Prerogative of the whiteman. This fellow looked at least part Mohawk, last of the braves mayhap.

"Why don't you wind up that buggy of yours and I'll get out of your hair. How's that sound, grandpa?" I asked.

With nary a word nor glance he pushed away to put on a blue Mackinaw jacket and a flat cap. I turned the fork around the plate and swilled coffee, yenning for tobacco. Nothing doing until I'd left this wigwam far behind. From outside came the sound of an engine starting. I hurried out to see the codger behind the wheel and climbed in beside him. My devil's luck. Out of a disaster some advantage. Try not to get shot out here. Let them kill you in town, if they must.

We turned around and drove along a cracked path, then out onto a gravel road. The country was flat and grey now, treeless farmland of blank fields bordered by long wire fences. Were I alone and walking these parts I'd stand out powerfully. End up dead in a ditch. A fluttering of my pulse restored anxious fear. There could be lookouts, a dragnet. Get to a train and bolt yourself in the lavatory.

"What's the closest town with a station?" I shouted over the motor.

"Napierville."

So, still in Quebec, *grâce de Dieu*. Maybe this oldtimer could drive me all the way back to the city. He kept his gnarled hands on the wheel and stared at the uncoiling road. If I'd been smarter or crueller I'd've tied him up and stolen his truck. This was no time for pity. Remember what happened to your last chauffeur.

The sky cleared, hard fields stretching nowhere. After awhile I made out a dark line on the horizon. Getting closer it became a freight, headed the way I wanted. A decision.

"See that?" I pointed. "You pull up at a crossroad. If it's slow enough you can let me off and go on home."

The old man cleared his throat and spat out the open window. As he shifted gears his hand shook with a mild palsy, either St. Vitus's dance or fear of the armed stranger barking orders. Keep him in your thrall. We braked at the tracks. The train was moving at a walking pace. Without another word I leapt out and ran up the grade to grasp a ladder, hauling myself up. The boxcar's door was closed so I climbed up to the roof. As the train retreated I watched the old man reverse his Chevrolet and power away.

My perch provided a wide vista about midway along the 'cars. I resolved to stay wary and keep my eye out for railway bulls or brakemen. The freight picked up speed. I rocked along and lay flat to lower my profile and watch the clouds above break apart. For several hours we swayed forward, the train passing Podunk towns and lonely crossings, heading inexorably north. Superstitious, I crossed my fingers. Sometimes it would slow and halt in that baffling way of all trains, only to eventually lurch alive and groan on. The wind turned easterly but then would box the compass and send sooty engine smoke over me. It whipped leaves along the hard-packed earth and bent double spurts of yellow grass hanks tangled with rubbish. I turned to look ahead and was rewarded. Montreal. The rough hump of the mountain sat stark and Cyclopean against the surrounding plains.

We chugged through Brossard and I pressed my luck to the Victoria Bridge crossing. We shuddered onto the Eighth Wonder of the World, as it was once known. From my viewpoint, for a fleeting moment, I commanded it all: the river underneath with boats working the seaward current, the train en route to the smoking yards, the city huddled and steaming in the pale fall sunshine. My heart lifted and despite the danger I felt a thrill. This would never have happened without Jack. My eyes smarted but I blamed it on smoke and too soon we were slowing to nothing. The freight readied to stop and be shunted or broken apart so I gripped Fortune's forelock and slipped down the ladder to the oil-soaked ground. A rich reek of creosote greeted me as I stepped over rails to bracken and shrubs bordering the tracks. I heard a hoarse shout behind me: "Hey, you!"

I ducked through a hole in the fence past a mangled "No Trespassing" sign to a city street, low brick buildings, and urchins playing stickball. I strode along, looking for a corner store, a tavern, and a tram stop, in that precise order. It was short work to find all three on Sebastopol. At Lucky's I bought a fifteen of Buckinghams for a pair of dimes and an afternoon *Herald* for two coppers. Across the street a tavern advertised clean glasses. It was well past the yardarm, near three in the afternoon, and for all my efforts and the miles I'd travelled I deserved a drink.

After quickly draining one Export I ordered another and went through the 'paper. The Tories were looking for a new leader. Prime Minister Mackenzie King was headed to the Imperial Conference in London. Edison believed that there was life after death. Relics from the Franklin Expedition had been discovered in the high Arctic, deep in the Northwest Territories. Babe Ruth would be in town tomorrow, tickets starting at four bits. Nothing about a gunfight in the woods along the American border. I doubted that the morning *Star* or *Gazette* had reported anything; it'd been far too late to meet their deadlines. The French afternoon 'paper was similarly uninformative, devoted almost entirely to a headless torso found in Repentigny.

No news was bad news. This pointed to the worst option: the ambush had been a business vendetta. Jack and myself were betrayed and I wasn't safe, not by a long chalk. If he'd been snared they would murder him but first turn the screws. Names of colleagues and accomplices. Jack knew where I lived, how I moved about. I was a loose end. I'd be tied up in a shroud.

Unless Jack had been killed in the fusillade. I shuddered. He'd told me to give him a week on the outside if anything went wrong. A week was too long and ninety-odd dollars and change would leave me with only enough for a ticket out. No. The danger was real, and my mouth went dry.

The next beer came lukewarm. The 'tender gave me the evil eye. Turning to the fight pages I smoked, drank, and thought, feeling a total wreck. Split the difference and give Jack three days to resurrect himself. Three days underground. First order of importance: new lodgings. Felt myself nodding over my cups and killed the ale. When the barkeep came again I paid and asked for a spool of twine, which he foraged for with an ill grace. I went to the jakes and wrapped the Webley in newspaper and tied it so the package looked like meat from the butcher's. I went out to the street.

Across the way a carbuncle of people waited for a streetcar and when the trolley crashed to a stop I joined them in getting on. We went over the canal and I jumped out at Peel. There was a bathhouse nearby with a tailor's attached where I could have my suit mended while I made my toilette. After that I'd find a new place to stay. It wasn't advisable to return to my old flop, considering. I'd only left behind several textbooks, a Gladstone bag with a change of clothes, and my overcoat. No, Goddammit, something else: a tintype of Laura and myself on College Street, hidden between the pages of *The Mauve Decade*.

We'd been walking down the sidewalk last year, early September, when a shill outside a camera shop snapped a photograph and handed me a card. I'd had no mementos of her. She'd never written me a letter, never compromised herself in any way. What's to compromise? I'd asked, we haven't done anything scandalous. Only ever with extreme reluctance would Laura meet me and only after continued persistence on my part. I didn't see it then, how little she cared. I'd returned to the studio a few days later for the developed print.

In the photograph she wore a silvery sable fur and a cloche hat like Theda Bara. I was in my three-piece suit, since pawned, and spats. She'd turned to the camera with a look of withering contempt, an expression I'd get to know too damn well. By Thanksgiving it was all over between us, such as it'd been. Burned to the ground. As a solace I began my other pursuit at the hospital. Incredible what a mere year wrought. Who was responsible for my fate? I'd thought that I was myself, until I fell in love.

At the bathhouse they issued me a towel and the key for a locker. I undressed, stored the package with the gun, and had the porter send my suit, shirt, and collar next door. In the hot room a burly lazar slept and an old bird peered at a wilted *Police Gazette* through steamed-over spectacles. I sweated out every atom of cordite, cocaine, and booze and then went for a cold plunge. Refreshed, I prepared to leave; my suit came back in decent trim with a note apologizing for not being able to remove tree sap from an elbow. I tipped a quarter in gratitude that there hadn't been any brain or bone in the wash.

SATURDAY NIGHT IN the metropolis. Neon signs came to life on St. Catherine Street, syncopating light and music, red, green, and blue splashing in time with hot jazz from gramophones. I floated along with a suppertime crowd in the direction of Phillips Square. A vendor roasted chestnuts. Morgan's department store was closed. Pigeons landed and shat on the head of the Roi Pacificateur behind me. Taking it as an augury I ambled to the Hotel Edward VII.

Hanging in the lobby was a portrait of the dead Emperor in his admiral's rig.

"Who's that, the Kaiser?" I asked through my nose like a Yankee.

The clerk pulled a face as I forged a signature in the register and forked over a dollar for the night. I went up to the fourth floor and entered a clean, bare room. After the day's efforts some rest was prescribed me. Propped a chair under the door handle, unwrapped the Webley, took off my boots, and stretched out on the bed, the gun at hand. After dozing and mumbling and fading away a sudden fastball struck the pillow next to my face. Hypnic jerk. I started up and rubbed my eyes clear, then went and doused my head in cold water. Quarter to nine by the clock on the dresser; for our King the time at Sandringham was set a half-hour earlier than Greenwich Mean for the pheasant shooting. Jack had said quarter past nine every evening at the Dominion and this was the first night.

By the time I returned to its dirty streets the city was really starting to enjoy itself. Past the railway terminal on Dorchester smoke rose from the wide cut in the earth where trains marshalled below the street, readying themselves to scream north through the tunnel under the mountain. Stopping at an Imperial Tobacconist I bought Juicy Fruit and chewed it, crackling bubbles between my molars. At right was the largest building in the Empire, more massive than St. Paul's or Canterbury Cathedral, the wedding-cake Sun Insurance behemoth. It anchored Dominion Square and had next to it the small tavern where Jack said he'd leave word if anything went wrong. How little he'd known.

I pushed my way into the crowded saloon and stepped up to the bar. Men were jawing politics or sport. Next to me a chap with a tin of Puck at his elbow gobbed tobacco into a spittoon at his feet between freshening gulps of beer, a disgusting choreography. I added chewing gum to the bucket of brown slime, bought a quart of Export, and retired, my back to a wall where I could watch the door. From scarlet faces came shouted scraps of talk.

"Redmen'll top the Argos one-legged this year..."

"Bennett can't make more of a mess of Ottawa than that straw man Meighen..."

"Went to her sister's and won't come to the door when I call..."

"Fired six good men for jack shit..."

The whole panoply of masculine weltschmerz. My problems were deeper and deadlier. I leaned back, drank, and scanned the room, waiting, watching. Next to me an old cove wearing a ratty beard and with a dead wet hand-rolled in his yap mauled a 'paper. So as not to be too noticeably alone I offered him a Buckingham.

"Thanks, sonny."

He was thumbing the sports pages so I chose that as a topic.

"Looks like the Canucks are trying to buy a championship this year," I said.

The cove turned to me and I continued: "Too bad about Vezina dying. Least they've got Howie Morenz, for starters."

He put down his 'paper.

"I don't care who wins as long as it ain't them blasted Maroons," said the old goat.

"I hear you. Had money on the Cougars to win last year. Now look where they are. Sold them all off to Detroit."

"Is that so? So you're not from around here?"

"No. Western League. Good teams there. Seattle Mets. The old Millionaires were my club."

"I was a St. Pats man myself," the old man said.

Already I regretted my decision to palaver. Relief suddenly arrived in the form of a familiar figure coming through the door. My heart leapt for an absurd instant, but it wasn't Jack. Brown, the little Customs man. He was living up to his name with a brown hat, brown suit and brown bowtie, carrying a furled umbrella and wearing a sticking plaster on his cheek where Jack had laid him open. This was not a chance entrance.

Brown went up to the barman and asked him a question. The 'tender shook his head. I was with child to know what was asked. Brown took out a small change purse, picked inside it for a coin, and paid for a bock. He looked around and for an uncomfortable moment I thought he recognized me. Couldn't be, as I'd been behind him when he had his little colloquy with Jack in the alley. I shammed some more with the bore.

"You're not from here if the Pats are your team," I said.

"No sir, I'm up from Toronto to visit my daughter Dorothy. She's a typewriter at the O'Sullivan school."

Brown finished his beer and left. I excused myself from the fascinating repartee and made a beeline to the bar. I put down a half-dollar.

"That fellow ask after anyone?" I asked the barkeep.

He took the coin and answered: "Yeah. A Godfrey."

"Godfrey?"

"Yeah."

"Any message for Sam from Pete?"

"Nope. None I know."

Snookered. Jack hadn't been here. I hurried out after Brown to see where he went. He was crossing the square in the direction of the Windsor Hotel. Jack must be using the Dominion as his letter drop. Shades of Junius and the coffee shops in the days of George III. Brown hadn't received a message and neither had I. The little man quick-stepped it to Cypress and I followed, stalking in darkness. At first it looked as though he was headed for the Metropolitan newsstand but he turned into the doorway of a forbidding building. With entree to that particular address I learned the Scotsman's vice. Not drink, as his purchase at the saloon had made clear. The building he'd gone into was a gambler's hell, specializing in barbotte and chemin de fer. He'd be throwing the dice all night. As it was a private club I abandoned my pursuit. Unlike Jack I detested games of chance. My tastes were other. Nonetheless, I now knew how Jack and the bootleggers owned Brown. They'd probably bought up his debts. Did Brown know anything about the debacle in the woods? Had he been the one who tipped off the enemy? I had questions, but I didn't half like the idea of being noticed skulking about. Besides, I was wrung out with the day's events. I resolved to wait it out and try the Dominion again tomorrow.

Back in my hotel's lobby the bored porter sat reading Oscar Wilde. I went up to my room and listened in the hallway before carefully opening the door, diagnosing myself with tachycardia, tenth occurrence of the day. The room was empty and very gradually my heartbeat slowed to normal again. I put the revolver under my pillow after checking the sturdy lock on the door, propping a chair once more under the knob. Nervous exhaustion kept me twitching in the bed for a spell. A flooding taste of caramel filled my mouth while my floating mind went through the procedure of preparing a shot of morphine, the precise and sinister ritual. Presently I faded away to the sounds of bawdy shouting and the snatches of drunken song, wood breaking, mirrors smashing, and the city tearing itself apart.

SUNDAY

PEALS FROM EVERY spire around downtown roused me. What had Mark Twain said about this city? Couldn't throw a rock without hitting a church window. Morning bells are ringing. Sonnez les matines. Are you sleeping, Brother Jack, or mouldering in a shallow grave? Knowing him, Jack had slipped out from under and was in the arms of a tender dollymop. French church bells sounded different: ding dang *donc*. The two hanging and ringing in Notre-Dame down at Place d'Armes were named after Victoria and Albert. Dong.

Outside was grey again, threatening rain. I put myself to rights and whistled downstairs, tossing my key to a new pimp at the desk. Hung-over wet-haired American businessmen booked out after weekend benders. Bought the 'paper off a boy outside and determined to eat at Windsor Station Grill, checking the scheduled departures just in case. The station was near my old digs. Beyond pulling up a pew there wasn't much doing of a Sunday morning.

My landlady would herself be kneeling with the Paddies at St. Patrick's right about now. I could chance ducking back into the rooming house for my remaining effects. I decided to risk it and so hiked over to Stanley and a file of nondescript row houses. I climbed the steps of the third from the end and tried the latch. It gave. I slipped in. The stand-up clock in the foyer ticked but its hands never moved, a distillation of the state of affairs at Miss Milligan's. As there was no one stirring I took the stairs two at a time to my room. Someone had been in it, the bitch rummaging after I'd failed to show two nights running. I filled my Gladstone with books and linen, grabbed my overcoat and gloves, and was back outside in no time flat.

I took my bag to the station and ate ham and eggs at the grill. The morning *Gazette* had nothing on Friday night's fracas in the woods. This only confirmed my fears. To distract myself I thumbed through the classified notices looking for a cheap room that didn't require references. Seeking quiet Christian gentleman, call UPtown 283, one week includes board and bedding. Sighing, I lit a cigaret. If there existed any toil more tedious than searching out lodgings I didn't know it. How many times had I moved in the last year, ahead of the duns? Verily, it was a science unto itself, choosing the choice moment to slip cable. And so here I was back to the round of 'phone booths, wasted nickels, shoe leather burned, lies told to suspicious landlords. Still, it might be worse. At least I wasn't looking for work.

The best prospect of rooms to let was in lower Westmount, or perhaps I could go native on the east side amongst the Frogs. There I'd stick out, a square-headed peg amongst the peasantry. No, I wanted to remain near the train stations and the river. It was far too easy to get trapped on this island in the St. Lawrence.

The concourse at Windsor was crowded and noisy. I noticed no police presence save a sole bobby pacing along with his hands behind his back, nodding pleasantly at unattended women. On the board I considered prospective destinations, all uninviting: Ottawa, Kingston, Niagara Falls. I should head over to Bonaventure Station to locomotive south. Winter was coming. The

Florida land boom had busted and I could tend the greens of a
golf course rotting away into mangrove swamps and live off alli-
gator meat, oranges, and malaria. Sail away to Havana and die.
Too much to ask for on a mere hundred dollars. No, ninety-seven
now. How much would be enough? Have to see.

I walked over to the waiting room. Inside, tramps warmed
their feet at the stove, smoking sweeps from the floor. It was over-
hot and brutally close, so I turned around and checked my bag
for the price of a dime. Exiting the station I nodded at the bronze
Lord Mount Stephen, a statue everyone mistook for King George.
It was the beard. This was George Stephen, father of the railroad
west. He'd started his rise at a haberdasher's back in Edinburgh,
picking a pin up off the floor and tucking it behind his lapel for
use later, impressing the bosses with his perfect thrift. From
there to the Bank of Montreal and the CPR and now he was dead,
his mansion converted into a private club for those who couldn't
cut the mustard with the reviewing board of the Mount Royal
or St. James. You couldn't turn around in this town without tripping over a striving clerk from the Old Country made nabob
and knight in the New. The earthly paradise was a reading room
where one could snooze over three-day-old copies of the *Times* in
an overstuffed chair.

As if to illustrate my point St. George's across the street dis-
gorged its parishioners. Out came barons who'd traded the kirk
for a well-carved Anglican pew. I saw Sir Rupert Irons, Holt, a few
Molsons, and that fat bastard Huntley McQueen shaking hands
with the reverend. Today's sermon had no doubt been on how
the rich could enter heaven by forging a needle out of Ontario
steel large enough for a dromedary camel to stroll on through.
These were the men to do it, our captains of industry, plutocrats
in the Commonwealth's service. Inside the church a plaque
commemorated an Irishman killed in Quetta, India, due to a

mishap playing polo, fondly remembered by his regiment here in Montreal. There was Empire for you, binding soldiers, financiers, priests, politicians, aristocrats, and its discontents. Myself.

An itch played in the palm of my hand. Money coming my way. I scratched a lucifer on the rough stone of the station to light a smoke. Ninety-seven dollars and change. Now what to do? Might ride a trolley across the island and back. Instead I remembered what I'd read in the 'paper yesterday and hied uptown to mooch in the little park beside the new Forum.

WHEN THE HOUR came 'round I dropped fifty cents for a seat in the stands at Atwater Park to see the ball game with Ruth and his ringers playing for both sides of two local all-star teams, a sort of Vaudeville turn. Assembling to watch, we were a good-sized crowd, it being the last time to enjoy outdoor sport before the weather turned completely. Before us was Ruth at home plate, warming up by blasting baseballs out of the park, one after another. Scampering children beyond the right field fence fought over each ball like dogs for a crust.

I was wedged in between on my left a thin man like Jack Sprat with a wife who ate no lean and on the right a file of French factory workers. Light rain fell, then quit. The band came out and we stood for the anthems: "God Save the King," the American number, and our other tune. Through a loudhailer a lady soprano sang: "In days of yore, from Britain's shore, Wolfe, the dauntless hero came, and planted firm Britannia's flag, on Canada's fair domain. Here may it wave, our boast, our pride, and joined in love together, the thistle, shamrock, rose entwined, the Maple Leaf forever."

Half the crowd was mum, thinking on Montcalm and the fleur-de-lis or perhaps plumb not knowing the words and merely humming along, holding their hats. I piped up for the hard part:

"Our Fair Dominion now extends from Cape Rock to Nootka Sound. May peace forever be our lot and plenteous store abound. And may those ties of love be ours which discord cannot sever, and flourish green o'er freedom's home the Maple Leaf forever."

Applause. All hats back on. The audience sat for the ceremonial toss of the horsehide by the mayor. With that the game began and a cold wind blew down from the north. The first pitch. Urban Shocker from the Yankees was tossing for Beaurivage and Ruth played for Guybourg. Two strikeouts and a fly ball to deep left and the sides changed before we'd even settled in our seats.

Ruth came on the field and took his position at first base. He doffed his cap and the crowd cheered. First a strikeout, then an easy infield fly, and third a sharp rap to shortstop that was winged back to first. Ruth almost bobbled it but managed the out and we went into the next inning straightaway. Ruth led off, fouled twice, and then hit one deep into centre that was snagged by the fielder at the track. The next batter made it onto first but then got caught in a double play.

I rose and went for a Frankfurter covered in mustard and onions, followed by a Coca-Cola. I wiped my mouth and drained the green glass bottle. As I stood and watched the next inning a short Jew in a raccoonskin coat sidled over. Unbidden he offered me a small cigar. He waggled his eyebrows and smiled.

"Did you see the Babe hitting them out of the park?" he asked.

"Sure did."

"Too bad he couldn't do that in the series."

"I thought he had three homers in one game," I said.

"One game. Then he loses the whole damn thing trying to steal second. The Cards nailed New York to the cross, you'll forgive the expression."

I laughed and looked at him, blowing smoke.

"Well, someone's always the scapegoat."

He hiccoughed. I asked him his line of work.

"Brassieres. A very uplifting profession."

I laughed again and he winked back. The Beaurivagers had a rally at the bottom of the second and were up three runs by the end of the inning. Ruth moved to shortstop and barehanded a fast zinger to beat a steal at second to end the run. He struck out his next at-bat and someone shouted: "*Va chier,* Babe!"

There was a tremor of nervous laughter. The Jew pulled out a flask and offered me a slug. I croaked it down and asked its pedigree.

"A special mixture."

Playing an American I asked him if I could get it in the States. He told me that I could, in the Middle West. Some countrymen of his ran it down from Regina.

"Where's that?" I pretended.

"Saskatchewan."

"Man alive. How'd they do it?"

"It's classed as a patent medicine, for doctors to carry a bottle in their black bags. If you're interested maybe I can facilitate an introduction."

"Swell. Can they get into Vermont or New York?"

"That I don't know."

"I know some folks'd be happy for help, if you know what I mean."

"Tell you what," he said, "I'll give you my card. You can come by to talk."

"I'm not here too long."

The strange import of that phrase suddenly struck me.

"Well, neither are they. Come by and talk and I'll call Solly. You can speak to him."

"Solly?"

"He's the smartest of the brothers."

"Brothers?"

"Three of them."

"Oke."

I took the card. This was a mere coincidence in a crowd. There was no hint of a provocation. It was that phenomenon where you'd never heard an arcane phrase before, then upon learning it you overhear it in conversation at the next table in a café. Bootleggers. Maybe I looked the part. The weight of the gun now at the small of my back, changing my carriage, lending me an air. If I met some other exporters it could throw a little light on Jack and the organization he was involved with.

Over the years I'd taken it as a given with Jack. He'd vanish, cook up a scheme, materialize with money, a 'car, a girl, the latest joke, a yarn. It was in stark opposition to myself, his hustle and drive. I'd brood, my mouth shut. He was outgoing, gregarious, a good time. Well, it wasn't too late. The circumstances demanded an effort on my part. I was mixed up in trouble and I cursed myself for not pumping Jack when I'd had the chance at the Derby or in Griffintown before we rode off into the woods. Now I might never find out what had led me to this stand.

There rose mingled cries and loud cheering and I saw a player running hell-bent for leather, sliding safe home to a roar and a tiger. Guybourg had scored two runs. I shook the Jew's hand, pocketed his card, and resumed my seat.

Next time Guybourg came up Shocker tried to lay down his teammate. Ruth fanned on the first pitch, fouled the next, and with a crack banged the next ball over the left field fence into a tree, startling a flock of pigeons. For a heavy man he skipped nimbly around the bases, to the crowd's delight. This was what they'd paid for.

Back in the dugout Ruth was handed a beer and emptied it in a swallow. He started signing programs and photographs, laughing and chatting with children, drinking some more. The game stayed tied through the end of the sixth.

The Guybourg pitcher blew out his arm the next inning so Ruth stepped in and retired the side. Later, a nasty foul tip clipped the ump and knocked him out; for sport Ruth put on the official's pads and called the game while his own team batted. It didn't help Guybourg one whit. At the change during the stretch there spread a ripple of merriment through the crowd at some jape Ruth was up to. He couldn't get out of the umpire's pads and was struggling on the ground, cracking wise to the nearby fans.

"What's he saying?" asked Jack Sprat next to me.

His wife sat nibbling Turkish delight.

"He ask Houdini to help him escape," said a dark ferret on my other side.

The eighth was a washout for both sides. Calcium spotlights were lit against the creeping dark and a sharp wind scraped across the diamond. The *mobile vulgus* contracted at this grim taste of winter, steam and smoke rising from the pinched crowd as it tensed against the chill. At last came the ninth, the score still knotted.

Ruth got up. The Beaurivage pitcher was an amateur from town with his family loudly rooting for him to fan the big-leaguer. It didn't work out. The local boy threw three pitches wide and then Ruth fouled twice for the full count. The next ball floated over the plate and Ruth pounded it out of the park. The diamond exploded and the Babe grinned like a happy hound as he rounded the bases for home where his team waited to clap and pound him on the back. The recovered umpire went over and talked to both sides' managers and then they beckoned the announcer, who joined their consultation for a minute, then went to the loudspeaker.

"Ladies and gentlemen, we wish to inform you that the game has been called at the top of the ninth by agreement, the

Guybourg All-Stars winning four runs to three thanks to a solo run by Babe Ruth."

A general huzzah.

"Mr. Ruth has, through the pre-game demonstration and this contest, now hit thirty-six balls out of the park and exhausted both clubs' supply. We wish to thank you for your attendance today and please join us in three cheers for our visitors to Montreal!"

The crowd did better than that, breaking into "For He's a Jolly Good Fellow" and then for good measure "God Save the King" again. Ruth and his compatriots doffed their caps and a friendly mob swarmed the field. He signed a dozen autographs and was finally helped out of the throng and into a taxi that had been let onto the field to take him back to his hotel. I ran into the Jew again in the crush leaving the park.

"Another Exodus," I said.

He clapped my shoulder, red-faced and daffy with hooch.

"The old Babe'll be swinging his bat on Bullion Street tonight," he yowled, making an obscene gesture.

The gate separated us and I was let back out on the mercy of the city. I started to feel like going on a tear of my own. The noise, movement, and temporary camaraderie had jazzed me. I could walk to Laura's house and say goodbye. Get it over with. The way things stood my last friend in the world was gone, dead. Laura had probably been affianced off to a moneyed heir. Perhaps I could bury myself in some small Ontario town, play with a crystal set in the evenings trying to pick up signals from Texas. Crunch through blue snow at night to romance a cross-eyed librarian, become a clerk at a hardware store and sing in the Methodist choir, march in the Orangemen's parade every July. I could do any number of things, but paramount I would find a saloon open on a Sunday on St. Catherine Street. After that I just might end up in a whorehouse on Bullion like Mr. Babe Ruth.

IN THE TAVERN my Frankfurter indigested so I ordered a Vichy water. A dwarf sang in Italian to a fat man beside him. The record was turned and the machine let out jazz, Roxy and His Gang, hometown boys like the Guybourg All-Stars. I started to think about Jack, and Laura.

He'd introduced me to her back in '24. Jack was being political on campus and she was bucking patrimony, seemingly. Laura Dunphy, the devoted only daughter of Sir Lionel Dunphy, Q.C., Privy Council, past president of the Liberal Party, a real tyee. Jack had played Pied Piper and led a group of us to a Bolshevist meeting soon after Lenin's death. An incomprehensible Glaswegian gave a report on factory conditions in the Ukraine and glorious future prospects for same. In attendance were myself, Jack, Laura, her inevitable plain friend Margery, Smiler, that prick Jerome Martel, and some clinging dishrag girls. Jack and Laura, a pair of redheads, strange portent. After the lecture a firebrand gave a stemwinder of revolutionary oration, and at its end we were all communists, marching out onto the street dead earnest, singing "The Internationale." In a café the collective solved the world's problems over egg creams and french fries. As we broke up for the night Laura put her arm through mine, announcing that I would be the one to escort her home. The look on Jack's face was difficult to read, that secret amusement. Jerome Martel's feelings were plain as day, and I gloated as I carried Laura off. I was done, easy as that. She had me by the time I walked her up the steps of her father's mansion on the hill, still humming "The Internationale," what the dwarf was trilling to the fat man at the end of the bar right now.

I gave them a mock salute with my seltzer and said: "Viva d'Annunzio." It shut the little man up. He turned to his comrade and they looked daggers at me. I could just as easily have toasted Mussolini. That would've been splendid, fighting a midget. A long way from sparring with Jack when we were young. He'd fought in the army, taking an inter-regimental belt at Valcartier before being shipped to Europe. We'd even picked it up again as recently as last year before once more drifting apart. Jack an irregular comet. Where'd he been since then? Where was he now? Sizing myself up in the mirror, dark and different, my reflection hydrocephalic and clouded in the glass, I had to ask: Where was I?

From the bar I bought a pack of Consuls and wanted whiskey but the law allowed only beer and wine unless you knew where to look. At least this province was better than the rest of the country, dry for most of a decade. I'd hunt up a government licence tomorrow for something stronger. The record stopped playing, the beer arrived flat, and I began to fill with regret. My mind turned to bygone failures, weakness, a misspent past, the decay of my medical studies, Laura lost forever, Jack maybe dead. The Pater, polishing his barometer and returning to his desk to read Scripture. The dwarf and his partner left. A new record played an Irish lament, "Turn Ye to Me," sung by John McCormack. Tired-looking whores sat at a table for a warm up, on a break from working the Sabbath. Near nine I made my sortie, dumping silver and ashes on the bartop.

Outside, it was raining. I turned my collar up against the elements. Old newspapers clogged the gutters. Crowded trolleys glowed by, windows steamed with human exhalation. Neon reflected off the empty wet pavement. My boots filled with ice-water, my bare head soaked. I'll catch pneumonia and die, came the thought. A right on Metcalfe to the Dominion, which was closed. Damnation. All lights out, the dark window advertising a plate supper of pork knuckles for a quarter-dollar. I pounded on the door. A black figure came towards me. Through the pane I heard: "Closed."

He was the same barman I'd tipped the night before. In this world it proved impossible to have anything done without laying out the rhino. I held up a dollar bill. "A question."

The door unbolted and the barman looked up and down the street, then hustled me in. He was bald and stank of rum.

"Is there a message for Sam, from Pete?" I asked.

He nodded, went behind the bar, and handed over an envelope. It was the kind used for bank deposits. I tossed him the buck.

"Way out back?"

He pointed a wavering finger to the kitchen where I pushed my way through piles of dirty plates and empty bottles and opened a gummy door onto an alley filled with rubbish. Outside once more, I tore open the envelope to read: "Loew's, last show tonight," written in Jack's hand.

Walking in the direction of the theatre I felt elation. He was alive. He'd made it out somehow and was back to his old tricks. There was a chance this could play out. By the time I reached the cinema I was wet through. The marquee advertised *The Trap* with Lon Chaney, and I blanched. What was I walking into? There was no one at the entrance so I quietly slid into an empty lobby filled with the smell of burnt popcorn. It was eerie. No ticket-tearer or usher. From the atrium I could hear a piano playing. I climbed the stairs to the balcony for a better viewpoint. I'd seen the picture when it first came out. Not nearly as good as *The Unholy Three*.

Through thick smoke the projector cast its light. A piano player laboured over suspense. There was quite a bit left to go, another reel or two. Two miners competed over rival claims, the scenario a pastiche out of Jack London or Robert Service. My mind wandered until a woman gasped as Chaney fought a wolf. The finale treated us to a tender moment with a baby and it all ended happily and for the best. With a flourish the house lights raised. Women fingered on gloves and the murmuring audience unclotted. There: down and to the left, two men in hats seated together, smoking. I gave a low Scout whistle. Jack turned around and pointed a finger at me, a cocked gun. With him this second, younger fellow. They came up through the thinning crowd and we met in the aisle.

"This way," said Jack.

We took a short stairwell leading to the projection booth and Jack opened the door to what turned out to be a janitor's cubby stuffed with torn publicity sheets, creased photographs of movie stars, ripped bunting.

"Do you have a handkerchief?" Jack asked once we'd fought our way in.

I shook my head.

"Then take mine. I'll employ another principle."

"What's that?" asked the other man. He was a pretty blond, shorter than me.

"The memorable distracting detail," Jack said.

The stranger began tying a cloth over his nose and mouth.

"What's the gag?" I asked.

"Money," Jack said. "You want some? Bob here does."

The third man nodded.

"Bob, Mick. Mick, Bob."

I looked from Jack to this Bob and back again, reeling my Irish in, that hot surge of fury. Without a by-your-leave or a word of explanation, as though my sentiments or any possible objections were not even in consideration. But it was too late. I couldn't lose face. I was worse than any Chinaman. Jack handed me the disguise, and I put it on.

"What'd I tell you?" Jack said to Bob. "Mick's our man."

"I still say it's a two-man job," brayed Bob.

"Three's safer. It's my caper. Equal shares."

Bob gave me a dirty look. I was cutting into his portion. Already I didn't like him much.

"There's the watchman, the manager, and a girl," Jack said. "Three's best."

"Third murderer," I said.

"No rough stuff if we can help it. You still have your cannon?"

I opened my coat.

"How much do you reckon?" I asked.

"There's a whole week's receipts on a Sunday. Maybe more. We'll see. You ready? I'm Pete, you're Sam and Ed. Got the rope?"

Bob took a big coil out from his coat and looped it over his shoulder. Jack checked his wristwatch.

"Half-past ten."

He opened the door to near-blackness softened only by the red of an exit sign. I went cold with fear. This had the taste of desperation to it, that familiar flavour of fear. My hair steamed as we made our way down a steep flight. Ahead of us was an illumination, a door ajar. Jack eased it open, revealing a man in sleeve garters and a bowtie dipping a pen nib into a bottle of ink. Before him sat a ledger. Jack clucked his tongue and the man looked up.

"What's this?"

Jack raised a finger to his lips.

"Who are you, sir? This theatre's closed."

Bob and I entered the office, guns in hands.

"Good Lord. What is the meaning of this?"

The man snatched off his pince-nez and began to stand. He had pluck, I'd give him that.

"Do not test our resolve, sir. We are here to relieve you of your pecuniaries."

Jack parodied the manager's Southern drawl creditably.

"But sir, you cannot. I must insist you disengage!"

"I will ask you to be so kind as to hold your tongue. We desire the contents of the safe," Jack said. "Samuel, Edward, locate the watchman and the lady. Take care that the doors have been locked and search for any telephones, like so." Jack picked up the Bakelite machine on the manager's desk and ripped the cord from the wall, then dumped the disabled works on the floor. At this, the manager stood a moment, then sat again suddenly, pale, confused. Bob left the office and I followed.

"I'll check the lobby," I said. "Try the back exit for the guard."

Bob slipped off, saying nothing. I headed down a passageway, my stomach sinking away, bowels frozen. The hall opened on the shadowy lobby, where an older woman in a cardigan fussed behind the candy counter. I walked to the doors and checked that they were locked from within. Turning my way, the woman went saucer-eyed. I caught my own reflection in a dark mirror, a menacing masked figure with a gun. I'd do whatever I said, for fear of worse.

"Come with me, madam," said I.

Some of Jack's mock gallantry had worn off on me. At present Bob was an unknown factor but seemed a cold, bloodthirsty, greedy little bastard. What we were engaged in was a felony. Should something go wrong, it would be the rope for us. Trust Jack, I reminded myself. Why? Because you always have, you fool.

"Where's the 'phone?" I growled.

Nothing. She was frozen. Get her out of here. I grabbed at her elbow and steered her backstage towards the office. My captive moved jerkily, like an automaton. We ran into Bob, lashing a uniformed geezer's hands to a ladder. He stuffed a wadded playbill into the watchman's mouth. *Quid ipsos custodes custodiet* indeed. Pre-medical grounding in the Classics is a requisite. Some Latin, less Greek, like the Bard. Remembered peppering my Juvenal with accents, playing the Eton swot for the Pater. He watched, bearded and severe as Jehovah, never sparing the rod as I tripped over the dative case. Jack slung the bat with ease, another of his gifts, beaming at our schoolmaster, never an apple polisher but genuinely likeable. People took a shine to Jack, I never knew why. The manager had probably already opened a bottle of sourmash, the two damning reconstruction and toasting the immortal memory of Robert E. Lee. I poked the woman into the room and Bob followed. The woman cried: "John!"

"Mary?"

Bob sniggered. I almost agreed. Who were these people?

"May I assume that you two enjoy the sanctity of the marital bond?" asked Jack.

The manager choked.

"Now see here, you ruffian," he said.

"For heaven's sake, John," wailed Mary.

"Yes, John. For your own sake and that of this good lady, be kind enough to open the safe. We desire no harm to befall the missus," said Jack.

John goggled. John Adams, I saw painted on the frosted glass of the office door.

"Sir, I beseech you, as a fellow Southerner, please..."

"John!" Mary shrieked.

Adams deflated. He swivelled his chair towards a Chinese screen, which he pulled aside to reveal a squat iron cube, then spun the dial and opened the safe. Jack sat on the edge of the desk, all taut attention and eager amusement, humming "Dixie." The manager took out a bound pile of notes, a sack of silver, and a fat bag stuffed with loose bills. He passed the lot to Jack.

"Thank you kindly," said Jack.

Bob pushed the woman down into a chair. I went to check our hogtied nightwatchman and from him smelled sharp sweat and urine. His eyes were shut tight. Disgusted, I returned to the office, where Jack was emptying a valise. He placed the money within and gave the case a heft. Bob's eyes glinted and he looked over to me. Ice-cold and hard. Mary Adams was pale with fright. From his pocket Bob took out a blade and the woman whimpered. He cut fabric from the hem of her dress and her eyes went to mine, terrified. Bob balled the muslin and roughly shoved it into her mouth. He took sticking plaster from the desk and put it over her lips, then grabbed the last of his rope and with Jack's help bound her and her husband's wrists and ankles to their chairs. My heartbeat steadied. Jack straightened his cravat.

"We thank you for your very kind indulgence in this matter. Now don't you go being over-hasty in attempting to extricate yourselves, as we have compatriots observing each and every egress. Do take care now, y'hear?"

With that we hustled out the back door to the alley.

"Where now?" I asked.

"Bob's."

We hotfooted it to Sherbrooke, avoiding streetlamps, walking in a staggered file along the pavement, with Jack ahead, Bob watching him and his cargo, and myself covering our rear. Bob's place was on Prince Arthur, in the student ghetto. It appeared my life had become a series of traverses from room to saloon to shitty room. What pattern was I tracing on the face of the city? We took the stairs to a standard two-bit garret with stains on the ceiling and spilled paint on the floorboards. Interestingly, large canvasses were stacked face first against the walls. Bob left, returned with a bowl of cracked ice, and pulled a bottle of whiskey from a boot by the bed. Jack checked his 'watch.

"Nice work, boyos."

I lit a cigaret, my hands spiting their training, shaking with a minor tremor. Tension. The puncture points along my arm gave a phantom throb. My teeth tasted chalky. I wanted something, morphine, opium, oblivion. Bob portioned out the gargle. Nausea rose within me to be chased down by antiseptic liquor.

Between Jack and Bob there ran a current of excitement, their grins lupine. Lon Chaney in *The Trap*. Jack poured the contents of the bag onto a ratty Chesterfield. Bob nearly ravened at the sight of the cash but restrained himself with an effort. Jack lit a cigaret. I tapped my ashes into a half oyster shell. What was I playing at? It'd happened too bloody fast for real fear to grip me overmuch. Fatalism. Jack regarded me. I spat a shred of tobacco onto the floorboards while Bob counted the money. The coins rang as they struck each other: nickels, dimes, quarters, dollars. Copper, silver, gold.

I fixed Jack with a look and we regarded each other, unblinking. I broke first. "What was that distracting detail you mentioned?" I asked.

"The accent. Our friend John'll remember nothing about me except that I'm a Confederate, you wait and see. One of your countrymen, Bob."

"What's that?" Bob asked.

I placed his nasal bray. New England somewhere.

"A Johnny Reb," said Jack. "The war of Southern secession."

"Fuck that," said Bob. "I'm Irish."

"Oh really? From the Free State are you now?" mocked Jack.

"What in the hell are you talking about?" asked Bob.

"You don't sound Irish," I said.

"Boston Irish," Bob countered.

"Bob's kinsman ran for governor of Massachusetts," said Jack. "Why'd he lose again?"

"Never mind."

"Mick here's a Peep o' Day Boy," said Jack.

Bob finished counting and glared. Jack winked at me.

"What've you got?" he asked Bob.

"Twenty-eight hundred and thirty-five in bills. Maybe seventy more in change. Some Double Eagles. What're these?"

Bob held out a handful of gold discs.

"New Zealand dollars," Jack said. "Coin o' the realm. So, that's almost a thousand apiece. Not too shabby for an hour's work."

Bob spluttered: "Jesus, Jack, you said..."

"I said it was an easy score," Jack cut in. "You hear any sirens? Filth knocking at your door? You Yankee bastards are never happy."

"I'm no Yankee," went Bob.

"Right, you're some sort of shamrock-blooded Paddy Free Stater and a second cousin to Michael Collins. Up here in the Dominion you're a Yankee, son, both you and that gentleman we tied up, so pipe down and cut the pot."

Jack turned to me now, full flower. Amongst other questions, I wondered how much he'd taken on board. Drunk and garrulous it was best to let him wax eloquent.

"Did you know that John Wilkes Booth was here in this very town at the St. Lawrence Hall before he shot Lincoln? The bugger bragged all over town he was going to do it. Hell, Montreal was rotten with Confederates and spies and after the war Jefferson Goddamned Davis lived here and wrote his memoirs. There's something wrong with this city; it breeds treason. Benedict Arnold, Booth, Benjamin Franklin."

"Franklin was no traitor," interrupted Bob.

"Franklin was a bought and paid for agent of George III," said Jack.

Sullenly, Bob finished dividing the paper money. We each took our respective shares and I counted mine out: nine hundred and forty-five dollars in mixed bills. Not bad was right. It was more money than I'd ever held in my hands at one time.

"Give me the coins," Jack said.

"What're you going to do with them?" asked my avarice.

"Bury them under a sour apple tree. Can't trust that bag with either of you Micks. You'd probably off and tithe it."

"I take no orders from Rome," I said.

Jack just laughed, as Bob and I eyed one another across a widening divide.

Bob resembled a nasty schoolboy, with traces of breeding shining through an assumed coarseness. It was something I'd seen before, rich boys talking common. Arrogant and vindictive, and no new friend of mine. Still, there was more to the gladrag, that much was clear. Bob put an elastic around his money. I figured I'd unstitch my coat tomorrow and hide mine in the lining.

"You paint?" I asked Bob.

"Some."

"Bob's a Fenian and a Fauvist," Jack teased.

Bob ignored Jack's baiting. Jack hadn't touched his money yet, and I still had questions to put to him. What'd happened in the woods? How'd he gotten away and what had prompted this risky heist? I was close to asking when he rose and gathered his cash and the valise.

"I'd stay away from the Bank of England were I you," said Jack. "Try not to spend it ostentatiously. That son of a bitch Adams'll claim double what we stole to the cops and tell the 'papers the same tale of woe for his insurance. The world was ever thus. Now, I know a grand place to unwind, a favourite of the chief of police, but not of a Sunday. Come along, it's on me."

Bob locked up and we met down on the street.

"You certain this is a good idea? Shouldn't we split up?" I said. "They'll be looking for three men together."

"Not where we're going."

JACK HAILED A TAXICAB at the corner.

"Mountain," he said as we got in.

We drove onto Sherbrooke, passed the campus, and headed for the Golden Mile, making another right up Mountain. The district was beginning to fray at its edges as the city encroached upon it; all the rich families were abandoning the ancient preserve of wealth for Westmount and beyond. Good riddance. Jack barked a command and we stopped in front of a mansion that had seen its fortunes fade but was still in better than decent trim, almost respectable and discreet, with only the slightest piratical cast.

"Hell of a cathouse," I said.

"The best in town."

We mounted the flagged stone steps to a portal engraved with a coat of arms. In response to a soft bell chime a pretty house-maid opened the door. Our merry crew was received in a narthex of mirrors and ersatz gold. With this decor, there was no mistaking the nature of the house. Within moments a dreadnought of a madam steamed down the curving staircase to meet us. She bore an uncanny resemblance to Marie Dressler. Jack bowed and kissed a rose-gloved hand. Powdered and pink, the matron keeled and tittered: "You cheeky thing. It's been far too long since you were here. I'd almost given up on you. And how delightful, you've brought some gentlemen along. How very lovely."

The madam had a pleasing, musical laugh, wet red lips, shark's eyes. Her perfume began to provoke a sneeze.

"What would you wish for tonight?" she asked.

"Elope with me," Jack said.

She batted him away with a furled fan. Bob stood and postured to my right. The bouquet of the madam's toilet water was now creeping deeper into my olfactory apparatus. Hold it in. Hold it. I fumbled for a cigaret as our group was swept into a sitting room done up in the fin-de-siècle manner, with electric globes made to resemble gas lamps and a player piano. Bob headed to a long divan against the wall and lounged, his manner supercilious. I bit at a thumbnail. It'd been a tiring day by any measure. Thick nude odalisques writhed in heavy gilt-framed paintings hanging over the mantelpiece. Jack conducted a whispered business with the madam in the corridor, and I sneezed into the handkerchief he'd given me during the movie-house hold-up. I sat in my overcoat and with my palms rubbed at my unshaven face, feeling consumptive, rheumatic, hollow. As I lit my cigaret Jack entered the room with four trollops in tow. A maid brought a tray of canapés, followed by several buckets of ice and wine on a cart surmounted by an enormous bottle of Champagne. Nine hundred and eighty-five dollars was a good year's pay for some.

"Ladies," gestured Jack.

The four girls positioned themselves around the salon in studied artless arrangements.

"We are," Jack said, "representatives of a young men's Christian temperance society and have come here tonight to gauge the pernicious effects of this devilishly bubbly stuff on winsome young maidens. Would you care to aid us?"

The girls gave a united cheer of agreement. Each was done up in a manner anachronistic with the room's fittings. They sported kohled eyes and wore black stockings rolled down to the knee, slim-cut short dresses, high-heeled shoes, and long-looped paste pearl strands around lithe white necks. Jack began building a pyramid of crystal goblets, then uncorked the massive Jeroboam and with two hands poured its contents over the construction. Beside me the young blonde screwed a cigaret into her ebony holder. She was blue-eyed, her face made up into a pout, a tempting indifferent moue. It was rare I frequented whores, loath to catch syphilis. This time was different, somehow, Jack paying the piper and calling the tune, conducting a farce that might banish Laura from my thoughts. Always she'd played prude with me, during my failed courtship, but I'd suspected her nonetheless: she'd protested too much. Since last October, a good year ago, nearly anything might've happened. Who was she with at that dance Jack had mentioned? Where was she right now? I shook my head and looked over to my paid sympathizer. She looked back and blew smoke into my face.

Bob rose and revealed a talent besides painting and armed robbery, laying down jazz on the piano, singing out in a nice tenor: "I've got some good news honey, an invitation to the Darktown Ball. It's a very swell affair, all the highbrows will be there. I'll wear my high silk hat and my frock tailcoat, you wear your Paris gown and your new silk shawl. Ain't no doubt about it babe, we'll be the best dressed in the hall."

Wine went 'round. A pair of the girls got up and turned a two-step together. The one next to me emptied her glass in a swallow. I leaned over to fetch some more, charging her goblet and then my own, following her lead by pouring it down my neck. Jack took down a pornographic engraving from the wall and placed it on his whore's lap, the better to sniff cocaine from. My blonde went and joined them. Bob switched the player to a printed roll and the instrument churned out ridiculous hurdy-gurdy blather. Bob danced with the pair of trollops on the rug. My girl came back licking her lips.

"How much do you charge for a kiss?" I asked.

She eyed me, took a puff, and exhaled more smoke.

"What's your name?" I asked.

A pause while she thought about it.

"Celeste," she lied at last.

"Heavenly," I said.

I lit a Consul. Jack handed over the picture frame and I took some of the drug. The divine Celeste regarded me dully. The print on my knees showed a scene from the *Satyricon*, or the Bible.

In my mind molecules began to break apart like Champagne bubbles. What was his name, the fellow who'd split the atom? A Cambridge man, from New Zealand. He'd taught at McGill for some time. Rutherford. All we needed was a calliope and a dancing bear to complete this circus with the pig-faced woman from county Cork to round it out. Science baffled! Zoologists stumped! A wonder to behold!

"Hey," I shouted at Jack over the growing din. "The Midget King of Montreal has a son and heir. He's showing himself and the bairn at His Majesty's palace on Rachel, a nickel a gander. A toast!"

I raised my glass. Jack guffawed.

"I've seen him," said Jack's blonde.

"That so?"

The devil was on horseback in my bloodstream now. I drank more wine.

"The most darling little man," said Jack's blonde. "He's a count or a baron, I think. And his wife's from Europe."

"The Midget Queen?" asked Jack.

"I believe so."

Here Celeste turned and gave me a strangely sweet smile, one nearly genuine.

"Have you ever seen a ghost?" I asked her.

"A ghost?"

"Yeah. Been busy tonight?"

"I'll say," she said. "We had that fat baseballer in here."

"Who, Babe Ruth?"

"Yeah, him. They almost had to call the cops on him he was so drunk. What a pig."

"You ever been to Coney Island?"

"Where's that?" she asked.

"Forget it. Where're you from?"

"Not here, that's for sure."

"What was your name again?"

She sought it for a second, twirling her costume pearls.

"I told you. Celeste."

"Right."

"What's yours?" she asked, brightening.

"Michael," I said.

"And where're you from?"

"Far west indeed."

"You don't say," she said.

"I'm starving," I said.

"So eat something," she shrugged.

There was Brummagem trash on the plates, limp cheese on toasted crusts. Instead of food I chose drink. Jack started talking to his whore about a friend of his.

"He lost a hand at Wipers. The left. We met in the hospital after I was gassed. Bugger carved himself a new one from a piece of mahogany we scrounged from a church. Four fingers and a thumb, just like Captain Danjou."

"Who?" asked the whore.

"*Légion étrangère.* Anyway, we went to a party in Belgravia somewhere after we got out and he held it over a lamp until it caught fire, and lit the candles on a birthday cake with it. That was a great night. He was a hell of a guy, for a Hasty Pee."

Jack's whore laughed.

"Hastings and Prince Edward Regiment," Jack said.

"What happened to him?" asked Jack's whore.

"He died. Survived the Western Front to die of 'flu home in Berlin, Ontario."

There was one of those silences, Jack looking elsewhere. The brothel's electric current throbbed and made the light filaments flicker. We were in a stroboscope, spinning around.

"Did you ever see that Charley Chase where his best man tricks him into thinking his fiancée has a wooden leg?" asked Jack's whore.

Bob was with the two other girls and they lifted the Jeroboam and poured the lees into his yap.

"Your friend looks too young to have fought," said Celeste.

"He lied his way in."

"What about you?"

"I was on a troopship when they announced the Armistice, then I got 'flu myself. Almost croaked in hospital."

I drank more wine. Celeste was beginning to get on my nerves. Things were becoming crookeder, my resentments hatching in the amniotic cocktail of Champagne and cocaine. Too much happening. From another room sounded louder music, perhaps a bunch of aldermen whooping it up. This whorehouse felt in-between, like a limbo. Criminals, prostitutes, burghers, divines, here until our indulgence was paid for. Soon our bottles would be bottom-up in their buckets of melted ice. Dead soldiers. I wondered what'd happened to Jack's sharkspine stick. Bleaching bones in the sun. My own body one day hewn apart on the dissecting table, organs weighed and bottled in formaldehyde, the flesh sliced and boiled away. My scalp worn on an Iroquois war belt, finger bones strung on tendons to sound as they rattled together in a north wind outside the tepee, my knuckles used as dice by gambling savages. Bob and his whores were at the piano singing "It Ain't Gonna Rain No More." Jack was talking to his blonde about Freud.

My eyes glazed over. The drug and wine were working me numb. If one places a small amount of cocaine on the tip of the penis it aids reduction of sensation and prolongs coitus. I thought about the filthy Irish hospital that'd nearly killed me and a streetwalker I'd picked up along the bank of the Liffey who'd almost given me a dose. There'd been several weeks where I'd hardly breathed before finally passing my Wassermann test. Would Celeste fail the same? How many had she lain with so far tonight?

"How're you feeling, honey?" solicited Celeste, in her best professional manner.

"Every day in every way I am getting better and better," said I, and threw my Champagne glass into the fireplace.

She squealed, grabbed a bottle, and fell back in the chaise with me. Her face powder started smearing and I could see traces of cocaine around her nostrils. I put a wine-wetted fingertip to the drug and then placed my finger in her mouth and she looked at me as she suckled at it with her hot mouth and squirming tongue. A professional, indeed. I wanted to steal kisses with Laura again in the open yellow sightseeing trolley headed up the mountain in the spring sunshine. This one wouldn't kiss. I could tell. With wine back in her mouth I asked about it.

"Some do," she said, swallowing.

"Do you?"

"No."

"Why not?"

"It's unhygienic."

BOB AND HIS WHORES staggered out of the room. I wondered what time it was. The lights were low and through the walls I heard a gramophone skipping.

"Pete!" I shouted at Jack across the distance between us, about five feet.

"What's that, Sam?"

"Remember the Wolf?"

"The Wolf," Jack said, and raised his glass, spilling fluid.

Jack's blonde giggled and drank from a bottle's neck.

"What happened in the woods?" I asked.

"Later," he said.

"And what about tonight?"

"Worry not, my son."

"I was going to leave. Take a train."

"Don't worry about it."

"No future in this," I said.

"Not much."

"What happened to us?" I asked.

"We got old."

The door burst open. Bob being kicked backwards. The whores screamed. I pushed up from the cushions and woozed to my feet. Three men wearing suits and Mackintoshes forced their way in. Cops? Jack chucked a bottle and plonked the first man square between the eyes. The intruder dropped and his compatriot charged Bob and threw him against a wall. Bob in his shorts, his jacket in one hand, shoes in the other.

"Lousy fucking Frogs!" Bob shouted.

The Mackintosh hit by the bottle lay on the floor. Jack rushed the man pinning Bob to the wallpaper. Jack's whore screamed and pointed: "Dot!"

Celeste looked at the third man in the doorway and her face fell in shock.

"No," she mouthed.

The third man tensed for his move. I lurched at him and was met by his fist sinking into my gut. Down on my knees, I gasped and grabbed at his ankles, trying to pull him down. He kicked at my head but missed and stumbled onto his back. From behind Jack shoved me through the door. I stepped on my attacker's soft groin and my heel glanced a live throat. Jack kicked and Bob staggered behind, trying to pull his gun from his jacket pocket while juggling his wardrobe.

"My pants..." he gestured.

"Bob, no," Jack yelled, pushing the gun out of sight. "Go!"

Shouted curses chased us out. We blundered through the foyer and out onto the wet porch, pushing down the steps and trying to run at a pace. I gagged and retched. Jack held me up as we stumbled along. Bob swore.

"Cops?" I wheezed.

"Bob," Jack growled.

"Those lousy fuckers," said Bob.

WE ROLLED DOWN the street and turned left at Sherbrooke. Jack still had the money case of silver. My share was safe upon me. After a few blocks we came to the gates of the university and moved just inside the wall under the bare boughs of an oak. I lay in damp leaves, enveloped in the heavy odour of dirt and sweet decay, looking up at faraway stars visible behind breaking clouds above.

"Jesus, Bob. What the hell'd you do to them?"

"They were the ones came after me," he protested, "just as I was getting started. They called me something and stuck their mitts on one of the girls."

"Maybe they thought you were someone else," I said.

"It could have been a divorce set-up gone wrong. Wrong room, wrong party," Jack said. "Or a lover's quarrel."

"You need a motion passed in the Senate to get a divorce," I said, unheeded.

The punch to my stomach had sobered me up properly and still throbbed. I remembered the look on Celeste's face as she saw the third man. It was a lover's quarrel and we'd been caught in the middle, our luck.

"Well, at least they weren't coppers. But what'm I to do without my pants?" asked Bob.

"If anyone asks tell them you're training for the Olympiad," Jack said.

"Yeah, the hundred yard bum's rush," I said.

Bob gave me a dirty look.

"Go on home, Bob, and ring me in the morning," said Jack. "Cut through the grounds here and no one'll see you."

The pair shook hands with a solemn formality. I was propped up against the tree trunk now and nodded. While Bob hurried away Jack lit a cigaret and jangled the case full of coins.

"How're you feeling?" he asked.

"Better."

I extended a feeble hand to cadge a drag. Jack looked around.

"Do you miss this place?"

"I wasn't cut out for the healing arts."

"I'll say. A degree's not worth a damn these days anyhow. Regard this august acreage. Fancies itself a shining beacon. Damn spread's a charnel house just like everywhere else, an Indian graveyard. Look at McGill himself, that Scotch bastard. You won't find the story on the Founder's Elm of how he made his gelt and endowed this pile. You know what it was?"

"No."

"Black ivory. That's why I don't give a tinker's for the bootlegging. What's that compared to blackbirding across the Middle Passage? A joke. Nowhere near to. It doesn't matter, and that's the secret of our bloody Dominion: money buys respectability. Simple. Whole country's a monument to robber barons. All you have to do is found a library or endow a charity for strays. Yesterday's blackhearted thieves are today's grand old men. Just you watch: the Bronfmans and the Gursky boys will be held up as paragons of rectitude once Prohibition's over. Money's clean the more you have. That's just what I'm after. An honorary doctorate and a dean's dinner. Brandy enough to float you downriver. You wait and see. Where're you staying?"

"I'm between hotels at the moment," I said.

"Come on, then. I'll whistle you up a cot at my place."

We travelled along deserted streets, the city sawing logs. No traffic or noise. Jack had rooms at the Mount Royal Hotel.

"Isn't this a mite conspicuous?" I asked as we ghosted down its stately corridors.

"No. It's the same thing. Money buys discretion. I tip the house dick an extra sawbuck and it's as though I was never here. It'll be like that tonight at that knocking shop. The madam'll write us off and the girls will be told to forget. They're probably already with another group of upstanding citizens. Clergymen, say. What would your venerable father be saying about we two now, I wonder?"

"There aren't many passages in the Scriptures dealing with being turfed from a whorehouse," I said.

"On the seventh day, no less."

In our youth together Jack and I'd been abjured from turning a hand of a Sunday. It meant no baseball, no newspapers, not even a ride on a buggy or bicycle. Such were the joys of living in the household of a Presbyterian minister. The town had been entirely of my father's temper, with Lord's Day and blue laws that near enough shut Vancouver down 'til start of business Monday morning.

"Ach, lad, I'll not have ye eyeing strumpets at the kinema," said Jack, in a fair approximation of the Pater's voice.

From a bottle on his dresser he poured me drink. I swallowed a combination of whiskey and thick salt.

"What is this?"

"Mongoose blood."

"You jest."

"Not at all."

He sat on the bed across from me. Inevitably it'd been Jack who'd rebelled and challenged Jehovah. He vanished after lights out one Saturday evening and was not to be seen with the amah and myself in our pew for Sunday service. Instead Jack took his schooling on Skid Road amongst the loggers, Indians, and badmashes.

"Thinking on the time you stopped coming to the kirk," I said.

"So was I. Won two hundred dollars playing fan tan that morning in a den on Pender."

"The Pater preached the fourth commandment as his text."

"Which one's that again?" asked Jack. "Coveting asses?

I laughed and swallowed more of the awful cocktail.

"Let me see your arms," Jack said

I stood, shucked off my coat, and rolled up my sleeves. None of the marks were recent.

"Good. I want to make sure I can rely on you."

"Are you going to tell me what's going on?"

"In the morning. Get some rest."

Perhaps Jack's addition to the nightcap was a soporific. I faded away in my chair in fair imitation of death.

MONDAY

COFFEE CUPS CLATTERING on a tray woke me from an erotic reverie. My clothes were wrinkled and wet, a skin ready to be sloughed off. Muscles spasmed across my back, accompanied by a small hang-over. Jack was up and whistling, in the chips again. I had over a thousand dollars now when two days ago I'd been near my last buck. The Webley was on the table next to the coffee. I yawned, stretched, and asked the time.

"Time to call the tune," Jack said.

"Did you slip me a Mickey Finn?" I asked.

"Now that'd be apt."

"Chloral hydrate, I mean."

"I know. Get up, Hippocrates."

"I need a shave," I said.

"Surely."

I yawned again and took some coffee and a cigaret from a box by my chair. Having never made it to any cot I'd slept upright in third-class. Jack kept whistling "Annie Laurie." I smoked and thought.

"What's next?" I asked.

"You'll see. Get ready."

Less than an hour later the preliminaries were complete. I'd bathed and scrubbed my teeth with a cloth. Jack loaned me a spare suit and hat, both a mite large. My lips turned numb from bay rum the barber spilled on them. Ether would have been nicer, or morphine, bedamn. We left the Mount Royal and caught a streetcar east, turning northerly up St. Lawrence Main. It was a crisp autumn day, windy and fresh with great armadas of cloud invading the sky, a lively, peppery spice to the air. We stood holding the 'car's straps, jangling along the boulevard.

"See the 'paper there?" Jack nudged.

A wizened gent held a folded section to his face. I managed to make out that Loew's movie house had been robbed last night. Here I was in the news at last. Clip the article and mail it home to the Pater, for joy.

"I was right," Jack said in my ear. "The Southerner is claiming seven thousand was taken. As though a week of rotten Vaudeville and an old flicker or two could net that much!"

I squinted. "What else does it say?"

"He can't describe the thieves. Proves my point. The man doesn't want us caught. He'd lose four grand from the insurance company and be up on charges himself. You hungry?"

I was and said so. We hopped off near Duluth and went into a Hebrew delicatessen for meat sandwiches, the sausage sticks called nash, and more coffee. Jack used the toilet and met me back outside. On the boulevard an ice cart trundled behind a woebegone nag and kids fooled around in the gutter. Women walked by, resembling Mennonites in their odd poke bonnets. We passed an old Gypsy crone wearing a necklace of gold coins, Franz Joseph thalers. The street whiffed of coalsmoke, piss, horse manure, and burnt toast, that smell often a harbinger of a cerebral stroke. Trepan me with a cranial saw per the dicta of Dr. Osler, my brain simply the enlarged stem of the spinal column. Remove the offending hemisphere.

We walked onto Fletcher's Field past the Grenadiers' redbrick armoury and onto a greensward. Park Avenue and the mountain were ahead, a skeleton scaffold of an unfinished cross stark against the western sky. Before us an angel posed on a column, her arm outstretched to salute us as we crossed the turf.

"So tell me," I said.

Jack kept walking, hands in pockets, as he explained what happened. He'd gotten out by the skin of his teeth. The competition had been tipped off in advance. Jack was out five thousand dollars for failure to deliver. That was his reasoning behind the comedy at the theatre.

"It didn't seem quite your style," I said. The Webley was chafing me; I'd need a holster soon.

"Needs must when the devil drives."

"So you only have what we took last night? Do you want my stake?" I asked.

There was true gratitude in my offer. I'd be up queer street if not for Jack, despite the danger he'd put me in.

"Thanks, boyo, but it's not nearly enough. Hell, I bet on Dempsey to win in Philly last month."

That was bad. The Manassa Mauler lost his belt to Gene Tunney in a decision. Now the money we'd stolen was to go to work as a grubstake. Jack needed to find out who sang the tune on him, and Loew's would pay our way. Jack said that he'd always worked on the supposition that his higher-ups were the Chicago mob but in Plattsburgh he found out that the money and orders came out of New York.

"Plattsburgh?" I asked. "How'd you wind up there?"

"When the lights hit us my driver stepped on the accelerator and I shot our way through until we plowed into a tree. That did it for him, he was crushed. I got out and ran a circuit and came out behind one of their 'cars with a flunky behind the wheel. Put my iron to his neck and we got out of there. In Plattsburgh I learned who he was working for."

I knew Jack had been seconded to an English military police unit after being gassed. They'd taught him things, seemingly. Interrogation.

"Did you kill him?" I asked.

"No, but I'd hate to pay his dentist's bill."

The flunky was working for a New York outfit, competitors of Jack's connection. The rivals had been given a schedule and a map of our route and told to grab the shipment. The trucks and drivers for our convoy had been supplied by a Frenchman here in Montreal who owned a garage. It had to have been either him or our drivers who'd tipped off the opposition.

"Who's this Frenchman?" I asked.

"A lawyer and hustler in tight with the local politicos, a Grit bagman. He plays poker at the St. Denis Club and drops a bundle every weekend on the ponies. The garage isn't far. In Outremont."

"What's the idea?"

"Charlie mans the place alone every day at lunch. The two of us pose him a few questions. You game?"

Jack's suit was loose on me and I wore his hat. All I needed was to wear his shoes. How far was I willing to go in following him? The money on me wouldn't last forever. If I had more I could take another shot at Laura. Beyond those considerations was something stronger, something I'd nearly forgotten in my purdah. Jack had stood up for me my whole damned life and I owed him something. Moreover, life had become interesting again. I was curious to know what I'd fallen into. Besides, did I have anything better to do? How much of life is decided by that simple realization? I kept walking, which Jack took as my answer.

"It was strange you mentioned the Wolf last night," Jack said. "I've always wondered what happened to him."

"He's probably dead."

"I don't know. The man was one tough bastard. Did you know I saw him? Must have been in '16, just after I got in with the Dukes. Before shipping out I was down in Gastown for a spree and he was rolling around Maple Tree Square, spoiling for a fight. By damn, the man hadn't aged a minute or turned a hair. You remember how he taught us to scrap up in the camps? Where was that again?"

"Alexandria," I said.

"And hunt. Man, could he run down a deer. Never used a rifle. Caught them with his hands, like how your old man taught us to tickle a salmonbelly."

"Not us. Just you."

That set Jack back for a moment. He hitched his step.

"What'd the Wolf say?" I asked eventually.

"He was drunk and laughed at my uniform. Maybe he didn't recognize me. Anyway, he was shipping out himself on one of Dunsmuir's coal barges, to Yokohama."

"The Pater always had him as a dipsomaniac," I said.

"You know, I don't think he even knew there was a war on. He'd like this caper, though."

"The Wolf was crazy," I said.

"Damned tough, still."

We stopped and sat on a bench.

"What's the drill with this lawyer?" I asked.

Jack paused and offered me a Turk. Pressure might need to be exerted. We'd have to stay on our toes, as there might be employees about. The last thing either of us wanted was to attract the law.

"Are you off morphine for quits? asked Jack.

"You saw my arms."

"I need to be sure. We don't want any more surprises."

"Not from me," I said.

CONTINUING ON WE walked past the Young Men's Hebrew Association and turned up Park. The garage was a few blocks north and my role, as usual, would be to stand steady and watch Jack's back. It seemed simple enough. We continued until Jack indicated a corner filling station with a garage and house attached, the entire affair a collection of yellowing wood. The sign read "L'Etape Supertest Trudeau, Essence et Mécanicien." Jack checked his wristwatch. It was noon. I turned to face the sun above the mountain. The yard rested quiet, two trucks parked by a painted fence advertising Ensign oil. Through the glass of the garage door I spied an expensive Chandler sedan with its bonnet open. Jack considered the shop. Its door was locked and a sign read: "Fermé." The wind died and the neighbourhood seemed abandoned, a scene from a drowsy Indian summer afternoon in the country. The garage door had a smaller one set into it, that one ajar. We went through it to the repair bay's rear corner and a formal office. Jack stiff-armed the door to reveal a man standing and eating a sandwich over his desk.

"Assieds-toi, Charlie," said Jack.

I stayed in the doorway, my hand now on my gun in my overcoat pocket.

"Jack," Charlie said.

"Surprised to see me?" asked Jack.

"Non."

"Why's that now?"

"I hear about what happen Friday."

"Zut alors," said Jack, clucking his tongue.

Charlie was well-built and surprisingly dapper, with Brilliantined hair and a trim dark moustache. He had the narrow eyes and pointed nose of his race, a mixture of fille du roi and backcountry Huron. His posture was erect, defiant. Jack's tone remained playful.

"Who told you about it, Charlie?"

"I hear it from Martin," he said.

"Martin, eh? Let's do the arithmetic. One driver shot dead. That was Pollart. One driver with me died in a crash. That was Gellier. That leaves the one in the middle. Martin. So he got out. Very lucky for him. A little too lucky, *peut-être?* Don't you think so, Charlie?"

"I don't know," said Charlie. He still held his half-sandwich.

"Continue. You heard from Martin. *Et, comment?*"

"He call me. He escape, hitchhike. He demand from me some money."

"Did you give him any?"

"I don't see him. How can I?" asked Charlie.

"I don't like this story. Somebody told someone something they shouldn't've. *Comprends?*"

Charlie furrowed his brow, perhaps translating to himself. "*Oui.*"

"I think it was you," Jack said.

"What?" Charlie threw down his sandwich and pointed. "Why do I do that? I lose my trucks. I have police come here for to ask me questions."

"Police? What did they want to know?" barked Jack.

"The wife of Gellier, she tell them he work for me, now he depart and does not come home two nights. I pay her, she has three children. Where is my money, Jack? For the trucks, for me, *hein?* Where? I ask."

Charlie slapped his palm on the desk, eyes blazing.

"I want this Martin, Charlie," said Jack, unmoved. "You have three days."

"Why should I help you? You have not paid me!"

"Do you have insurance, Charlie? Smart lawyer like you, you should, in case accidents happen."

Jack turned and brushed past me out of the office. Charlie followed. In the garage Jack grabbed a long piece of iron like a tamping rod. I was now in the corridor behind Charlie, next to a door that must open into the house we'd seen from the street. I could smell Charlie's hair oil and sweat. Jack turned, the rod in his hands.

"Three days, Charlie."

He speared the rod through the Chandler's windscreen.

"*Hostie*," cried Charlie. He moved to stop Jack but I pulled out my gun and jammed it into his spine. The Frenchman turned his head and showed me pure hatred. Jack swung and smashed the side windows, beat on the sidings and ruined the metalwork. The door next to me opened inward and I kicked Charlie at Jack. Jack dropped the bar and connected a straight left to the Frenchman's jaw, dropping him. I spun and pointed my gun barrel into the face of a skinny little Indian-looking kid holding the doorknob.

"*Papa?*" asked the boy.

Charlie turned from his crouch on the floor.

"*Pierre, non!*"

I cuffed the child upside the head into a heap of tires. Jack lifted Charlie up by his shirtfront. Jack's skin was flushed red; he was angry, and when Jack was angry, he got mean.

"Three days, Charlie. I want Martin, I want answers, I want my money. Toot fucking sweet."

He let Charlie go. I put my gun back in my pocket and looked at the boy on the tires. He blinked tears from hot, angry eyes.

"Three days, Charlie," Jack repeated.

We backed out of the garage, and the boy ran to his father, Charlie nursing a dripping red mouth. The pair watched us leave with identical glares. This round was Jack's but the match wasn't over. We walked back to Park, where Jack hailed a southbound 'cab.

"The Ritz," he said, cracking his knuckles.

JACK SAT NEXT to me in the rear seat and played with a ring he wore on the small finger of his left hand. It was embossed with an emblem: a silver triangle in a circle. Something was bothering me as we drove back into town, but I couldn't place it. Something overlooked. My attention was quickly distracted by more pressing concerns, however, the peristalsis of my lower intestine. I had a vision of the perfect jakes the Ritz would have: spotless tiles and freshly scrubbed porcelain smelling faintly of bleach. There'd be milled French soap, hot water, clean white towels, and an underling to whisk my shoulders with a brush. As fate would have it traffic clogged Pine in a pack of stalled autos. I started to grimace. We waited fifteen agonizing minutes while Jack continued cracking his knuckles. I pinched shut my sphincter.

The hotel, at last. Jack paid the 'cabman and a uniformed Hussar wearing a tall bearskin hat eased us through the revolving door. We went downstairs to the bar and I shied off to the facilities. The gentlemen's convenience was better than could have been hoped for and I read a complimentary *Gazette* while I shat. Afterwards the aged attendant dried my hands and offered me a pastille. I checked my teeth in the mirror for caries and to see if my fillings remained. Gold from the entire map: the Rand, the Klondike, California, the tombs of Mycenae. I wondered if my grave would one day be robbed and the grains in my teeth melted down for jewellery, transformed into a necklace for a maiden's throat in nineteen hundred ninety-nine. I spat out the sweet; for the fossil's help I rewarded him a nickel and went to the bar.

An American sat talking to Jack about Coolidge's trade policies. At the snap of fingers a venerable sommelier ceremoniously opened a bottle of wine. Jack and I treated the Yankee, who saluted the liberal liquor laws of the North.

"It's what I like about your country," he said.

"What's that?" Jack asked.

"Well, number one, none of our Puritan hysteria. I tell you, sometimes it almost makes me blush to think of what they're trying to sell us in the States. Take that trial in Tennessee last year. Darrow showed Bryan up for a damn fool and the Bible for a pack of howlers, and he still lost! In the twentieth century! Evidence of science's progress everywhere around us! Now, lookee here, evolution's a fact, sure as this is fine wine, which I thank you gentlemen for. Now what are you going to believe, a book scribbled by Moses wandering in the desert three thousand years ago or one typed the other day by Mr. Einstein? What I mean is, we all know why the sky is blue, don't we?"

"Something to do with the sea?" I ventured.

"Precisely."

The American drank. I waited for him to lay out the second point of his argument.

"What're you selling?" Jack asked.

"I'm glad you asked, young fellow. Let's call it peace of mind."

"Jesus," Jack said.

"No sir, but I do know some Bible salesmen. Good men, most of them, but they dip into their goods too much. Wouldn't stand it in a whiskey merchant and it's the same damn thing with Scripture pushers, rots the brain. Now, I was in Burlington just last night at a commercial hotel and I met one of these fellows. Here, I'll show you what I mean. He sold me a book that you gents might be interested in. I have it right here, a real pip."

The American rummaged through his valise and found the volume in question.

"*The Man Who Nobody Knows*. Take a listen to this." Our guest opened the book to a marked passage and read: "'He picked up twelve men from the bottom ranks of business and forged them into an organization that conquered the world...

nowhere is there such a startling example of executive success as the way this organization was brought together.'"

Beet-red with enjoyment, the American took another mouthful and continued: "This, though, is a gem. Sums it up right prettily." He cleared his throat. "'He would be a national advertiser today... the founder of modern business, the author of the ideal of service.'"

He guffawed and pounded his fist on his knee.

"Can you beat that? The Messiah in a three-piece suit reading stock quotes on a tickertape? I don't know whether to laugh or cry. On the one hand we're the most advanced nation on earth, begging your pardon, and on the other we're superstitious as a bunch of Pygmies. Selling Jesus to the poor and needy in the guise of a Goddamn tycoon. The man would cast down the lot of them for profiting from the world's misery."

"We're not much better," Jack said. "We've got our own Prohibition and the Ku Klux Klan, and if you want superstition drive five minutes out into the countryside. Talk to the peasants out there and you'll learn Jews have fangs to drink blood from God-fearing Catholics and that the loup-garou roams the woods."

"Where're you from?" I asked the American.

"Baltimore, Maryland," he said. "Home of the sanest man in the Republic."

"Mencken," said Jack.

"Beano."

"Speaking of trials," I asked, "do you think they'll execute those Italians?"

"If they don't I'll eat my hat. The only thing the government's more frightened of than Reds is Anarchists. They'll make an example of that pair, count on it. Remember, no one ever caught whoever it was bombed Wall Street a few years back. If they want to keep the Babbitts and the booboisie happy and sinking their pennies into fly-by-night stock they'll gas them or hang them or put a bullet in their brains."

"What, no electric chair?" I joked.

"What brings you to town?" Jack said, sinking the last of his wine.

"Keep it to yourself but I've got a hot line on a dehydrated vegetable soup company. Thanks again for the tip-top tipple. Be seeing you, fellas."

He whistled a waiter over, settled his bill, shook our hands, and was gone, taking his bulk and gravity with him but leaving his book behind.

"Now Mick, me lad, you must excuse me but I've a few appointments to keep. Where can I reach you?"

"I'll probably get a room at the Occidental."

"What name?"

"I don't know."

"Use your imagination."

"Smith," I said.

Jack sighed.

"Well, if you need me I'm under Standfast at my hotel. Ring me tomorrow and keep the evening open. We'll meet. Oke?"

"You bet."

Jack popped his hat on and stood up. I showed him the palm of my hand so he shrugged and slid out of the bar. I quickly paid the tab and followed, wanting to see if I could shadow him and get a sense of the larger picture, his connections in this mess. I knew of Brown the Customs man, Bob, and now Charlie the lawyer in Outremont. There was the missing driver Martin and the Lord knows who else. What I really wondered about was the identity of Jack's bosses. How was he fixed up? I skulked out onto the street and watched Jack cross Sherbrooke only to climb the steps up into the Mount Royal Club, where the burly gorilla at the door let him through. Perhaps there was a way I might insinuate myself inside, fake moustache, tradesman's stoop. No. I had none of the play-actor in me. I couldn't pull off any foolishness of that sort. Theatricals were one of Laura's delights, a taste she shared with Jack: charades, dramatic readings, songs around the piano. A suspicion slowly metastasized within me, and I chewed off a fingernail, chopping the crescent of keratin between my teeth. Laura's father was a greybeard at the Mount Royal. I swallowed the nail and walked to the station.

THAT AFTERNOON WAS spent getting my grip and renting a room. I bought a sheaf of magazines from a newsstand to while away my life, the green-covered *American Mercury*, *Harper's*, *The Goblin* from Toronto for a laugh and *Black Mask* for thrills, plus a book of bathing beauty photos in case of self-abuse. At the Occidental I found a plain and quiet room where I put my few things in order. The hidden picture of Laura and myself fell to the floor. The snap was worn at the edges from where I'd handled it. A moment out of time.

I picked up the telephone and asked the operator to put me through to the Dunphy residence. A maid answered. My throat constricted and I severed the connection. I sat on the bed in my shirtsleeves with my head in my hands. Jackass. Too old to be playing childish games of love. She'd led me on, Old Nick knows why, and finally dropped me without a qualm after all the devious stratagems I'd concocted to slip her lovelorn letters, all the artfully orchestrated chance encounters in social settings. I'd been stealing morphine and selling it to finance my romantic campaign. Was it any wonder that after Laura pitched me I began taking my own medicine? Soon enough I was skipping lectures and duties at the Royal Victoria. The money melted away. I became careless and was caught out. Or near enough.

And no Jack to save me. Same as in the years after the war: he vanished. The Pater received postcards from San Francisco, Montana, London, then nothing. No one knew.

After I returned from service my father sent me to a local college where we adopted Oxford bags and played golf between semesters. I'd picked up enough chemistry and biology to be accepted for medical studies here in Montreal, just in time for Jack to show up out of the blue, claiming to be enrolled in Divinity, one of his jokes, belike, but one never knew. Perhaps the Pater's influence over him and a wish to atone. For what? Go ahead, Mick, and pound sand.

Jack and I were Methuselahs amongst the stripling freshmen two years ago but we weren't alone; my classes were filled with former soldiers playing catch-up after the war. Four semesters was all it took for me to be out on my ear, out in the cold. I was too damn old now, twenty-seven, child of the last year of the last century. No, that wasn't correct. The century properly started in 1901, the year Queen Victoria died and took all the old certainties with her.

Unconsciously my fingers mimed the movements of preparing a solution, muscle memory. A steel hypodermic filled with release. Put the thought out of your head. Look at the marks on your pale skin. Smoke a healthy cigaret. Distract yourself. Think of what honourable work you can turn to, think about who you are, where you're from. You're the son of a Presbyterian minister born beside the Cariboo Road. You spent your childhood in mining camps and at the mouth of the Fraser, a motherless boy on the shore of the sea with a wild child for a friend, a changeling, a cuckoo's egg taken under the Pater's wing. Jack, brother and bane, wide and expansive where you're narrow and small. Do yourself a favour: stare out the window into the city and a world spinning out of control. You're nothing, not a mechanic of the human machine, not a son or a lover but a criminal, a short-term ex-soldier unbloodied in war, an Irish Protestant, the worst of all worlds.

I picked up the 'phone again and screwed my courage to the sticking place. Into my ear came the operator's nasal voice, an electric screech as the connection plug was fitted into its hole on the board and a click as the receiver was picked up at the other end of the line. The same maid answered.

"May I speak with Miss Laura Dunphy, please?" I asked.

"And whom shall I say is calling?"

"Professor Edwin Drood, McGill University."

"One moment, if you please."

The maid sounded like a Scotch domestic cleared from the Lowlands to serve different masters on the igneous North American rock. A new indenture, wearing wool while her mistress was clad in silk. Laura copper-haired and cool-eyed, the cat of the house. A muffled sound and then her, her voice low and thrilling.

"Hello?"

"What're you doing tonight?" I asked.

"Who is this?"

"It's me."

Silence. Then: "I thought that you would understand how I felt when I failed to accept your last invitation."

"That's the best you can come up with?"

"Honestly, this is too tiresome."

"Not like dancing," I said.

"I am sure that I do not know what you mean."

"Think about it."

"Michael, you are threatening to become a bore. Have you anything purposeful to say?"

"Laura, you're not talking to Little Boy Blue here. There's a strong possibility I might be leaving town for good and I'd like the chance to see you before I go."

"And where are you going?"

"Far away."

"I'm afraid that I am not at liberty to see you."

"'My love swears that she is made of truth, and I do believe her though I know she lies.'"

"Michael, stop this."

I hung up. Full stop.

Depression seized me. I opened the window and smelled snow. I thought of my revolver and my temple. It was already past dusk. Oh, but the poor chambermaid who'd find this ruined body. There'd be another girl, a knock-kneed number in a sunny small town. I picked up the 'phone again for the front desk and ordered coffee, then leafed through the magazines in search of some truth. Instead of revelation I found tooth powder advertisements and cures for halitosis. There was nothing real, nothing like Laura in a black coat, black gloves on her elegant hands standing beneath a tree amongst the fallen chestnut leaves, her long hair blazing fire in the October evening light. Or had that been a painting in the Museum of Fine Arts?

The coffee came but I sent it back down on the pretext it was stale. I started pacing, a kind of chattering voice chasing and echoing itself inside my skull. On the dresser was a wireless and I turned it on to the sound of a cat being strangled. The steel whisker went up and down the wire, picking up dance music, hymns, a snowfall warning for farmers, and then nothing but crackling. The empty skies were filling up with voices: Morse code, radio transmissions, unknown electrical rays. Airplane propellers drilled through the atmosphere. It was too much for one such as myself, raised in youth on the fixed verities to be found in *Chums* and the *Boy's Own Annual*, tales of the Raj where cricket-playing adventurers always triumphed over dusky Arabs, the shaven-headed Bosche, and any stray Bengali tigers. It was a world with Kim astride the gun, Richard Hannay thwarting the Black Stone, and a sundowner under drowsy punka fans your just reward. We have got the Maxim gun and you have not. All of which had been torn apart one August morning in 1914, mowed down by ranks of machine guns and plowed under by percussion bombs.

I resolved to walk and clear my head. I would hustle a game of billiards on the lower Main, see a moving-picture show, do anything but trawl through that sea of memory filled with lost loves, squandered hopes, wasted time, embarrassing drunken antics. I rode the lift down to the lobby and then, outside the saloon, hesitated.

"BEG YOUR PARDON. Would you happen to have a light?"

She was a little older than I, well made up and wearing a light fur and a black velvet ribbon with a charm tied high around her throat. I fumbled a vesta towards her face. She touched my hand as she lit her cigaret. A woman alone. I tried to picture myself as I must appear to her.

"Are you from around here?" she asked coolly, regarding me from her perch at the bar.

"Enough to know my way around," I answered, scanning the room for its few denizens.

"I see. Where are you from, originally?"

"That's a very good question," I smirked.

She laughed and I saw the smallest touch of lipstick on a canine. The colour of her eyes was difficult to tell in the light.

"Well then, how long is 'enough'?"

"Two years," I said. "Two years too many."

"Don't you like Montreal?"

"Not particularly," I said.

"Why not?"

"Do you know what it is? I can't stand the way people complain about the weather here."

"It gets pretty cold in the winter, doesn't it?" she asked.

I started to warm up.

"Yes, but they've known that for four hundred years. It isn't as if it's a surprise every autumn when the mercury drops. The 'papers are always full of it as though winter's an unusual hardship or some blasted thing."

"People like to gripe," she said. "It's the way of human nature."

"Like I'm doing right now. Would you care for a drink?" I asked.

"How nice."

I snapped my fingers, showed the waiter part of my breadroll and beckoned him to follow us as we floated deeper into the room. The steward came and filled the lady's glass, as though by telepathy. The power of money. The woman settled into the velveteen of a quiet settee.

"Why are you here if you dislike it so much?" she asked.

"War in heaven, evolution—take your pick."

I was perched on the edge of my seat, a dry vermouth in a cool glass in my dirty hands.

"Clever fellow, aren't you?" she mocked.

"I failed charm school," I said, and lit a smoke.

She touched her hair. A tell, primping for me? Or was she on the job, signalling a watcher? What we had here was no randy young widow looking for kicks, that was for certain. She drew on her long, thin, perfumed cigarette. I became interested.

"And a lovely young lady such as yourself, what brings you unchaperoned to this church bee?"

She laughed and threw her head back. Her bosom swelled.

"I'm working."

My eyebrow raised itself.

"No, not like that. I'm in town for a show at the Palace," she said.

"Which one?"

"*So This Is Paris*. We're here 'til next Thursday."

"And they put you up in this dump? Why not somewhere decent, like the Windsor?"

"This isn't such a bad place. You're staying here, aren't you?"

"How'd you know that?" I asked.

"It's raining out. You're dry. Besides, staying here I can save a little money and get away from the rest of the company. When you travel in a group it's nice to be on your own once in awhile."

"And no show tonight?" I asked.

"The house is dark on Monday."

"Well then. Do you know Montreal?"

"A little. I've been here on other tours. It's changed. New buildings, new life."

"It's all the liquor money. Do you like jazz?"

"I play a character who does," she said.

"My name's Michael, by the way, but for some reason everyone calls me Mick."

My hand moved to hers. The bar was now deserted. A moustached bartender wiped a glass with a white cloth. It could be anywhere on earth.

"Lilyan," she said. "Lilyan Tashman."

"Charmed," I replied.

"*Enchantée*," she returned.

"So your character likes jazz but you don't?"

"No. I mean, yes, I do, of course, but not as much. She's a flapper, a real minx."

"That must be quite a stretch for you."

She narrowed her eyes and wrinkled her nose fetchingly. "Sauce. Buy me another drink and you can get away with that."

I bought her a drink and sat with her in our cozy nook, drawing in hints of her perfume. The low light favoured her features and I pegged her in her late twenties, early thirties. She was well put together and smiled ever so slightly as her eyes met mine— blue-green, I could now see, flecked with flaws. There was an amber spark as one facet refracted a mote of light. Lilyan opened her soft scarlet lips.

"Michael, what type of business are you in?"

"Wholesale freight."

"Meaning what?"

"Export trade, mostly."

"Anything in particular?"

"This and that. What the market wants."

"How evasive," she said.

"Do you like to dance?" I asked.

"I sing and dance for a living."

"I mean for your own amusement."

"From time to time."

"What's your next stop?"

"Detroit."

The minion poured another drink, and I purchased Sports- mans off a young girl walking past our table. Lilyan had slipped one shoe off and had her stockinged foot resting on a seat. I began to tingle.

"There's more to you than you're letting on. You're being dis- ingenuous," she said.

"We've just met," I said.

"Don't you trust me?"

"My amah taught me never to speak with strangers."

"What a thoughtful woman."

"My mother died when I was born," I said.

"How sad."

"So you'd think. Say, what's that scent you're wearing?" I asked.

"Lavender."

"It's lovely."

"Listen, Michael. Are you going to invite me up to your room now or later?"

"Now, I suppose."

"Bring a bottle," she said.

I waved the hovering waiter over to settle the bill and ordered booze be sent up on my tab. I crushed a ten into his hand to grease the gears. Miss or Mistress or Madame Tashman gathered her things and walked to the lift without turning to see if I'd follow. I made haste to join her and we were pulled up to my floor by the machine. In the hallway she curled her arm through mine and leaned into me, her walk a trifle unsteady. Who knew how long she'd been at the bar before I arrived. I unlocked the door to my room and turned to kiss her. She responded, putting her arms around my neck, returning my embrace with sweet slow kisses. I felt her warmth and tasted her painted lips. We broke apart.

"Not bad," she said.

She walked to the stuffed chair, trailing her fur over its shoulder, and curled up into the cushions like a little cat, her shoes kicked off to the floor.

"Music?" she asked.

I wrestled with the wireless to find some pleasant sounds. There was a knock at the door. My senses became alert. Perhaps it was the copy of *Black Mask* I'd been reading or just a general fear spooking me but in this part of the story the hero's distracted by a conniving female and doesn't keep his wits about him. It's always a set-up, and the next thing he knows he wakes up tied to a chair, seeing stars. I took my revolver out of the dresser drawer and held a towel over it. Lilyan's eyes widened but she sat perfectly still. I opened the door to a service cart loaded with iced Champagne and a pair of goblets. I signed for the goods and tipped the teenage porter a quarter-dollar in relief, then pulled the cart in and uncorked the wine.

"Export trade, my foot," Lilyan said. "Who are you really?"

"I'm nobody," I say.

"You act like a gangster. All jumpy. That's what I said to myself when I saw you downstairs."

"But you still approached me. What kind of dame are you? Are you on the make?"

"Would I have kissed you like that if I was a working girl?"

"Good point."

My hands poured wine and I passed her a glass. I tossed Jack's hat across the room and made to sit on the bed. My life had become a series of encounters with people in taverns, movie houses, hotel lobbies, and at ball games. Don't you have anyone of your own? Laura. No, to hell with her. Christ knew who she was with right now, frequent speculation. What had Jack said about seeing her at a dance? For that matter, where was Jack? The Mount Royal Club, the mayor's house, a gambling den, or penthouse suite? His course was impossible to imagine. Same as mine. Who was this woman sitting opposite? What was I doing?

Lilyan smiled and waggled her glass. When I came over with the bottle she reached up and pulled me to her. The lovely creature kissed me, and I kissed back. Softly she pushed me away to pull off her hat. I lifted her up while she peeled away her gloves. We locked together, swaying and turning with the music from the wireless, a low piano rag. She kissed me in the French fashion and stuttering black-and-white Nickelodeon images played out on the screen of my mind's eye. Lilyan moved in just such a way as to reacquaint me with the erotic reality behind feeble half-remembered pornography.

She anticipated me and somehow floated us elegantly to the bed and onto it, so easily, so smoothly, unfreighted with hesitations or fears. This was the modern age of love as finally revealed to me, with a modern woman who knew what it was she wanted.

She had none of the inhibitions of others I'd known. Lilyan pulled herself back by her elbows and propped herself up on the bolster, looking at me with sleepy blue eyes, her hair a dark blond unpinned and falling around her face, her full bosom respiring and breathing deeply, her throat flushed hot and pink. That black ribbon with a charm on it tied around her supple, delicious neck.

"Do you have a French letter?" she asked.

"*I grec*," I said.

"Ha-ha."

"I confess I don't normally carry a prophylactic on my person. I know I should. I was a medical man, after all."

"Were?" she asked.

"Not anymore."

"And what are you now?"

"I'm currently without portfolio."

"You're strange," she said. "But I like it."

"If you want I'll go out and see if there's a chemist's or barber-shop open. There must be somewhere."

"Why don't you hand me my purse?" she interrupted.

"You've done this before."

"Why not? It's legal and it's free."

Rummaging through her handbag Lilyan found a tin disc, a Merry Widow. A black bottle dropped to the floor and I picked it up.

"What's this?"

"You'll never believe it," she said.

"Try me."

"Belladonna."

"Nightshade? What on earth do you need that for?" I asked.

"Trick of the trade. We put a little white make-up at the corners of our eyes and a few drops of the stuff in. Makes your peepers look bigger and brighter."

"You'll go blind. It's poison."

"So's everything," she laughed. "Come on."

My boots were off and I poured more cold Champagne. The radio played a peppy number by the Happiness Boys about a man and a canoe and a cherry phosphate and what was the girl's name in the refrain?

Laura. I froze solid.

"What is it?" Lilyan asked.

"Nothing."

She drank my proffered cup of cheer and coaxed another kiss, more deeply now. She was right. We were two taxpaying adults of voting age. Together, with eager fingers, we unbuttoned my shirtfront, unhooked her corsetry, her tresses loose and tangling between our lips as we kissed, our lips together, mouths open, her tongue darting hot and wet into me and then she slipped from her underclothes like a hand from a muff and I felt her warm powdered skin beneath my hands as I caressed her. Her fingers were toying with me. There were light brown freckles on her heavy, swollen breasts. Her warm breath, her wet lips, her tongue again, lavender and wine. She looked at me with kind, amused eyes. I was rusty, out of practice, but she guided me out of my clothes and under the covers, teasing me, laughing, whispering in my ear: "Where's your gun, Michael?"

The wireless played a tone and retreated to a sea roar. A shaded electric light burned over the dresser. Lilyan helped the preventative device onto me and we began to fuck. I didn't care if it was going to cost me or not. I closed my eyes and got lost in her for as long as I could.

"So this is Paris," I said.

She laughed softly and sighed.

AFTERWARDS, SHE TOLD ME about her life.

"I'm from a small town in Illinois. Everything was peaches and cream growing up. We're Episcopalians and I remember church socials and watermelon and cake on the Fourth of July. I knew I wanted to be an actress after we did the manger scene one Christmas when I was ten. I was the Virgin Mary, if you can believe it. Well, since then I've done everything short of murder to keep clear of the life my parents were preparing for me. We were quality people, respectable, you know? There was a sweet boy they wanted me to marry, he's a dentist now, but I convinced them to let me go to a finishing school in Chicago first and live with my aunt. When I got there I was your standard moonstruck small-town girl milling around the stage door, desperately trying to get noticed. I sang, I danced, I did anything I could. After awhile my folks became suspicious and demanded I come home. Of course I couldn't. For them an actress was little better than a prostitute and in those days, well, anyhow, maybe they were right. But I stuck with it, and eventually I started to get a few small parts and my name in reviews. Just Vaudeville turns, but I wanted to be a real actress, like Sarah Bernhardt or Lynn Fontanne, you know, cosmopolitan, sophisticated. I made a little money in a couple of revues and got by teaching singing and the piano to rich little boys and girls. But it was a hard life, oh boy. And the men, well, they thought the same thing as my parents, that we were all just roundheels. This was before the war. That changed everything. My little brother was killed in France and I think it broke my folks. Then I told them the truth, that I was going to try my luck in New York and that was it. They told me they never wanted to see me again. Oh, but I had stars in my eyes back then, I doubt I'd recognize myself now if I climbed into Mr. Wells's time machine. I wish I could too, sometimes. Do you know New York? It's no place at all to be broke and alone so I got married! He was a swell fellow, a songwriter and we lived in a little apartment and I went out for auditions and honestly I don't know what happened. One play after another and parties and gossip and out-of-town revues and somehow ten years went by and here I am on the road again, babbling away. We're divorced now and I don't know how long I can hold down parts with all the young girls coming up to take the ingénue roles and soon enough I'll be playing mothers and spinsters and then what?"

She'd been kind enough to relate all this, considering at some point in the night my vigour had flagged, draining to nothing, and I'd withdrawn from her body ashamed and impotent. We'd lain together, smoking the rest of my Sportsmans as she plied me with tender gestures to placate the shame that moved through me. It happens all the time, she said. But hollow anger simmered. I wanted to break glass, destroy things, apologize on my knees. Pride prevented me, another weakness.

"And what about you honey, what's your story?"

It came out, halting at first. I omitted Jack. I was a backwoods boy, born in the Far West of mining camps and switchback trails through black forests. My father was a preacher of the Word in saloons and mess halls to the scourings of mankind, sinners lusting after gold, whiskey, and women. Finally he'd been given a summons to respectability from his elders down the river. We'd had a house in the West End of Vancouver by the sea, with my amah bringing me tea and our Japanese gardener bowing over flowers in the soft grey rain and cutting away Scotch broom and blackberry thorn. I watched Empresses at the port steaming away to Honolulu, Yokohama, Sydney, and Hong Kong, and CPR silk trains being loaded for back East. It was a youth of stolen firecrackers in Chinatown, of jabbering Cantonese and Chinook with the other boys, running wild. In the summer we swam in the cool water off Third Beach by Siwash Rock.

"What's that?" she asked.

"A faithful Indian turned to stone by a spirit as reward for his virtue."

The Champagne was long gone. It was perhaps now two in the morning. Lillian tried to tickle some more life out of me but her ministrations failed. Nitrates could help, chemicals from the dispensary or extracts by Chinese apothecaries: ground bear testes, rhinoceros horn, goat glands. My body betraying me. The humiliation forced a curt, cruel word to slip out and Lilyan flashed on me.

"Listen, you. I liked your look from the get-go and was feeling blue and lonesome and thought you might be good company. Now you hand me this guff after all I've done tonight. I'm not some floozy you can pay to go away, you know."

"I know. I'm sorry, it's just that . . ."

"What?"

She waited for my response.

"Christ, nothing."

"All right. I understand. It's not easy for a man."

"Please stop."

"What is it? Is it me?" she asked.

"No," I said.

"Because if there's anything you want me to do to help I will."

"You've done enough already. It's my fault. I've had a tough day, that's all."

"Doing what?" she asked.

"Nothing."

She left the bed, grabbed her shift and started to dress. I lay where I was, silent, biting my fool's tongue. She put on enough for propriety's sake and gave me a dead glance, then opened the door and exited without a word, stage right, down curtain, no applause. I got up and threw my cigaret in the toilet, closed the light and beat the pillows into a different shape. The sheets still held her scent. I went and opened the windows wide into the cold October air and stood naked and alone in the blackness of the night.

TUESDAY

THE NEXT MORNING I checked out of the Occidental and into the Wayside, nearer the station. There'd been something not altogether canny about the manner in which Lilyan Tashman had inveigled me into sharing her company. She had finagled herself quickly and efficiently up to my room, too sudden a seduction. My erotic appeal was not that strong, and yet she'd ended up leaving in what seemed a genuine huff. Was it really genuine? The woman was a professional, it would be wise to remember. Everything she'd told me might be a pack of lies. Since then, however, no danger had befallen me, none I knew of. By cultivating the notion that I was being singularly targeted I aggravated what the psycho-analysts would term a complex: paranoid persecution. Its symptoms were characterized by an unreasoning suspicion with regards to the malevolent motivation of others. Considering the circumstances, this conviction didn't seem entirely unhealthy. At the very least I was wanted by the police for robbing the kino, never mind my participation as accessory to other crimes. I knew a medicine I might take to palliate my fears: the analgesic morphine. I hankered after it with sharp pangs of need and hunger.

It was past time to purchase a proper suit and hat so I walked to the Old Town and found a three-piece worsted at the Hudson's

Bay Company in addition to a box of cartridges for my revolver. If inclined I might purchase pemmican, snowshoes, a muskrat skin. I wore my new habille out of the store and had Jack's duds sent to the Mount Royal Hotel. It was now noon and I felt a respectable member of society once more so I grabbed a newspaper and hunted up a cup of java.

In the broadsheet I read nothing but breathless copy on the queen of Rumania in Philadelphia. Turning my mind to the current situation aggravated doubts. There was more to Jack's scheming, larger plots, entangling deceptions. He was using me for some reason, as a penance or salve to his conscience, while at the same time manipulating me. If this criminal course continued, it'd behoove me to ferret out any potential dangers. That raised the question of where to begin my investigation. As it happened, and as always, idle speculation led me to preoccupation with Laura, her elegance, presence, her charm. My love curdling to sweet hatred.

Turning back to the *Gazette*, I sought anything further on the movie house robbery, but the story'd fallen out of the 'paper, its column inches now occupied by advertisements for cold creams and Hallowe'en stout ale.

I lit a cigaret and again attempted to puzzle out Jack's actions, but with such scant information it was too much to ask of my brain. Coffee rolled in my stomach so I got up and left a few pennies on the table by way of a gratuity, starting to feel ill and jazzed. While walking St. Catherine west one of Robert Service's poems rhymed in my head, perhaps prompted by the rhythm of my paces. Fugitive pensées straying, my parasite flicking its tail. Kill it with a dose of hard brandy, bite at a thumbnail and notice your trembling fingers. My hands were clean as I moved lightly over the sidewalk, stepping nimbly between pedestrians slowing to gawk at displays in store windows. I went into Morgan's and bought a snappy new brim, fifteen dollars for grey felt. Put Jack's in a box. Across the street in the square the Salvation Army murdered a hymn.

At the Mount Royal, Mr. Standfast was not in. I left Jack's topper at the desk and at last placed his alias, from the novel by John Buchan. Lingering awhile I thumbed through an antique, greasy copy of the *Canadian Illustrated News*. Later, something in the newspaper raised my ire. From the desk I cadged pen and paper and wrote:

TO THE EDITOR, *The Gazette*

Sir,

It has been said that an Irishman's only political plank is the shillelagh; nevertheless, an item in today's edition prompts a response. The Native Sons of Canada have yet again put forward a motion to adopt a new flag. The Red Ensign, it seems, is no longer good enough. Very well. This being the case, here is, and with all apologies to Dean Swift, my own modest proposal for Canada's banner. Simply, it should be a revised coat of arms, viz,

The shield: a potato on a bed of rice, symbolizing the country's two founding races, Irish and Chinese, supported by one pig sinister, for Ottawa, and one dexter beaver biting off its testicles, for the taxpayer.

The wreath: celluloid poppy flowers, symbolizing industry. The crest will be a carrion crow atop a battle bowler, our blazon resting on a field of green, for the almighty Yankee dollar.

The motto: *Proximus sum egomet mihi.*

Once unfurled, this new Canadian standard will surely fly forth proudly and lead forward this great Commonwealth we call Empire!

Yr. humble servant, &c.,

Mr. Charles Uxbridge Farley, Esq.

Montreal, Canada

I licked an envelope and sealed the little humdinger. Instead of a stamp I put down the *Gazette* office as a return address. It'd take time to get there, but I'd saved a penny.

When I left the hotel I dropped my epistle into a blue Royal Mail postbox, its coat of arms—a lion and chained unicorn—the English again, sticking it to their defeated subjects with every common appurtenance of authority, this year in the reign of George V. The King's name prompted the memory of hearing his high, quavering voice coming out the funnel of a phonograph player somewhere by Phoenix Park. I'd been let out of hospital at last, recovered from the 'flu, taking in the city's sights: the post office still a ruin from the Easter Uprising, Parnell festooned with ivy, Nelson's Column. A crowd stood near the Castle and listened to their sovereign, the first time his voice had ever sounded in public. Beside me a drunk punter blew a raspberry in derision and staggered off. The drunk was followed away by a sober man in an overcoat, Holy Ireland an island of informers, spies, Black and Tans, Republicans, myself in the year of Our Lord nineteen hundred and eighteen.

Before being demobbed I received my back pay and a wire transfer from the Pater. With a few pounds to spend I foolishly used them to travel up to the family's old stomping grounds in the north, in January, most miserable of months. Belfast had been bad: grimy, stony, cold, soaked in inky rain. Londonderry was worse, to my mind, crowded, closed off. I visited a maiden great-aunt and sat in a stuffy parlour drinking weak, milky tea in gloomy silence. She hadn't taken to my colonial accent, notwithstanding my uniform and pip. Perhaps it'd been the Maple Leaf at my collar or the fact that I'd started smoking asthma cigarets to strengthen my lungs and asked her for a whiskey against the damp.

The visit was your true eye-opener, and I understood a little of the Pater and why he'd left the Old Country. For a spell

I regretted he hadn't lighted out for an American territory but the old man had always been loyal to the Crown and pink parts of the map. Upon reflection, my fate might've been worse and I could have been born near the tailings of Ballarat or Dawson just as easily as the panned-out wash of Williams Creek. Then my mind returned to its jumping-off point and the Service poem, with its strange things done 'neath the midnight sun. Purposeless speculation, I thought. Might've this, might've that. If the Pater had stayed in New Westminster instead of following his ministry upriver my mother might've lived. Every turn of the paddlewheel led the poor woman closer to her grave, to my life in Alexandria, to Jack. Mine was a makeshift story. The sound of a police siren brought me back to Montreal and I stepped on a man's shoe at the corner of Guy. The stranger spat: "*Connard!*"

Taking that as a cue I got off the street and went to sit on a bench at Canada Place in wan sunlight. This city hated me. It was the same thing, the same damned streets, same rotten cafés and hotel rooms. Winter would worsen Montreal, make it even more petty and constricting. We weren't a generous people, by and large. Ours was a second-hand country with second-hand sentiments for second-hand subjects. The sheer vastness of the land did us in. Canadians were wards with no true say in the world, under the control of the Colonial Office, Whitehall, Parliament, the Privy Council, the Court of St. James's, the Crown on high. Maybe Borden had gotten us a seat at the table at Versailles and into the League of Nations but it was as though my countrymen were children wanting to dine with the grown-ups. We still jumped to attention at the red-tabbed brass's trumpet call, the "Ready, Aye, Ready" ethos of Laurier and Meighen. One would think that that spirit had been ploughed under at Vimy, but it hadn't, and now there were new pipers for us to follow, the banshee song of the south. It was ever thus, the Dominion pulled between paladins of Empire and plutocrats of the Republic, always in between and with no say in who ruled us. Canadians, it seemed, had inherited the worst characteristics of the English— snobbery, priggishness, supreme self-satisfaction, and purblind righteousness—and we'd combined them with the lowest Yankee traits: money hunger, small-town boosterism, false piety.

I was a welter of history with too much time on my hands. I picked myself up and walked back towards the main artery. Artery. The trembling one felt as morphine pulsed through the fibres on its royal road to the mind, there to soothe and unfold thought in all its textured variety. My use of the drug had never been emotional, leastways not at first. It had been an aesthetic addiction, a way to turn this brutal colonial city into a palace of memory and wonder, history and art. Here for example was Old Tomorrow in knickerbockers and robe, holding a scroll, the twin of his contemporary Disraeli. Across Dorchester stood a monument to Strathcona's horse against the Boer. I read its lapidary inscription, so very fitting: *Imperium et Libertas*. For that we'd fought Fenians and Louis Riel, had sailed up the Nile with Garnet-Wolseley to save Chinese Gordon at Khartoum and battled Ruskies at Archangel. Empire and liberty had put me in the itching wool of a Seaforth Highlander and sent me off to follow Jack in France. Two years ago it'd nearly led us against the Turk at Chanak until Rex King had done something no prime minister ever had before: politely declined the invitation.

Stopping at a stand I picked up another 'paper, the afternoon *Herald*, to read in the lobby of the Mount Royal. Splashed across its front page was an exposé of fraudulent spiritual mediums. A reporter had gone to a séance asking about an invented dead wife and from the seer received soothing messages from beyond the grave. The entire story had a phony wash to it. Betimes it clicked: Houdini was in town and this was manufactured publicity for his show. For an hour I lounged and read and watched a fat house detective with a short cigar stuck into his face lean against a column. The dick's lazy gaze at last left me to take in a tall blonde sashaying unevenly across the lobby's parquet. My ears pricked up when I heard her ask loudly for Mr. Standfast and I was just in time raising the 'paper to shield my face. It was the actress from the night before, Lilyan Tashman.

She looked grand in a plaid suit and skirt, wearing a Gloria Swanson hat and with some creamy silken stuff bubbling around her throat. She carried her handbag in one hand, and I'll be damned, a feather duster in the other. The house dick targeted her. He moved the wet stump of his cigar from his mouth to a dirty box of sand. A toady held the lift open and as Lilyan swept along the detective moved to intercept. She stuffed the duster in his face and twirled it 'round. The dick's hands went up and he pushed away, his piggish snout a rictus of disgust. Lilyan entered the lift. The uniformed cretin inside closed the door and cranked the lever while the dick sneezed sharply, once, twice, thrice, and reached out to steady himself on a wingback. I waited for the elevator to stop and noted the floor, then went and again asked at the front desk for Jack. The staff feigned ignorance, money sealing lips. I sidled around to the stairwell and climbed up to the sixth. When I reached it, panting, the hallway was empty. I couldn't remember Jack's room and so marked the doors one by one. Behind 618 came a familiar trickle of laughter. I waited five minutes, pacing back and forth, long enough to smoke my last Sportsman, then knocked.

"Who is it?"

"The Duke of Connaught," I said.

"Son of a bitch."

Jack opened the door. Lilyan was spread out on the chair I'd slept in the other night. Jack stood in his undervest.

"Thought so," said Jack. "You know the hatred I have for that bastard."

"Fine way to speak of your Grand Master."

"So it'd appear. Come in."

"Don't let me interrupt."

"Interrupt what? Look at her," Jack said.

I went into the room. Lilyan Tashman was glassy-eyed and had a shoe and stocking off.

"I didn't realize you two were familiar," I said.

"Friend of yours?" asked Jack, arching his eyebrows, all innocence. I smelled liquor wafting from him. He smiled expansively.

"We struck up an acquaintance last night, but you know that damned well."

"How'd it go?"

"Swimmingly. What's she doing here?"

"See for yourself."

Looking closer I noticed a glass ampoule, a length of cord, and a hypodermic.

"You won't be getting anything from her for awhile," said Jack.

Suddenly I was in thrall.

"What is it?" I asked, eyes fixed on the vial.

"I think you know," he said.

"You have any more?"

"Wrong question."

The bastard. My mouth flooded with chalky saliva and my gastrointestinal tract squealed. It was desire, not for the woman, but for the companion racing through her veins.

"Where'd you get it?" I asked.

"Ah, well, you see," said Jack, "this young lady is what you'd call a friend of a friend. Yesterday you seemed down in the dumps so I sent her 'round your way."

"I'm touched, really. It's a side I've never seen of you before, pimping."

"Goods satisfactory or money refunded."

"I'll take a rebate, then. In kind."

"It'd do you no good," said Jack.

"How do you know that?"

"Experience."

Jack's eyes narrowed. When drunk he was foxy.

"Come on, let's go for a wet."

"What about her?" I asked.

"She'll be fine."

I went and checked her pulse and breathing. She stirred and tried to focus on me. "Well if it isn't Mr. Nobody," she said, then her eyes rolled upward and she was gone into that world, feeling nothing but the warmth and glow of a false flame. I envied her. She'd be out for an hour or two. Her shoe and stocking had been removed so the injection could be made into her foot; as an actress Lilyan couldn't mar her arms with evidence of the spike. I'd noticed nothing the night before, more fool me. I lifted the pale warmth of her leg and placed it on a quilted rest. Jealousy wouldn't do—it merely fed Jack's amusement.

"What do you think?" he asked from the toilet.

"How is it you know her?"

"She moves in certain circles. You remember Bob, I'm sure. He's one with the theatre folk as well as his painters and bootleggers. We were introduced when her revue came to town last week."

"And you fixed her up," I said.

"More or less. For a price."

Jack re-entered, wiping his hands on a towel, then pitching it to the floor. The room had a heavy musk to it, an animal's lair.

"I'm touched you considered my comfort," I said.

"You have no idea, old salt. *Alors*, let's gargle."

In the lift I asked Jack if he'd gotten his suit and hat and he replied in the negative. He seemed complacent, unconcerned, and for a moment I entertained the thought he shared Lilyan's vice.

When the lift's doors opened, the lobby buzzed. The fat house detective had pinned a man to the floor as photogs popped flashbulbs. We sidestepped the tumult to a service door and a warren of hallways that emptied into a back alley. Around the corner was a low dark bar. Inside Jack absented himself for another piss. Flat beer was wearing on my palate and I wanted an astringent. Fielding a discreet enquiry the bartender agreed to let me have a bottle for two dollars as long as it was kept beneath the table, for form's sake. It was that kind of place. The bottle's label claimed that the hooch was Haig & Haig, which I considered almost plausible until the liquor peeled a layer of plaque from my teeth. After two glasses I felt I was in a coffin ship scudding under a hard lee wind. The tavern helped reinforce the sensation: instead of electric globes there were old gas jets that quavered in some unstopped draught. Places like it were salted away all across the country, remnants of a different age. It captured an echo of the mean twilight of the nineteenth century, now overwhelmed by the clean chrome of the twentieth. The other patrons appeared to be navvies or breakermen muttering over their poisons, with Jack and I visitors from some future age of airplanes and the wireless telegraph.

Jack returned at his ease and I said: "Sometimes I feel I was born in the wrong age."

"How do you mean?"

"It's because we come from the edge of the world. Back there we were Adams with every day the day of Creation. Some parts of the bush had never been trodden by whiteman or Indian. Imagine that! Your footprint the first one in all of time. No trails, no history, no ruins or monuments. Now I feel like I'm stuck in a machine. There're railways for the bloodstream, the telegraph for a nervous system, and hog rendering plants the stomach. I just don't feel a proper part of the whole system, like there's no place for me."

"Well man, it's high time you get used to it," Jack said. "It is a bloody machine, and there you've said it. If you're not damned careful it'll grind you up and feed you to some fat bastard as a Salisbury steak. That's what they did to us in France. A good thing Kitchener crashed into the North Sea or someone was going to put a bullet in him down the line. Both him and Haig, that whoreson."

"Ha!" I laughed. "It's his whiskey you're drinking, seemingly."

"Pah!" Jack spat. "We ship the stuff south but I won't drink the rot."

He sniffed suspiciously, picked the bottle up, and gazed at it, then laughed.

"No it's not. You almost had me there. If it was I'd black your eye. Never forgive the cunt for Passchendaele. If not for Currie I wouldn't be talking with you here now. You know what? I saw him a few weeks back when they were laying a cornerstone on the campus. He was in his chancellor's robes. Almost went up and shook the man's hand."

"You could've asked him about those mess funds he embezzled when he was with the militia back in Victoria."

Jack laughed again. "Water under the bridge. Ah, fuck it. I'll drink, but only with a toast. To Sir Arthur Currie: may he roast Douglas Haig's balls on a spit in Valhalla."

We drank. Jack looked at me. Against my better judgment I admired him. He was near-faultless in clean linen and a trim dark suit, with a gleaming crimson cravat and cool blue eyes. Irritated, I fingered my collar, already grimed after a day. There was always something about Jack, a distinction, with his height, features, red hair, and sang-froid. His person was coupled with a strange mutability, the chameleon's concinnity. Jack had no side to him. He possessed a taste that commanded each situation and never called attention to itself, was never garish or awkward.

Whereas I was ill at ease wherever I went, overdressed at a dive, underdressed at high tea. The rustic clung to me in my wrinkled wool. I looked like I'd stepped out of a daguerreotype of Ulysses S. Grant in his creased day coat. Jack was a creature bred for this new age as I was not. He knew me better than any alive and still I couldn't confide that shortcoming to him. I turned inward and worried at metaphoric scabs of resentments. Jack took another drink and began to wax expansive. In this mood I knew best to humour his vanity. It might lead to some answers.

"Where'd you get the dope?" I asked.

"Braced some Chinks for their deck. Same place I got the shooters, a fan tan parlour. Chinatown's rotten with hop. There was a raid coming up and I wanted to snaffle a few things before the police scooped it all."

"How'd you manage it?" I asked, impressed despite my worser devils.

"Sheer brazen cheek. It's mostly a matter of confidence. Convince yourself of your own authority and others will share your delusion. People want to believe what they're told. I learned that from the Pinkertons."

This was new to me.

"You were an op?" I asked.

"Aye."

Jack took another drink and filled me in. He'd answered an ad in San Francisco back in 1920 and with his service record they'd hired him on the spot. It'd been small potatoes at first: divorces, employee fraud, small-time shitwork.

"'We Never Sleep,'" I quoted.

"Truer than you realize. There were times."

"When?"

"Not supposed to talk about it. I was seconded to do some strikebreaking at the Anaconda. Don't want to even think about that. That was pure poison. Poisonville, another op called it. This was in Butte, Montana. Too much axe-handle work for him, I reckon. No stomach for it. Later on he and I worked on one of the strangest cases the outfit ever came up against."

"What happened?" I asked.

"Someone stole a Ferris wheel."

As he spoke, my thoughts drifted back to morphine, and Lilyan Tashman. Jack switched tack: "There's trouble ahead."

"Pardon?"

"My masters aren't pleased. I've been given a stern lecture. They don't like my explanations or my progress and're going to send someone in," Jack said.

"That's not good."

"You ain't whistling. They don't trust me. They think that I have something to do with that cock-up in the woods, that maybe I pulled it over their eyes and pocketed the take. These are some close sons-of-bitches I'm dealing with. They're not Bob's Irish gang or Hebrews like the Bronfmans or Gurskys, these are Sicilians, the worst kind of Guinea. Chicago's mostly Neapolitan, and that's a world of difference. I've heard there's another shipment due soon that'll head upriver and be portaged somehow to Detroit, maybe for the Purple Gang. They don't like the old route into New York anymore. Well I'm not point man and bearleader for this show, and that means I've been crossed off the list. I was their man here as long as it went and now I'm out in the cold. Therefore time is, as they say, of the essence. I've learned that they're going to make the transfer here in town because Montreal's still neutral ground."

"How do you know all this?"

"Brown. Remember him?" Jack asked.

I did. The Scotsman at Customs.

"Barbotte," I said.

"How'd you know that?" Jack fired, now sharp.

"I've got eyes."

"Do you now? Well, I still own him. I bought all his markers and he's mine, top to bottom. But he only goes so far looking the other way. The shipping schedule's wired down from Quebec and this boat's a known quantity. It hasn't touched land and won't do so until it gets here but they have to send a manifest ahead in territorial waters. Brown got his copy and gave it to me. The *Hatteras Abyssal* out of Rotterdam. It's here they make the trade-off."

"Is that normal?"

"Difficult to say. There're ten to twenty ships docking here every day from all over the world. This one's mine."

"So what do you want to do? Hijack the booze?"

"No. Too difficult, too unwieldy."

An understanding came.

"No," I said. "No."

"We have to," said Jack.

"Christ." The cash.

A tremor ran along my fingers and hand and transferred itself to the tumbler of whiskey as I raised it to my mouth. The spirit burned its way over my tongue and down my esophagus, with some catching in my throat. Jack offered me a cigaret and I shakily lit one. These were the same hands trained to operate on patients made pliant by the anaesthesiologist in the clean confines of an operating room. Thank the Lord I never got past unfeeling corpses. They were far more forgiving of mistakes, and the shakes. I saw my dissecting partner Smiler jabbing me with a scalpel and then pinching the severed optic nerve of an eyeball with a clamp, laughing as he swivelled it to look at me. Our professor chided us and tubthumped for Drs. Livingstone, Lister, and that excellent field vivisectionist Jack the Ripper, never mind Dr. Crippen.

"It takes it to their front doorstep," Jack said.

"That's what you want? Isn't it enough that the cops are probably on our trail? Now you want to rob gangsters. It's madness."

"Better than knocking over movie houses," Jack said.

"For movie houses you go to gaol. Gangsters'll feed us to the ravens. Don't you have any better idea?" I asked.

"No."

"Nothing?"

"Jesus, Mick. This is our chance. I mean, look at you. What are you going to do next? You want to sell insurance policies or deliver the Eaton's catalogue? I for one am tired of taking orders."

Jack was right. I was a good-for-nothing and not getting any better. Here was the kind of reckless, foolhardy proposal that great men accepted. It was a challenge. All of my scrimshanking would be forgiven by this dangerous test. I'd been on the line already, and they'd come for me after doing nothing more than riding shotgun on one of the Frenchman Charlie's trucks. It was time to choose sides.

"They shot at us, killed my driver," I said, convincing myself.

"And they're coming for me," said Jack. "I know it. Now Mick, you could walk away right now and leave me to my fate. I can take care of myself. They don't know you from Murphy and that's that. So."

"Let me think about it."

"Don't take too long. This is it, this Saturday, and I need to work out a plan. Something simple. These pishers are damned suspicious but sometimes they overlook the obvious. I've got a couple of cute ideas."

"Oke," I said.

"Oke you'll help me or what?"

"Oke."

"Oke then," Jack said.

He stood up and buttoned his coat.

"Let's go check on that dollymop," he said.

"If you insist."

We left the hole in the wall. On this continent cheap buildings were thrown up in haste and razed soon after; it was a wonder anywhere remained extant. The dictate was bigger, newer, cheaper. In England one drank in taverns haunted by ghosts of Cavaliers raising bumpers to King Charles. Here you were lucky to stumble into a saloon in some boomtown that'd burned to the ground only twice before, coming up again each time like scrubweed in an architecture of crooked joists and warped beams. Foundations would be busted to aggregate and used to macadamize country roads. In parting from the bar, the bottle under my coat, I expected to never see it again.

The hotel was dead quiet when we returned and upstairs Lilyan Tashman slept in Jack's bed, her clothes puddled on the floor. Jack took the Haig, filled glasses, and sat himself on the chair that held Lilyan's scanties.

"Take a look at her, make sure she's all right," he said.

I checked her pulse and the dilation of her pupils. She was still well in the depths of a jag. Every one was different: sleep, wild energy, equipoise. Lilyan was gone away. Simply seeing her had me lusting for a taste.

"Let's get some grub," Jack said, inverting my appetite.

He called up room service and ordered roasted chicken, spinach greens, fried potatoes with mustard. We chewed away and after the meal I cleaned my Webley. It was a pretty tableau vivant, I thought, two criminals and a drugged moll. There was an odd sordid undertone to the scene as Jack took out a knife. He threw it in the air and caught the blade between his hands, an old trick from the mining camps.

"Once I knew a scout who could catch a knife between his lips," he said.

"Practice makes perfect," I said, and added: "Where'd you hide that bag of silver from Loew's?"

"Somewhere safe," he said.

"Does that bastard Bob know?"

"Oh, aye. You don't care for him, do you?"

"Not half. Is he being brought in again?"

"Maybe."

Something nagged at me.

"What's his story, then?"

Jack told me how Bob held up the end for a fellow Irishman, a Yankee. Usually booze was brought in by fast boats to small coves on the New England seaboard and Bob was part of King Solomon's gang but they were backed by a ward boss from Boston, Bob's kinsman, a fellow by the name of Honey Fitz. Fitz was an old pol, once the Beantown mayor, then a representative thrown out of Congress. Bob was here in Montreal keeping an eye out for Fitz's son-in-law, a banker with his finger in the bootlegging pie. He made payoffs, twisted arms, and kept a line open.

"Do you trust him?" I asked.

"Who, Bob?"

"Yes."

"Not particularly. He can be useful."

"Like me."

"You sell yourself too short, Mick. You've got to exploit your talents better."

"Perhaps."

"I mean that. For instance, tell me how you managed to get out of school without a black mark. You said they knew you were dipping into the medicine."

"It's a matter of knowing where the bodies are buried," I said.

Lilyan Tashman started clawing at the bedsheets. Our heads turned to her.

"We'd best be out of here," I said.

"Easier said," Jack went.

She began to thrash. There was nothing on hand to soothe her but towels. I dampened them at the sink and held the coolness to her sweating brow, then sponged her sleek, beautiful nude body, enveloped by her warm live smell. I'd never seen Laura in the altogether except for a stray stocking-top or the hint of décolletage. Laura was of a higher degree entirely, a paragon, Lilyan a slattern compared thereby. The theatre coarsened femininity, I thought, turned it into an exaggerated burlesque. Theda Bara as Cleopatra was covered in paint but beneath the cosmetics and away from the hot cesium lights womankind was a different story entire. We ministered to Lilyan as her convulsions waned. With other men this state would invite a rape. Gentlemen both, Jack and I struggled to dress her, now that she'd become a potential liability. In the end it was too much and we gave up with half her combinations twisted 'round her torso.

"I'm better at getting their clothes off," Jack said.

He looked at me and I laughed. We drank more whiskey and waited for the drug to run its wicked course. Another day in the life. In less than an hour Jack and I were thoroughly drunk. When Lilyan finally came to she groggily gathered her dress and things.

"What's the hurry, Mistress Scurry?" Jack mocked.

"No hurry," she said in a faraway voice.

"Do you have a show tonight?" I slurred.

"I don't know."

"So this is Montreal," I said.

"What?"

I lit one of Jack's cigarets. He staggered off to the lavatory. Lilyan began the complicated process of buttoning eyelets and lacing stays, the difficulty compounded by her haziness. I watched her and became stupidly aroused. Usually disrobing was the stimulant. This was a reverse striptease, if you please. The toilet flushed and Jack returned.

"Where're you going?" he demanded.

"Nowhere," Lilyan said.

Jack turned my way.

"Mick, meet me at the Five-Minute Lunch tomorrow at one."

I stood, my stomach tightening with a nauseating jealousy. Jack opened the door and I exited, with one look of parting. His fly was still unbuttoned from pissing and Lilyan was on her knees in the middle of the bed looking up at him with a bovine unawareness mixed with resigned expectancy. I managed to make it to the fire escape stairwell before vomiting up everything I could.

WEDNESDAY

NEAR ELEVEN THE crenellated cells of my body screamed me awake. Today was rain and disgust. After drinking weak water from the tap I made my hasty toilet and went to meet Jack at the restaurant. The man was winding me up, testing me. My motives for continuing on this path were unclear. It wasn't merely the sight of morphine last night, the money or the girl. I felt a dark awakening. For half an hour I waited at the Five-Minute, chewing over a Western sandwich, swilling muddy coffee, smoking fresh cigarets. Jack never showed.

The next block over three golden balls swaying above a pawn-broker's dripped rain. I'd mislaid the stub for my father's hunter during a move and so the timepiece was now lost forever, saving if I bought it back at face value from the Shylock. When I'd detrained in '19 the Pater and I'd taken a 'cab to the courthouse square and then silently eaten Mulligatawny soup together in the dining room of the old Hotel Vancouver. He'd given me the 'watch, a Longines, and solemnly drank a glass of loganberry lemonade to my return. It was now six months since I'd last written him. Secretly I was waiting for him to die. That was, of course, if I didn't first.

I turned up my collar and slogged back to the Wayside where I played Napoleon patience with a deck of cards from the bedside table. It was after losing seven games straight that I got the bright idea to count the pasteboards. Fifty-one, with the eight of spades missing.

Furious rain against my window woke me later that evening. Restlessness and hunger drove me from the room and into the wet. Outside the hotel an elderly couple huddled together at curb's edge waiting to cross the street as motors splashed by. As the man's foot descended into a puddle the woman said: "Don't step in it, it might be Lon Chaney."

Only two nights ago I'd seen *The Trap* and helped stick up the Loew's. My cut of the cash I'd hidden on my person, a thick wad protected by the Webley I now gripped in my overcoat pocket. Chutes of water sluiced down from storefront eaves. Across Cathcart cantered the police: two mounted constables. The officers ignored me as I slouched along, thinking on Chaney and disguises. I pushed down my hat brim and became simply another anonymous pedestrian trying to stay dry. What had Jack said, though? The memorable telling detail, overwhelming accurate perception of identity. Something obvious and discardable: false eyepatch, scar, outlandish moustache, curious manner or limping gait. Chaney as the Phantom of the Opera, the Hunchback of Notre Dame, or that film where he'd been a crime boss with his legs amputated above the knee.

The most demented of Chaney's pictures had been one where he'd played an evil ventriloquist who dressed as a grandmother and was in league with a circus strongman and a nasty midget disguised as a baby. The trio ran a store selling caged birds as a front for more larcenous activity. People came into the shop and Chaney the ventriloquist would throw his voice to make them think the birds could speak. The bird's voices were drawn on the screen like speech balloons in the newspaper funny pages, Jiggs or the Katzenjammer Kids. The customers would purchase what they thought were talking birds, only to return complaining that they no longer spoke. Chaney, in his grandmother get-up, would then visit and case their houses. Later he'd burgle the homes, aided by the strongman and the midget, the lot of them refugees from some travelling carnival of tattooed women, sword-swallowers, wild men, and Siamese twins. *The Unholy Three*. I'd seen it at the Pantages, a long time ago. I had a confused memory of a complication with a girl and the requisite hero, an innocent charged with murder after the strongman and the midget killed a homeowner during one of their robberies. Remembered the midget disguised as a baby smoking a stogie and plotting with the circus strongman against Chaney. And the best part, the very best part of the whole shooting match, had been the grand finale. The crew escaped to a secret hideout with the girl as a prisoner when out of nowhere a gorilla showed up and killed the giant and midget. Chaney turned repentant and hawked joke books with his ventriloquist's dummy at the courthouse before being sent to gaol. And here I was thinking my current circumstances were unlikely. My mind wheeling around, the pavement unsteady, I banged my shoulder into a passing Indian.

"Beg your pardon," he said.

On the sidewalk someone had dropped a jar of preserved tomatoes and the mess resembled burst fetal masses. In order to offset their fees fellow students of mine at the hospital would perform illicit abortions and run stills for bathtub gin to sell across the border in Ontario. My morphine trading had been nearly amateur in comparison to those felonies, with the only difference being that I'd nearly been pinched. My only protection from an open scandal and possible arrest had been knowledge of the school's immemorial practice: sincere imitation of those resourceful men, Burke and Hare of Edinburgh. Well, let them try to touch me, the bastards, I thought, and watched reflections in storefront windows to see if shapes followed me. With my weapon clenched in my fist I was the anarchist in Conrad's *Secret*

Agent holding his India rubber bulb wired to detonate. The bullet would burn a hole through my topcoat on its way out.

Behind the desk of the Wayside the pander handed me a message. I read: "Union Hall, nine o'clock. Hannay."

Jack and his John Buchan turn again, *The Thirty-Nine Steps*. Wait. How'd he know where you're staying? You told him you were at the Occidental under Smith and here you were at the Wayside under Magee. Dammit, another illustration of Jack and his methods. The bastard said he was with the Pinkertons, the unsleeping eye. Stay ahead of him from now on. He's using you, trying to twist you in the wind. Stay awake, boyo.

A shiver wracked me, and I collected myself. Jack's dispatch wasn't coded and so must be a safe summons. It was nine now by the clock on the wall. The question posed: stay or go? Jack's play with Lilyan failed to arouse in me refusal; I was deadening somehow and animated by a deeper impulse, a low concupiscence. It was all one. At the rank I hailed a 'cab and made a reluctant return to campus. Montreal was a graveyard of memories. My mouth suddenly parched and I thirsted after warm tea with lemon to soothe it.

The taxi dropped me at the Roddick Gates, each of the four clocks telling a different time. I walked alone in the dark under elms spattering rain down my neck. Ahead blazed the hall. A sign gave details:

Medical Students' Union

A Discourse Upon Spiritualism and the Scientific Method

— MR. H. HOUDINI —

Commencing 8 PM

Something was afoot. At the door stood an unctuous pup I recognized from the pathology lab, a shifty little informer right at home amongst diseased tissue samples and eviscerated corpses:

Lubie by name. Resentments erupted as crimson boils on his ugly phiz. Lubie'd been two years below me and had puffed himself up since, gatekeeper and tattletale, all rheumy eyes and dirty suit aswarm with bacteria.

"Ticket," he grunted at me.

"How much?"

"Union member or guest only."

"I was a member," I said

"Current Medical Union members only," the blackguard said.

I was a step below him. Several options presented themselves to me: a quick punch to Lubie's tiny testicle, the Webley's barrel shoved into his gut, a tactical retreat. I turned to see if anyone was watching, and turned back to "Here's his ticket."

Jack handed the bastard a stub. Lubie snorted. As I climbed by I elbowed him hard in the kidney. Lubie grunted and doubled over. I felt a mite better.

A reedy voice could be heard in the hall beyond the reception. Jack and I went into the room. It was a swelter, the seats filled with heavy men in damp coats with hats on their knees, thick womenfolk wrapped up in drab shrouds. The lamps' iron filaments flared with an uncertain electric current on a man behind a lectern onstage. Before we sat down Jack steered me out again and into a dirty water closet. He took out his small vial and spilled cocaine on the platinum cigaret case. In a gesture of conciliation for the previous evening he offered me the salt first. One sniff of the drug and a cold finger touched my hypothalamus. When we returned to the hall Jack and I sat near the rear. Nearby a clutch of sniggering students fooled in the corner and moved like drunks.

The man onstage spoke: "Inasmuch as notions of the possibility of communication with those who have passed from the terrestrial sphere have been studied using empirical methodology

the results have unequivocally tended towards the uniformly negative. This would lead one to suppose that in our present age of
scientific development the means have not yet been devised to
establish whether such a removèd plane can be revealed by any
rational process, or contrariwise, whether such a supposèd realm
can be considered to verifiably exist.

"Notwithstanding the concentrated combined efforts of the
most stringent scientific disciplines there continue to remain
charlatans without number who, contrary to all received proofs,
aver an ability to communicate with the loving departed. These
same predators feed not only on the naiveté and credulity of
those poor sufferers left behind, but do so for the basest pecuni-
ary motives. They are wastrel wolves extracting a toll far dearer
than money. These fiends tax the remaining hope and spirit of
bereaved survivors. My own researches into and well-publicized
exposures of fraudulent mediums and hoaxers have been legion.
This chapter of my life is well-documented and I hope familiar
to this learnèd audience.

"My own career should provide proof enough of Spiritualism's
falsity. As part of my showman's training very early on I myself
learned the secrets of their pernicious practice; I have never
claimed to possess powers verging on the supernatural, as many
wicked practitioners regularly do. The study of conjuring, stage-
magic, and legerdemain has allowed me to reveal to the public
every method employed at so-called séances by erstwhile mediums, or media, to be pedantic. These mediums ply their trade
with the sole purpose of defrauding the poor, the grief-stricken,
the sick-at-heart. I do not consider it a violation of the magician's
oath to unmask these parasites. A true magician seeks only to
enlighten, amaze, amuse, and entertain, whilst mediums, seers,
psychics, and prophets are mere confidence artists in pursuit of
monetary gain based upon the exploitation of sorrow. Therefore,

in addition to my speech, tonight I shall conduct a small experiment with random members of the audience gathered here and thusly demonstrate how easily trust and hope may be abused by the skilled mountebank. This portion of the discourse, I must add, is currently part of my performance at the Princess Theatre, tickets there starting at the very reasonable price of fifty cents, ladies and gentlemen."

Houdini smiled. The audience tittered and applauded politely. Houdini cleared his throat and shuffled the papers at his lectern. He took a sip of water and grimaced. I'd never seen him before in the flesh, only depicted in newspapers and on hoarding posters. He'd suspended himself upside-down from the cupola of the World Building on Pender Street in Vancouver and escaped from a straitjacket but I'd missed that, down with the chicken pox. Houdini wasn't overly tall and was surprisingly thick. He had an enormous flattish head with greying hair parted strictly down the middle.

The cocaine was providing me what I was pleased to pretend were insights into Houdini's personality based upon his physiognomy. The man's entire career was perhaps what they termed a compensation for his diminutive size, his physical bulk the result of the highly developed musculature necessary for the tremendous exertions demanded by his trade as escape artist. In Houdini's movements were the grace of the practised showman and performer, even in the gentle manner with which he set down the water glass. From the man's face, however, I thought to glean the most about his psychology. His features were marked with the striving of an absolute will. A commanding visage, well-nigh imperious and trained to be such in order to overawe and cow recalcitrant audiences into submission and credulity. Houdini could hint at intimate knowledge of the *arcana mundi*, show wonders, make an elephant disappear before our eyes.

The massive brow denoted a large cerebrum. The magician would be a phrenologist's delight. It couldn't be doubted that he was intelligent, his fame resident on escape from impossible scenarios. Therefore: cunning, craft, a genius for self-promotion. If not for their total difference I could be describing Jack beside me.

Houdini began to speak again in his high-pitched voice, the sole incongruity in an otherwise distinguished make-up. My interest started to sparrow around the room. On the far wall a gigantic oil of Lord Dorchester peered down on the audience nearsightedly.

"What're we doing here?" I whispered.

"Came to see Smiler, for one."

Jack tapped the breast pocket of his coat meaningfully, the place he'd hidden the vial of cocaine. That little bastard Smiler. Here I was expelled from the school and Union for suspected narcotic theft and in my absence the rotten piker'd horned onto my racket as a going concern. I shifted uneasily in my seat, conscious that former dons might be amongst the crowd and recognize me. Looking for Smiler I found his smug face just offstage right, seated on a cane chair as part of the group that'd enticed Houdini to give his lecture. Smiler pulled at a chain to palm a 'watch from his waistcoat pocket and another bolt of envious fury shot through me.

Houdini raised his hands and suddenly there twinkled something silver between his sinister thumb and forefinger, a needle. His oration continued: "Many if not most Spiritualist practices originate from the Indian subcontinent, where the ignorant and gullible are legion, prey to shamans, fakirs, and other so-called holy men. Some of their claims are preposterous enough to be seen for what they are and rejected outright. Others may be easily demonstrated and thus discounted. Numbered amongst these latter are claims of complete mastery over pain and bodily discomfort through supernatural succour. We see it in such explicable activities as walking over hot coals unshod or the piercing of the flesh with skewers or needles, like so."

With a swift motion Houdini plunged the needle into his cheek. The audience gasped and a woman let out a small cry. He pulled another pin out of thin air and stuck himself again, seemingly. Houdini smiled and even from the furthest corner of the hall I could see how wan and aged he looked. The hard bone of the skull was visible beneath the stretched skin. Heavy creases marked his forehead. He wore an air of exhaustion as he summoned Smiler to pluck the needles from his face. At this we all clapped our hands together.

My thoughts once more fixed on that bastard Smilovich soaking in his unearned applause and I began gnashing my teeth, the chemical flavour of the drug dripping down into my pharynx. Houdini moved on to something about Theosophy and faery photography, chiding Sir Conan Doyle for his credulity. He then commenced a mind-reading display. Another of my former confederates, a chemist named Jacques Price, helped Houdini with his mentalism. Various things happened: a man was told he had a pomegranate in his pocket, another what he'd eaten for luncheon at Hausmann's, for a third Jacques Price wrote a phrase in Italian on a chalkboard.

"Should you be so kind as to attend my performance this week I will be able to demonstrate further," said Houdini. "You will forgive me for not revealing the means by which I was able to demonstrate mind-reading here tonight but please rest assured that no occult power was invoked. The abilities claimed by mediums are no more than the stock-in-trade of the magical arts from the time of Moses to our present day. With sufficient training any one of you here could accomplish the same feats as I ..."

I felt Jack tense next to me of a sudden, his interest sharpened.

"On the other hand ..."

There was a flash of light and Houdini was gone. For near on twenty seconds we sat dumb in shock until another startling explosion heralded the man's return. He roared: "This week at the Princess Theatre you will see a complete medium's séance with clear explanations of such erstwhile supernatural phenomena as table-rapping, the ringing of phantom bells in enclosed spaces, and ghostly apparitions including ectoplasmic forms. I will also then field a number of questions, as I do now. The floor is open, ladies and gentlemen."

The first question came from a weedy-looking shrimp who stood and asked: "Mr. Houdini, what have you to say about the unusual occurrences recorded by the American Charles Fort?"

"It is my belief that Mr. Fort is in fact as skeptical of any dubious claim as I am and his documentation of the inexplicable is in aid of scientific truth and not sensationalism."

"Mr. Houdini, do you believe in reincarnation? In life after death?" asked a thin dark girl in spectacles.

"I do not. Consider this: in almost every instance a medium will aver her client the returnèd incarnation of Caesar Augustus or Marie Antoinette, never slave or village idiot. Draw what conclusions you may. As for your second question: I have left secret instructions to be opened upon my death. Every year on the day of my passing a series of particular questions that only I know the answer to must be asked at a séance. Should the response be correct then we may say there is a world beyond and that Houdini has escaped from it!"

"Mr. Houdini, are you a Jew?"

"I am. My father was a rabbi. What possible relevance your question may possess is beyond my ability to descry."

He stood erect, all majesty, his hands now gripping the lectern with enormous force. It was strange; not the magician, but Jack. Why'd he risen and posed Houdini that particular question?

The session tailed off with a few pathetic queries on ghosts and vampires, questions Houdini batted away as equally insignificant. It was a poor showing from a supposedly well-educated audience. Houdini bowed stiffly to our applause and gathered his papers. He walked to where Smiler, Price, and others were milling in a group. Smiler was spouting philosophy, a regurgitated piece of conventional wisdom. Jack went towards my former companions. I followed, and saw their surprise as I approached. Houdini's face tightened when Jack came to him.

"What may I do for you?" asked Houdini, coldly.

"Your servant, sir," Jack said. "Pray forgive the personal nature of the question earlier. I wonder, Mr. Houdini, if you will be patient with me."

Very slight stress on the word "patient" and when Houdini gripped Jack's proffered hand the escape artist's attitude shifted.

"What may I do for you?" Houdini asked once more.

"I'm given to understand that you own a copy of *The Curious Experience of the Patterson Family on the Island of Uffa*," Jack said.

"I do," said Houdini.

The group had fallen silent, entranced by this cryptic dialogue. I saw Smiler glaring at Jack. Price had hands in pockets and was surreptitiously scratching at his groin. Jack squared his feet and continued heedless, he and Houdini sharing an understanding.

"I've long wished to read the account but have never been able to find it. Have you a copy with you here in Canada?"

"I do," said Houdini, reluctantly.

"I'm a quick reader and would esteem it a high honour should you lend it to a poor widow's son. I'll happily provide you with any surety you require."

"None will be necessary," Houdini said.

"Very well. Where may I call for it?"

"The volume will be left for you at the front desk of my hotel, the Windsor. Your name, sir?"

Jack gave one.

"Thank you, Mr. Houdini."

They shook hands a last time. Smiler escorted the magician away. Sycophants dispersed. Jack stood still as though mesmerized.

"Jack," I said.

"Eh?"

"Let's go."

The hall echoed as we returned to the rain. Lubie squatted on the steps, snuffling like a swine. Jack broke from his trance.

"Come on," he said.

"Where to?"

"You'll see."

We walked quiet in the dark to the gates on Sherbrooke. True to form Jack was plotting, and I could almost hear the gears at work.

"I've never heard of that book," I said. "Who wrote it?"

"No one."

"What?"

"No one wrote it. Well, someone did, but he doesn't exist."

"Who?"

"James Watson," Jack said.

"Dr. Watson?"

"The same."

"I don't understand," I said.

"But he did."

"The other thing, your calling him out as a Jew and that. He's on the level."

"And the square," Jack said, hailing a taxi.

The 'cab went uphill and along Pine to a large stone house, all stern wealth. We curled along a drive and under a porte-cochère, where Jack paid off the driver. Here spread an aroma of the nearby mountain green and rich, wet red leaves soaking in the dark, the dim spread of the city below with a suggestion of the river beyond. Not for the first time I yearned for the clean vastness of the sea. I felt a deficit of fresh oxygen in the East and I sucked up two lungfuls, closed my eyes a moment, and tried to simply exist.

Jack whistled, gestured from between the white pillars of the portico and without further ado opened the front door, from whence issued the smell of strangely scented cigaret smoke, cloves, and a sweetish spice. In the vestibule a pretty girl tottered towards us, giggled, and vomited into a large Chinese vase. Behind her followed a tuxedoed blade, his white tie askew. He grinned stupidly and dragged the girl away. We followed a noise down the hall to its source in an expensive salon. Fifteen or twenty people made up the party and a Victrola played jazz, with barefoot couples dancing on the Turkey rug and gin bottles piled on a table. They were all young and loaded, high society nitwits. Eyes turned to Jack as he entered and swept off his hat in a gallant gesture. There were squeals from a few girls and a mild tumult.

I hung back and scanned the vapid faces of the bright young things. Louche forms in short dresses and bobbed hair draped themselves over Chesterfields. Quasi-Valentinos wearing pulled-apart eveningwear drank and puffed at little cheroots. On a far chaise in the corner I recognized Bob's blond head. He was talking to a copper-topped woman, her back to me and his hand high up on her thigh. As I was about to turn away I heard a laugh like a cork pulled from a bottle and felt my scrotum constrict. A face revealed itself, throat extended, mouth open with pleasure, lips a red circle. The eyes opened and looked into mine and it was her, Laura.

I stepped into the room.

"And what's this?" drawled a lazy voice.

A ponce wearing a monocle stood before me, cocktail glass in his soft pink hand.

"He's with me," Jack said.

"Does it have a name?" asked the invert.

Fury, embarrassment, and fear clammed me up. I went dead cold.

"How very gauche," the monocle said. "Send it away! Back out the tradesman's entrance!"

No one spoke. The only sound was a scratching from the Victrola's funnel. I was being looked at and felt a flush of heat in my damp suit, followed by a quick, choking rage.

"Easy, Roger," said Jack. "Welcome your guests. Be a pal."

The eyeglass turned to his coterie and their murmur. Someone changed the black disk and I saw Bob smirking my way but his hand was gone from touching her body. She looked in my direction, not at me but at Jack. The needle found its groove and out came Jelly Roll Morton. I could feel myself an object of scorn, persona non grata, a goat. Roger the pederast looked poison at me and his sentiment spread through the room. My true talent, Isis unveiled, the ability to provoke an instant dislike and to return the sentiment with interest. Weight of the Webley at the small of my back, six bullets ready to release. I opened my case and lit a cigaret. Jack had his overcoat off and was being poured two drinks by a flirt. He brought the mouthwash over and handed one to me, took the cigaret out of my mouth and placed it in his own.

"Trials of Job, Mick me lad," he said.

"Why'd you bring me to this fandango? There's a time you'll go too damn far."

"That I'd like to see. So far you're rock steady."

"I'm being tested," I said.

"You might call it that."

"And who are you to set the examination?"

"Calm yourself, Mick. Play nice with others. Talk to some girls, make her jealous."

Again that amusement in his eye. He wanted me uncomfortable and off-balance. Winding me up like a tintoy. Why did I put up with it? Because he delivered. I was in the same room as she.

A pretty little number dragged Jack off to turn a hoof. I went to the bottles by the window box and poured neat gin, my back to the revelry. I saw my reflection in the glass darkly, and felt my heart beating like a malfunctioning furnace. Ignore your parasympathetic nervous system, the baiting and humiliation. Forget it all, turn, and look at her from across the room. See her here, now. Drink it all up. Raw spirit burned going down.

There was Roger the lord of the manor covered in his leeches, Jack with another twist dancing close to a slow foxtrot. A roar of laughter, the tumble of bottles. Laura was gone. She'd left the salon, and so had Bob. A nerve jumped along my face and twitched at my left eye. The cigaret coal burned at my knuckle and I let the stub fall, let it smoulder and burn this house down and all within it. I cut out to the hallway to find the once-retching girl passed out on the marble with her idiot chaperone beside her. The front room was empty; another door was locked with no light through the keyhole. Had they left the house together?

Above my head the ceiling moaned. I climbed the carpeted stairs carefully, flanked by hanging tapestries: brass rubbings from Crusaders' tombs. It was too dark to see until the second-storey corridor. This wing had bedroom doors left and right, all locked tight except at the end. I could hear quiet voices and a muted squeal, a grunt and a gasp. The door was open a crack and a line of light led me as I came closer. Sway of a single candle flame with shadows thrown on the wall. A canopied bed. They were on their knees on the fabric spread in an indecent posture. I felt myself looming and fading into nothing, dead. My gun was infinitely heavy, too heavy to lift. Out of the orange glow I sensed the gaze of an eye pierce out and it was hers but I turned away and walked back from the gallows. She'd left the door open. She'd wanted to be seen.

Without knowing how it happened I found myself down in the cellar, somehow having passed through the kitchen and entered this subterrain by a fatal gravity, seeking a grave. A deep must and fungus filled my nostrils and around me 'ranged in racks were cobwebbed bottles from before the war. I wanted one, wanted an oblivion, anything but this numb agony. I selected a vintage and cracked it open with the butt of the Webley in lieu of a corkscrew but the whole thing splintered and broke, coursing staining wine over my hands as I dropped the mess to the flagged floor. Wine dripped from my fingers and mixed with blood from where the glass had cut my hand. An animal reaction guided the wound to my mouth and I tasted salt, copper, rot, death.

It was her pure hypocrisy, her feigned virtue and purity that wounded most. All that prudery, the dry passionless kisses and timid caresses broken off. There'd been no moral principle at work in her repeated denials, her frigid refusals, her contempt. It'd simply been me, me and me alone. She'd lie with others, but not with me. The wicked, evil, two-faced liar. The love of my life, squirming with another. The whore.

There was a thump above my head as they danced a Turkey Trot. Hunching in the basement I turned small and cold. I staunched the flowing blood with a rag. To the left was a passage elsewhere and I picked up two bottles to take with me. I followed the tunnel to an old barred door, locked from within. Wrenching the rusty bolt open started the blood again and my concern turned to a fear of contracting tetanus. Ozone poured over me. I was out on a street sloping downward into the city. There was a wind up, blowing east. The windows behind me filled with silhouettes swaying and moving. I took out the Webley, taking careful aim at a black figure in the window. Roger, fate willing. Instead I turned my back on them, pushed the cork down one bottle's neck, and drank until near-bursting.

On the march back to the Wayside a dirge welled up from within, Omar Khayyám by way of Fitzgerald: "A flask of wine, a book of verse—and Thou beside me singing in the wilderness, and wilderness is paradise enow."

On an empty curb at midnight, broken and destroyed, I collapsed and croaked. I crawled on hands and knees to a wall, propped myself up, and emptied the second bottle. There was a light in a lobby—my hotel. By some remaining instinct I managed to get to my room and enjoy a drunken sleep filled with nightmares.

THURSDAY

MORNING WITH THE sun back out. Chimneypots poured forth smoke and steam. From my window I watched slow trains pull into the yard by the river. Soon I was out on the street where frosted red leaves scratched along the pavement. The fresh wind snapped my mind into place and cleaned away any lingering shame from the shadowy night. I primed for action and walked to Windsor Station for a quick cup and smoke. Clear the decks and run up the colours: it's time to attack. Jack had been bossing me, keeping his movements dark. I'd walked blind towards the enemy trench and if I kept following orders without direction of my own I'd catch shrapnel or worse. For too long Jack had twisted my tail; it was time now to do a little twisting back.

There were precious few candidates for pressuring: Brown the wee Customs man, that rat-bastard Bob, and oily Charlie the French mechanic-cum-lawyer. No, on reflection it was someone else who might provide a few answers: Harry Houdini. Jack hadn't gone to the Medical Union by accident or merely for Smiler's cocaine. There'd been the series of riddling questions, the unusual request for an unwritten book. If I entered at that angle and discovered Jack's vector it might give me an inkling of the conspiracy I was now part of. Firm in my conviction I walked to the Windsor Hotel. It was near ten-thirty, earlier than the noon hour appointed for their rendezvous. I could intercept the flash, read the book or whatever it was and put it back. It was a start. At the front desk I spoke to a pockmarked clerk.

"Mr. Houdini has left a package to be collected here," I said.

"What name, please?"

I gave the one Jack had used the night before.

"One moment, sir."

The clerk picked up a receiver and whispered something. A moment passed in the murmuring lobby and was marked by the single chime of a bell. The clerk sneered and said: "Sir, Mr. Houdini left specific instructions that he wished to be informed the moment this package was collected. He will be with you directly."

Merde. This was not anything I wanted part of. All I'd imagined was a peek at the book or message from Houdini Jack was after to see how it played into this malarkey. It was too late now to cause a scene ducking out. Remember Jack's words: sheer brazen cheek.

Hell and damnation gang aft agley. What was I trying to accomplish, sniffing around the edges of his scheming like this? Parity, information, intelligence. The way he'd sicced Laura and Bob on me at the party and used me as an idle amusement: Jack was wrong. I was a free agent, unaccounted for and independent, with the power to alter events. This was something I'd forgotten while devoured by my inward world. Some message had passed between Jack and the magician and I, as always, was cut out. Later I'd been exiled from the gin party. If I was enemy, let me behave as one. Even now Jack was in all likelihood bedding a twist from the shindig whilst I waited amongst rubber plants and geraniums. Another clear bell sounded and the lift doors slid open. There was Houdini foursquare in the box. His gaze pierced yours truly and he marched straight over.

"Who are you?" he demanded. "You aren't the man I spoke with."

"No," I said.

"Well, what the devil do you want? If you're another crawler bringing warnings I advise you to push off."

"Warnings?"

"State your business, man. I've no time for triflers. Mrs. Houdini waits upon me."

"Mr. Houdini, I mean no offence. Please, if we might speak privately for a moment."

A spasm of nervous constriction crossed his face and he tensed up. I fancied I saw his biceps flexing beneath the fabric of his morning coat. There was no wish on my part to tangle with the man; he was strong and a mite fearsome, though I'd a few inches and twenty-odd years on him. Houdini sighed impatiently. From so close he appeared worn, his movements stiff and pained.

"Very well," he said, "but with some haste if you please."

We drifted to a pair of wingbacks shielded by aspidistras from the desk. I gestured Houdini to sit and he did with an ill grace, pinching the crease of his trousers to keep their knife edge.

"Well?"

"Mr. Houdini, I came for the book."

"Don't be a fool. There's no such thing. What do you want?"

"I want to understand what's happening here. You say you've been warned. Was it by the man at the Union last night? The one I was with?"

"Ah! You're an ignorant pawn. I expected better."

"From whom?"

"From your masters! Ha! Warned, yes I've been warned, but it will take a power mightier than those behind your companion to stop Houdini! The truth will out, sir. The truth will out."

"What truth?"

He barked a laugh.

"You think to draw me? Tell your masters that Houdini reveals his secrets to no man. He will not be drawn."

"Have you been threatened?"

In Houdini's hard glare there was a fierce suspicion.

"Who are you?" he asked.

"No one. No one of importance. I'm part of something I don't entirely understand and beg your indulgence to allow me to ask you a few more questions."

"Are you a reporter?"

"Lord no."

Houdini snorted decisively.

"As I have said in the past I will have neither truck nor trade with fakers and charlatans. My exposure of the medium Margery in New York illustrates this point. Now, when I come to this fair Dominion with knowledge that may save her honour my sacred duty is to reveal the truth.".

The man's intense manner was difficult to counter.

"You've learned of a false medium?"

"Far worse than some sham humbug. No, there's a danger to this country. I provide a tit-bit for you to carry back to your masters, errand boy. When in London I learned the name of a highly placed official of your government who subscribes to superstition. Imagine the harm that may befall your people in these unsettled times, the danger to your sovereign. It is my duty to unmask these—"

"Who is this official?" I interrupted.

"Ha! Imagine my telling you! Inform your betters that none can stop Houdini, no gag, no chain, no fetter, no lock, not even death itself."

He held me rapt, his eyes unblinking. Quick as thought now he stood and strode towards the lift's closing doors. Their course was halted and they re-opened for him. Houdini ignored the elevator boy and entered the chamber and was gone. I remained seated, surrounded by the lobby's confusion. Someone was watching me. There: at the front desk the pockmarked clerk pointed in my direction and with him Jack. Damnation. Jack came over and clapped his heavy hand on my shoulder.

"Well, what've we fucked up now, boyo?"

No humour or pleasure in his tone. Through a subtle physical coercion that I attributed to his training with the Pinkertons Jack directed me out of the hotel and onto Peel.

"Sticking your nose into where it doesn't belong," he said.

"Don't you look at me. You're the one who tied me up in this bloody tangle."

"And I thought you'd manage some small competence. Jesus, Mick, you don't have half an idea of what's going on."

"And that's just the way you like it, me in the dark. The party last night with Laura and that bastard friend of yours. Nice of you to keep it under your hat."

Jack stopped cold. His eyes shifted and he looked at his shoes.

"That one I didn't know. Believe me, I had no idea at all," he said.

"Bollocks. First it's booze, then it's Bob, and now Houdini. What are you trying to do? Flush him out or scare him?"

"Perhaps a little of both."

"At whose bidding? This can't be your idea."

"That I can't tell you," Jack said.

"Well I've got a damned good notion now."

"No you don't. You have no idea, Mick."

"I think I do, especially after what the man said."

"What was that?"

Jack was all attention now. I could almost imagine the pressure he was under, and in a certain way I'd accomplished part of my goal. Let him hang out to dry for once.

"Your Houdini told me that a highly placed member of His Majesty's government here was messing about with soothsayers and faeries and talking to spooks from beyond the grave. He thinks it'll leave the Crown open to manipulation by the Bolsheviks or the Bavarian Illuminati or the Goddamn Japanese, I don't know. Houdini's going to spill to someone, the 'papers or the horsemen or the Prince of bloody Wales."

It's difficult for a redhead to turn pale but Jack was doing a fine job of it now.

"That's what he said? Are you certain?" he asked.

"Sure as the pound sterling," I said.

"Who is it? Who's the official?"

"Houdini found out in London so it must be someone high up. That's all I know."

"Ye Christ."

"Who is it? Don't pretend you have no clue," I said.

Jack took off his hat in agitation and ran his hand roughly through his hair. He looked at me.

"Listen: wait here. No, there. Across the street, in the square. I'll be back in half an hour."

He grabbed my shoulders, fixed me with a stare for a second, and pushed off. It amused me somewhat to see him on fire. Jack's oblique route away took him towards St. George's but then he turned right on Dorchester in the direction of the Grand Lodge. For the moment content, I opened my case, lit a Sportsman, and waited on a bench beneath the bare trees, watching pigeons peck the ground at my feet. They were joined anon by wild starlings, no doubt of it with that iridescence on their plumage. Here was a bird out of Shakespeare and Olde England, not New France. A pigeon took my tossed cigaret stub and ate it up.

THE DAY WARMED and the monument behind me became a sundial with the shadow creeping my way. It occurred to me I was hungry. Wistfully I looked at the Dominion Hotel and its attendant public house, a haunt of newspapermen, printer's devils, proofreaders, and advertising salesmen, but not hellbound editors, publishers, and owners. The window advertised *verres stérilisées* in lowercase cursive neon letters: red, green, yellow. I carried silver in my pocket.

Inside the saloon I ordered an ale and took a seat by the window with a view back on the square. On the bench I'd vacated lazed two Siwashes furtively passing between them a bottle of what looked like salty Chinese cooking sherry. On another bench a codger old enough to've fought the Boer himself fed crumbs to gulls. The Dominion was thick with blue tobacco smoke from midday topers here for the free lunch of pickled pork knuckles, spuds, and Liberty cabbage. My stomach yowled so I joined the line-up and was back at my perch with a steaming plate and another schooner of Export, its price now twenty-five cents. No such thing as a free lunch, never.

Dollars danced in my pocket and the wad of folding-money rested safe and sound in my autumn coat, as did the loaded Webley. The wool of my half-decent new suit itched and the reversible celluloid collar bit. I wore clean undergarments, rain-polished black boots, and a maroon necktie to complete the disguise, an impostor posing as a normal human being. I touched and thus dirtied my freshly shaven face and with a slaked thirst lit another cigaret, then with a shinplaster two-bit note bought one more *breuvage*.

A sharper shoved me and I went rigid. You never knew who you bellied up with at a bar and anyone here could be a plainclothes-man on the trail of the cinema-heisters or bootleggers. This narrow orbit was one of habit; in a city large as Montreal you kept to known watering holes as a creature of the forest. But it would be wiser to change hotels again, pay cash down, no questions asked.

Making for the outdoors, I pushed my way through massed shoulders, crushing broken peanut shells underfoot. Clouds now shifted across the face of the sun and rain threatened. Jack stamped in the square, waiting for me for the first time in his blessed life.

"*Salut*," I said.

"Mick, dammit man, we've got to move."

"*Où?*"

Jack shagged down a 'cab. We got in.

"Outremont," he said.

"*Quoi?*"

"It's been three days," Jack said. "Charlie at the garage. He's got to give up Martin."

"*Qui?*"

"Martin, the third driver on the woods. The one who got away. Shape up."

"Never."

THE TAXI BEAT AGAINST a flood tide of city-bound traffic en route to Outremont. Ultramontane, with Pius XI on Peter's throne. Park Avenue cut Fletcher's Field off from the Cartier angel, which stared at the flapping pennant of St. George above the Grenadiers' armoury. Very quietly I sang and Jack, despite himself, picked up the tune.

"Some talk of Alexander and some of Hercules, of Hector and Lysander and such great names as these, but of all the world's heroes there's none that can compare, with a tow row row row row row to the British Grenadiers."

The 'cab had an open top and we smoked and sang. Fast sunshine after a squall was Jack's mood, the cheerful sod. The beer had done me good and I felt better than fine. With some care I checked the cylinder of my Webley and thought on the full box of cartridges I'd hidden above the cistern in my bathroom at the Wayside. What now? Another draw of tobacco while Jack

whistled "In the Clover" as we cut along past Mont-Royal Avenue. I saw well-to-do women shopping at dressmakers' and one
comely creature caught my eye. She wore an insolent pout that
slew me where I sat. Who the hell needed Laura? I could buy
myself a sloe-eyed vixen and have her crawl for me. The 'cab's
speed and rushing air mixed together in a delicious tonic and I
felt exhilarated, alive. Colours leapt out in the crisp afternoon:
the green of a tailor's sign, a blue scarf on a Jewess, shining red
apples in a barrow at the corner.

Our taxi swung into the bay of the filling station and Jack and
I hopped out, full of beans and raring to go. His great capacity
was to relish each new encounter. It was what divided our natures,
but for the present I felt a part of what he must sense most days.
We shared a glance and became kids again in Chinatown or on
the mudflat houseboats of False Creek.

The garage was shut once more and wore the same sign:
"*Fermé.*" It was my hope that Charlie hadn't prepared for our
return and was alone again with his sandwich and flask of coffee.
Jack went around to the rear of the property and I followed.

Out back a ratty scrub yard led to two doors of the complex, one for the house and another that seemed to open into a
connecting corridor. From a maple bough hung a despondent
innertube at the end of a rope. Gallows and hangman's noose.
Leaves littered the dirt amidst a stench of old oil and rancid
petrol. We tried the first door close to the garage and found it
locked. Jack picked up a rock but I stayed his hand and turned
the handle of the door to the house. It clicked open. Quietly we
went into the kitchen. From our previous visit I recalled the little
Indian-looking kid who'd popped out of nowhere, Charlie's son.
The violence had taken place the same time of day as now and
the tyke might be home from a Jesuit school for luncheon with
Papa. We crossed the threshold, adding to our infractions.

"Breaking and entering," I said to Jack.

Jack took his Webley out and held it in his left. "Carrying a weapon," he said. Carefully, we tiptoed through to a hallway, a staircase, and the front door. Next stop was an empty sitting room filled with pale white curtains, a black crucifix on the wall. Jack pointed upstairs.

"See if we're alone."

I went up to the second floor on creaking runners and poked through several bedroom doors: a baby's room, the parents' with another crèche, empty. *Revanche des berceaux*. In the boy's room I was touched to see a lithograph of Wilfrid Laurier next to one of Ignatius Loyola. Back downstairs Jack stood by a door that aligned with the rear of the garage.

"Ready?" he asked.

"Steady," I said.

"Go!"

Jack kicked the door open and went in, holding his revolver with both hands.

"*Police,*" he shouted in French.

The office sat empty but Charlie lay under the busted Chandler on his back. He was slow getting up and Jack was on him, his gun in the Frenchman's face. With his right he grabbed Charlie's collar and kneed him hard in the gut. Charlie went sideways and retched over the floor. Jack stood back and belted his Webley.

"Mick, the hose."

I uncoiled a length from the wall and turned the handle, mixing water with purpling petrol and oil on the cement before reaching Charlie's face.

"Hey Charlie, *comment ça va?*"

Charlie spluttered and gasped. Jack grabbed him and shoved the man up against the sedan, his elbows on the running board.

"*Je voudrais Martin. Donne-lui à moi,*" Jack said.

"Jack," coughed Charlie.

"*Maintenant.* Now. Martin the driver. *Où est-il?*"

Charlie spat.

"Mick, toss the office."

In the office I gave Charlie's desk and files the once-over. There were piles of paper, a photograph of the ugly family, Paterfamilias Charlie with his thin dark moustache in the middle. A drawer held a few loose dollars, half a deck of Sweet Caporals, and a medallion of St. Benedict. I pocketed the lot.

"Mick! Done!"

Upon my return Charlie seemed freshly kicked about the head. Jack trained the hose over him.

"We have an address and a ride, right Charlie?"

The lawyer-cum-mechanic pointed to a set of keys on a hook. Jack tossed them to me. From outside I heard the snarl of dogs fighting. We left Charlie on the floor. At my last look at him I could swear he was smiling at Jack and me.

In the lot were three automobiles: a Locomobile, a Ford, and an Auburn. The keys fit the last, a right-hand drive. I pushed the self-starter and the motor rattled to life. The auto had a left-hand brake and gear-shifter and right pedal accelerator. I released the brake and gave the engine petrol, lurched forward, and stalled. Bloody hell. Jack slid into the back through a suicide door. I pushed the starter again and heard a roar. My foot pressed the pedal and I pumped at the gear-shifter as we lurched forward again, this time over a curb and onto the road. How much horsepower in this beauty? The interior was all blond wood and soft tawny leather, a far cry from the Tin Lizzies I'd learned on. Couldn't remember the last time I'd been behind the wheel. We swayed and bucked as I pulled into a lane, thieves and bandits both.

"Where to?" I asked.

Jack read from a wrinkled scrap of paper:

"*Numéro 1302, coin de Mont-Royal et Chambord.*"

I cranked left at Mont-Royal, one hand clenched around the steering apparatus, the other clumsily grinding from gear to gear in an attempt not to stall again. East past St. Denis the city turned French-Canadian. On a rattletrap iron staircase that twisted down to the street stood a big-breasted black-clad matron cursing out children fooling in the alleyways. On another stair an old crone beat at a rug. A rag-and-bone man pushed his cart past three whiskered old worthies headed into Chez Normand's Bienvenue aux Dames to sprinkle salt in quarts of flat Molson's. My eyes moved between jaywalkers, horses, competing motorcars, darting urchins, and two elegant women walking arm-in-arm into a boutique.

"Here we are," Jack said.

Number 1302 had a kind of pus-yellow painted thistlehead turret at its top corner with the rest an artificial blue. It was an unsightly, unlucky combination of colours, a poisonous warning. The Auburn choked to a stop and I resisted the urge to sound the horn. I left the keys in the 'car and we got out, Jack squaring up at the entrance, his boxing posture.

"Second floor, looks like," he said.

"Oke," I said.

A steep flight of stairs pointed up. I thought about our chances. The only entrance or exit was this spinebreaker. We made it to the top and a door.

"One more time," Jack said.

"Ready?" I went.

"Steady," he said.

"Go!"

Jack shouldered the door and it splintered open on a weak lock. He burst through and tripped flat on his face, with me stepping nimbly over him onto the empty level, my gun at my side. It was hot, with a dark hallway facing a kitchen to the left. Jack stumbled up behind me. I walked into the room and from the opening to the right a rude shape crashed towards my head. Then a blackness absolute.

FROM THE BOTTOM of the sea I rose, my ears ringing and eyes red. Chin on my chest and blood on the white linen of my shirt, head heavy, and a thick taste of copper and salt. Thirsty, tied upright to a chair, my hands lashed behind my back to the rear legs. A crushing headache and something sticky on my face. Blood, more blood. I straightened up and next to me a shape like me, bound, eyes open, Jack with his own bloody mouth. His eyes motioned mine forward and I complied groggily. Two tough louts leaned with their backs to the wall. On a low table before us rested our guns, the display a taunt. Jack hacked up and spat out a suspension of reddish fluid onto the linoleum. We were in the wrecked kitchen of a flat, a dirty place with a Virgin on the wall. The toughs looked like farmhands tricked out in city clothes. One raised an apparatus to his face and there came an explosion of light. He'd taken our photograph. Jack cursed at them. They didn't speak.

Time slowed and the quality of light changed to a thin dimness. My hands ached and Jack seemed to slip in and out of consciousness. They'd given him a good drubbing. I closed my eyes and rested. Both trapezius muscles began to spasm. From a place came the laboured sound of heavy breathing. When I opened my eyes a fat man in a three-piece houndstooth-check suit sat behind the table. A little terrier bitch rested on his lap and one of the toughs handed him a bottle of Vichy water. The man wiped his neck with a silk handkerchief. He was curly-haired and covered in a fine stipple of freckles. My soul lusted for a drink of that water. He saw this and chuckled with a lazy wet mouth.

Make no error, boyo, those eyes are hard and black as jet. The fat man turned and spoke to my companion.

"Monsieur Jack," he said.

"*Enchanté, Sénateur*," replied Jack.

That was a genuine surprise. Now we were moving up in the world. One of the toughs crossed his arms and I revised my opinion: they weren't farmhands but hockey players, though in Quebec the crushers were usually one and the same.

"You have been very foolish, I think," said the Senator.

"You might say that," said Jack.

"You disappoint me. This wildness. It is not good. Time for it, I think, to end."

"Now that I'm of no use to you."

"It is true. This business with Charles Trudeau and Pierre Martin is how do you say, irresponsible. These man are innocent."

"So you say. I say they sold me out."

"Impossible. For them I vouch. For you that is enough."

"Or what?"

"I am not so cold. For what you have done in the past I am willing to turn the blind eye for this indiscretion. An opportunity of grace, I think."

"Mercy buckets," said Jack.

"You will stay away from Monsieur Trudeau and Monsieur Martin. I protect them."

The Senator stroked his terrier. I couldn't help but think we were Bulldog Drummond before Fu Manchu the way he gloated. My life had become a story from *Black Mask*. The Senator motioned to his toughs and spoke a fast incomprehensible quacking French, the sort from up in Gaspé. It was pure Greek.

Jack turned his head to me, looked down, moved his right boot and looked back up. There was some weapon there, I surmised. Our Webleys remained on the table before us. The Senator said something to the farmhand who'd photographed us;

the brute picked up the camera and left by a different door from the one Jack and I'd used to enter the apartment. The odds were better now. I flexed my bonds as the dog on the Senator's lap yapped then curled a hind leg over its head to lick at its vagina.

"*Alors*, what is it we will do with you, I wonder," the Senator mused.

"You could recommend us to Mackenzie King."

"It is very droll, but, I think, unlikely."

"I know what," Jack said.

"What?"

"You could cut us in the line-up to fuck your wife."

"*Quoi?*"

"She's been had by every hack in Ottawa."

The Senator rose and his dog leapt. The remaining tough stiffened and balled his fists. My bonds seemed loose; they'd tied us badly, the peasants. My left hand slipped free. I waited.

"*Connard*," the Senator breathed.

"Yep, your missus is the biggest roundheel on the Hill. Takes it up the *trou* as well."

"*Infâme*," whispered the Senator.

There was no way of knowing what'd been planned for us. I couldn't see a Liberal Senator having us killed, unless he learned we were Tories. A good beating was more the Grit style. Nevertheless, Jack's strategy of provoking the man didn't seem the soundest. Even if Jack had a knife in his boot we still had to cut ourselves free. The Senator's dog scrambled to a corner and seemed to start laughing. The Senator, breathing heavily, placed his hands on the table before us. I could see his swarthy skin darkening with fury.

"Perhaps I am making a mistake with you, Monsieur Jack. The police will perhaps be interested in you and your friend here. Some information anonymous, I think."

"What good'll that do you?" asked Jack. "You were the Minister of Customs when this started. You think that because you're in the Red Chamber King'll protect you if I start to spill?"

The Senator motioned to his thug and the helpmeet came over and punched Jack hard in the stomach. Jack buckled and gagged. The goon blew his knuckles and turned to me. The Senator patted the thug's shoulder and brushed him away.

"This I find distasteful, as I do your treatment of Charles Trudeau. But you are fortunate today, I think. I am merciful. It is simple: you and your comrade will leave the city. You are allowed to live a little more, *hein?* You should, I think, be happy."

It was possible. My left hand was free and I could simply reach out and pick up my revolver. They'd been damned careless and arrogant, mocking us in our powerlessness. It was the same mistake we'd made with crafty Charlie Trudeau. Jack gulped air and the Senator loomed above me. I didn't like his smell, rosewater and dog intermingled. My mouth was parched and my head still repercussed with the blow that'd knocked me out. The dog started pissing against a rotting wall, distracting the Senator and his tough.

"Rex!" the fat man barked.

Very cleanly I picked up the Webley with my left hand and pulled back the hammer with my thumb. The fat man froze. The tough backed up against the kitchen wall. Jack laughed, and slowly the Senator joined him in a baritone.

"You will not shoot me," he said.

"You're right."

I pointed the barrel at Rex. The terrier came to me, interested.

"*Aimez-vous votre canaille?*" I asked.

"An Englishman would never harm an innocent creature," the Senator said, his eyes widening.

"I'm Irish," I said.

I pointed the barrel at the tough and fired. He dropped to the ground screaming: *"Calice! Calvaire!"*

With eyes screwed shut he grasped at his upper thigh. Lucky bugger. I'd aimed below the belt buckle. The dog skittered away in fear.

"You're next after all," I told the Senator. "Cut Jack free."

The fat man's skin had paled beneath his freckling. His dog and tough both whimpered. Smoke and a cordite reek hung in the close air. If the police caught me and I wanted to pass a paraffin test I'd have to scrub my face and hands with eau de cologne or an abrasive soap. The Senator moved stiffly to the countertop and found a rusty knife.

"Attention," I said.

Awkwardly I hopped the chair around to keep the Senator in my line of fire. With thick, stupid fingers he sawed at Jack's bonds. Partially free, Jack took the knife and finished the job. He stood, stretched, and gently prodded the Senator with his index finger.

"Get in the corner with your dog," Jack said.

The Senator complied and scooped Rex up. The tough was shivering and putting pressure on his thigh where dark blood oozed out between his fingers.

"Hurry up," I said. "We don't want a shooting match."

Jack cut me loose. I stood and felt my body itch and tingle upon its release. Jack's face swelled and my head was logy and sore, ears ringing, copper in my mouth, bladder fit to burst. I leaned over the man I'd shot.

"You'll need a doctor," I said.

His shivering redoubled. I'd used the revolver at last, a prophecy come true. The Senator tried to make himself small and cradled his bitch. Jack picked up his own shooting iron and turned to the door. We heard the hard pounding of feet up the back stairs. More trouble there. Jack went over, laughed, and snapped his fingers in the fat man's face.

"À *la prochaine, monsieur.*"

With that we scarpered. I started slipping down the stairs halfway down and rode the treads on my heels, turning backward at the door and bashing out onto the sidewalk. I landed on my coccyx but felt nothing save dizziness and exhilaration. Jack mounted the Auburn and pushed in the keys. A long black saloon 'car with chauffeur was parked opposite but the driver did nothing. He'd heard the shot and seen two bloodied men with guns come tumbling out of the building and decided his salary didn't include getting plugged. Wise bird.

Jack started the engine, choked into gear, added essence, and swung around into the black 'car, the fender screeching across the enamel of the Senator's ride. I jumped on the running board and waved my Webley.

"The South'll rise again! *Sic semper tyrannis!*"

Jack roared down Chambord and I crawled in a window. Perhaps my cerebellum had been damaged by the blow I'd received. I was having trouble thinking, and everything was hilarious: Jack lighting a cigaret while driving with his knees, the sign on a storefront of a gap-toothed idiot sucking up spruce beer with a straw, the startled looks of pedestrians as we rocketed along the quiet street.

My hands only started shaking as I broke open the cylinder of my revolver and removed the spent cartridge. Jack was driving erratically, weaving along and finally stalling out by Lafontaine Park. We traded places and I turned right on Rachel and then left to line up with the clock tower at Victoria Quay. We rolled along downhill and crossed St. Catherine, then worried our way in low gear westerly to Griffintown and Jack's hideout. I parked the motor on a dismal block behind a pile of empty chicken coops and kept the keys. The Auburn looked out of place in this part of town but we were too walloped to do much else. At a corner store I bought a bag of cracked ice and from under the counter a bottle of overproof rum. Jack sat on the curb in front of the building, his head in his hands.

"Come on," I said.

I helped him through the entranceway and up to the third floor. Jack managed to pull out the large key and open the door. He made it to the bed and fell into a swoon. I collapsed into a chair, where I sat still for a spell and blinked out.

LATER ON I heard a voice.

"Charlie got his revenge," Jack said.

"And how," I groaned.

"Should've known better, dealing with a lawyer."

"He was ahead of us," I said. "It was a trap."

"Didn't give him enough credit."

Jack nursed his face with ice balled up in a stained cloth. I lifted the rum bottle, cracked its seal, and added melting ice from the waxpaper bag to a chipped cup. George v's own. Dusk now upon us. Jack took out his medicine and rubbed cocaine powder on his gums to numb the pain. I sniffed a little for renewed pep. We were well-hid in this bolt-hole but it felt as though the other shoe was about to drop. What I'd liked least about the Senator's talk was his threat of the police; they'd been far too absent throughout our series of crimes. Jack and I had operated in a vacuum, abhorrent in nature. Bootlegging, armed robbery, and now a shooting. The man might bleed to death. Testing my sentiments I was interested to discover that I didn't care. Sensation had been dimmed by the shock of my beating, further blunted by the drug and drink.

"Do you think the Senator'll set the dogs on us?" I asked.

"No. His hands're too dirty."

"What about the shipment tomorrow?"

"He doesn't know about that."

"Are you certain?"

"Fairly."

"That's bloody reassuring."

Time slipped by as Jack and I coughed over Charlie's Caporals. I examined my fingernails and smelled my hands for tell-tale residue. There remained the faint aroma of gunpowder. Jack grimaced.

"Nice shot," he said.

"You ever plug anyone?" I asked.

"Germans, mostly."

"Maybe we should take the fat man's advice and get out of town while we can," I said.

"We will. After tomorrow. Now it's war."

"Plains of Abraham redux," I said.

"Best two of three," Jack laughed

We fell into talking Lower Canada: of English and French, Wolfe and Montcalm, Benjamin Arnold, Thomas Jefferson, Napoleon, Louisiana, and the Empress Josephine. To be followed by a little treason concerning the King and Emperor of India, and how we might depose the throne in the name of Marxism and an international revolution of the proletariat.

"That Stalin's a tough bugger," Jack said.

"United Soviet States of America," I said.

From nowhere a crow flew past the window, barely visible in the growing gloom. The bird the first *corbeau* I'd ever seen in Montreal, or the first I'd ever noticed. Its wings scratched like an umbrella opening and closing, or the black taffeta dress of a particular waitress at the Cherry Bank Restaurant long ago. What was her name? When it came I sang: "K-K-K-Katie, beautiful

Katie, you're the only g-g-g-girl that I adore. When the m-m-m-moon shines over the c-c-c-cowshed I'll be waiting at the k-k-k-kitchen door."

Jack lay on the bed, his necktie unknotted. I refilled my glass and swallowed more kerosene. I'd shot a man, and might be a murderer. I was a criminal. No more peace, order, and good government whilst Mick was around. The Pater'd be mortified. This drinking and fornication and more. And what was he doing on the other side of the Dominion? Three hours earlier there. Four o'clock. He'd be taking a nap.

"What're we up against with this Senator?" I asked.

Jack motioned for more rum. I checked his face. He winced as I touched the bloated flesh.

"How're your teeth?"

"Loose."

The glass protecting the print of St. Veronica reflected my own map back, eyes like pissholes in snow.

"Who is he?"

"A Grit," Jack said.

"That's plain."

"I was bagman for the party last election and did some other things as well."

"Such as?"

"Running a crew in the cemeteries writing down names of the recently deceased so we could use them to vote at the polls. That's a dodge old as Confederation. Our friend the Senator was a mere cabinet minister then. Customs and Excise."

Jack stubbed out his cigaret and leaned back on the bed. He reminded me there'd been a federal election last month; I'd been holed away at Memphremagog away from 'papers and the wireless. Mackenzie King and the Grits had been in a minority government with the Progressive party propping them up against Arthur Meighen and the Tories.

"Have you ever seen him in the flesh?" asked Jack.

"Who?"

"Precisely your reaction if you had. Rex King is the dullest egg in Christendom and you'd forget him five minutes after shaking his hand. In fact he's the foxiest bastard outside a briar patch."

As Minister of Customs our friend the Senator had been duly compensated for failing to curb irregularities at the port, Jack explained. No law in our country forbade the sale of liquor to the Americans despite their Prohibition. The risk only came when actually smuggling across the border. Bonded whiskey from Scotland arrived in Montreal earmarked for trans-shipment south to the States. All well and good, and no duties collected here for the Crown.

"However, most of the booze never made it out of the country," Jack said.

"Where'd it go?"

"Dry counties in Ontario, mostly. All the profits, fewer risks. Unfortunately for the minister, someone got wise."

The opposition Tories learned that Customs agents were being compromised and payoffs were going straight to the top. The scandal threatened to take down King's government. Our prime minister thus took preventative action against his minister.

"And made him a Senator. Saints preserve us."

"Better yet," Jack continued, "King formed a blue-ribbon Royal Commission to investigate the Port of Montreal. Hearings were held and detectives sent in to investigate."

"Meanwhile the world kept spinning and molasses flowed in January. I follow. Then what happened?"

Jack laid out the lineaments of a parliamentary donnybrook: Arthur Meighen and the Tories howling for scalps, the Progressives defecting from King's government, King visiting Rideau Hall and tendering his resignation, the Governor General weighing in on the side of the Tories, more shenanigans in the House of Commons, a midnight vote, a crisis of the Constitution and, after a summer election, Mackenzie King back at the top, his enemies defeated. Meighen was put to pasture, the Governor General on a slow boat back to Blighty, and the Customs scandal ploughed under entirely.

"Now Rex King's lecturing the Empire on Canada's sovereignty in London and it's business as usual in Sin City, as you see."

"And your role in this farce?"

"Can't you guess?"

"No."

"I was one of the detectives the Royal Commission sent to investigate smuggling at the port."

I burst out laughing. Lamp standards on the street now burned a soft gold. I opened a window and smelled impending snow. Before a stoop a bent figure sharpened knives on a whirling stone, spitting sparks.

"Pinkertons," Jack continued. "When King worked for the Rockefellers in the States he used the agency. I came recommended for this line of work."

"Naturally, with your gifts."

Did Jack hear the irony in my voice? If he did, he chose to ignore it. In front of the tavern across the street stood two men in black surcoats. Working for the government was how Jack had aligned himself with bootleggers, Charlie Trudeau, and the Senator. Fox guarding the henhouse. Jack divined my thoughts, his nasty habit.

"There was too much money to be made," said Jack. "If not me then who? The Senator still got his cut and Charlie Trudeau ran the trucks. The difference was I started smuggling to the States for keeps, and I was dealing with Italians across the border. Another world. Long way from Soda Creek. Which leads me to ask you, Mick. Are you still with me tomorrow night?"

I looked at the shabby brick tenements across the way and tasted coalsmoke. A child screamed from one of the rooms below us. A deeper cold fell and I shut the window. The two men in black did not look up. Was I with him after this? We'd come mighty far together.

"Pardon me," I said.

I went to the lavatory and had a good long gander at myself in the dim light. With a sliver of soap I washed and scrubbed my face and hands in the frigid water and slicked back my hair. Wild notions rose within: walk away this moment. Jack will be your ruin. Crime is punished. What would I do with myself? I had no job and wanted none, no friends save he, no family. I'd lost my love. In the vile darkness I pulled out the revolver and returned to the room. I could easily shoot him and then myself. Jack sat on the bed, his gun in his hand. He looked at me and smiled.

"I'll need another bullet," I said

"Knew you were true blue."

"*Alea iacta est.*"

We killed the bottle. The men in front of the tavern moved away. There came over me a flush of heat and cold commingled, of past, present, and future aligning, a fuse slotted into place. I'd never experienced anything quite like it and was at last allowed to identify the sensation: surrender. This was my fate, tangled in a skein with Jack's. I must follow the thread to its end, wherever it led. While Jack slept I spent a painful night upright in the chair, the Webley in my hand, waiting for the dawn.

FRIDAY

SOMETIME DURING THE long night it began to snow. I smoked the hours away and watched slow flakes fall from an iron sky. Near daybreak drays hauled wagons through the white. Plodders sloshed muddy footprints through the splodge and then came saltshakers, sandmen, and shovellers who cursed and huffed over heavy masses. By and by the sky unveiled blue and it became one of those sere eastern mornings I hated to admit I loved. By noon the city's heat and friction would melt the snow to dirty gutter runnels. While watching Montreal light up I faded. A voice woke me.

"Friday."

"Friday," I repeated.

Jack's eyes burned bloodshot and his face was raw, lip swollen. My poor body ached and itched, blood boiling from the rum and salt. The cardboard cigaret deck was crushed and empty, one bullet smoked for each regret. Jack sat Indian-style on the bed. On my sinister zygomatic ran a pulse of hot pain from the blow that'd knocked me out. The room stank of cordite, stale tobacco, and men, worse than a pool hall the morning after. Out the window fingers of ice weighed down telephone wires in the building's shadow.

"So, what's the interior of the Mount Royal Club like?" I asked.

"Pardon?"

"You heard."

"Clever brute," Jack said.

His eyes glittered out from beneath lowered lids, a colder blue. My own were brown near black with the pupils pinholes in the iris, stinging and sullen.

"Hungry?" asked Jack.

"Not half."

A gramophone wailed out Caruso from a downstairs room. I felt none too clean and in need of a cooking in the bath.

"Let's move the motor elsewhere," I suggested.

"Fine idea. We'll need it later," Jack said.

So Jack was determined to carry through his mad scheme. I noticed he hadn't answered my question. We creaked to life, my mind pinwheeling, an ache near the crook of my arm where the needle'd bit through the skin back in the day. An observant coroner would see the scar there.

Together Jack and I shambled down to the street and walked to where we'd left the sedan. I circled the block to make sure it hadn't been marked for a clipping. The Senator or Trudeau might've contacted the cops and given over our particulars, hoping the authorities were up to the task of taking us down. The force owned a fleet of five blue Frontenacs, and there were plenty more patrolmen on foot. The likelihood of our being rousted was low but we took meagre precautions nonetheless.

Jack suggested we leave the Auburn in a scrub lot on the back side of the mountain. I nixed the idea as obvious and with too many places for the police to stake us out, rifles at the ready. My notion was to scatter it as a leaf in the forest amongst other motors. Jack agreed, too tired to argue me, and we parked on a side street in east Westmount. From there we hacked it back into

town, Jack off to his hotel and I to mine after a stop at the tobacconist's for twenty Forest and Streams. We agreed to meet in the
Morgan's toy department at one.

With some care I approached the ancient 'hop in the faded
red velvet coat outside the Wayside and slipped him two dollars.
No sir, no one has been nosing around the hotel asking questions
about any of the guests lately and your room has been entered
only by the chambermaid. A nancy behind the front desk handed
me my key without any interest and I went up. In the lift a frost
seeped through me, a premonition, but the room proved to be
untouched. Before anything else I went to the toilet and urinated,
then refilled the Webley's empty chamber from the hidden box
of cartridges. I sat down on the bed in a cold sweat.

What was I becoming? One virtue of the recent activity had
been its usefulness as a distraction from contemplation. Now
that I was alone in a quiet room doubt made its assault. I was
a pathetic creature prey to the manipulation of others. None of
the fine qualities grafted onto me by my education and upbringing had flourished; I was no one's idea of a gentleman, with no
rectitude, no finer sentiment. *Mens sana in corpore sano,* my
arse. There was an infection working through me, corrupting
my actions, turning me into an antigen in the body public. I felt
the locus of an impending epidemic, society's immune system
battling what it saw as the wayward seed of a moral cancer. The
Pater, Jack, Laura, her father Sir Dunphy, the Senator, Charlie
Trudeau, William Lyon Mackenzie King, Lilyan Tashman, and
that dirty four-flusher Bob—they'd all die, I swore. I hadn't lasted
to take the Hippocratic Oath, worse luck for them. The Webley's
action was smooth, its weight heavy in my hand. With disgust
I put it down, tore off my collar and shirt, and threw them into
the hallway incinerator chute, then stripped, brushed my teeth,
bathed, and roughly scoured my nakedness with a cheap towel.
With care I fastened new cuffs to a freshly boiled chemise and

snapped a soft collar 'round my neck, then lay full-length on the bed. From the street came the sound of a woman screaming obscenities in French.

A reverie manifested from the future: I was a clerk quietly rolling pennies for the Bank of British North America, courting the fair stenographer daughter of a lumberman back in Vancouver. She and I would walk past the arch in Stanley Park and look across the inlet to the pyramids of raw yellow sulphur beneath the mountains on the far shore. We were engaged, and in love, and the Pater would officiate at the wedding ceremony. All my efforts at that hellish cabin in 'Magog where I'd wrestled away my addiction to morphine were rewarded, my trespasses forgiven. I'd turned over a new leaf and settled down.

It was no use. The Pater'd sniff out the corruption oozing from my pores. He'd recognize his son for a wastrel, a thief, a drunk. Jack was the true prodigal. It's the way of the striving Scotch-Irish: without a calling or a title or a bank account I was the worst of my class.

The only way I was headed back west was in a box. There were no further colonies to ship me off to and hide the family's shame, except the North. Fancy that, me manning a Hudson's Bay Company post on Frobisher Bay or the bank of the Great Slave Lake, the true *ultima Thule* of atonement and toil. No. Better off in the great Republic to the south, where I'd be snapped up in a trice, my villainy, covetousness, and hypocrisy rewarded and praised to the heavens. Look at Warren Harding, for Christ's sake.

With deliberate care I re-counted every banknote by denomination in piles on the bedspread, a finite amount shrinking nickel by dime. Tonight that'd change, should Jack's plan play out. Thinking on that, I smoked. Truly the essence of life was in this endless waiting for something to happen. All the interstices, the queuing for tickets, crowded bus trips, and painful midnight walks to empty rooms, all the moments that the mind wiped clean. Instead it crammed itself with detritus and reckoned up restaurant receipt totals. Unwanted snatches of popular songs reverberated. There's no drama in the quintessence, the eternal wasted moments like this point in space and time. The Earth was in constant motion and Einstein could do the maths. Was it possible to walk it all back, unshoot the Senator's thug and cradle Rex the dog? The poor bitch cowering in a corner. I closed my eyes to banish the image and unbidden Laura's shape materialized. I felt a tumescence of arousal and touched my erection. Humiliated, I rubbed my eye sockets and felt every dendrite fray, raw nerves spitting electricity. I rolled my money together and pocketed the gun. Animal vigour seemed the only real activity, a pursuit of appetite. It was time to go.

With my Gladstone carry-all I left the hotel but kept the key, having paid for three more days. From there I repaired to an old haunt on Craig Street for an ale. It was dark as sin inside, *comme d'hab*, low and mean and right. My skin crawled and my hands shook as I lit a match. In the *Star* I again read about the progress of the bloody queen of Rumania and a poor bastard who'd been struck down by a streetcar at the corner of St. Mark and St. Catherine. Still nothing on bootleggers, the Loew's robbery, Trudeau's beating, or a shooting fracas on the Plateau. To nourish my frame I ordered a Horse's Neck and followed it with another ale. The chatter in the bar quelled slowly and I looked in a mirror. I was pale and interesting from exhaustion. Jack's powdered pep would perk me up. He was getting it from Smiler, I remembered, and my humour leached of blood. Smiler and I had trained in leechcraft at the Royal Victoria Hospital. There was a Leachtown off the River Jordan on Vancouver Island; failed panners swirled for stray grains of gold there. Great rigs with thick cables were strung up to hew the forests down with a tearing and a rending, saws biting through wood as huge firs crashed down. There came a sharp cracking and the bar's windowpane showed a long white line. Someone had thrown a rock. The 'tender went outside to investigate and returned, shaking his head.

"*Personne*," he said.

A seedy egg in the back began blethering about the mayor so I killed the ale and left a little silver. While hiking away with my lousy bag I passed a pair of bobbies in leather Ulsters on the sidewalk and did not blench. Was any of this even happening? Was I being watched, an unwitting actor in a complicated conspiracy involving Jack and the Senator, an unknowing tool of some secret group manipulating my activities for occult reasons? Yes. It seemed clear to me I was being used to satisfy certain prophecies of the British Israelites and the Round Table to raise the Red Hand in Holy Ireland. I would rebuild the Temple in Jerusalem with an archangel's name and the caduceus of Mercury, then claim my crown. It was either that or sire the Moonchild and assist Bolsheviks in the service of Marx and worldwide revolution. My random crimes undermined capitalism and the bourgeoisie's complacency. I was fated to destroy the Commonwealth and the League of Nations. Do it, Michael. Be stern and cold, wield sword and cross.

I needed sleep. For a very few confused minutes I was at St. Pancras Station in London, then a Christmas panto in the West End with a chum from Victoria. My head spun as I dropped my Gladstone off at Windsor Station, under the angel guiding a dead serviceman to heaven, same as the one in Winnipeg, same as the one in Vancouver. With that reminiscence I completed a wide circuit to Morgan's department store. What I needed was hot tea and rest to rid associative thought of its power. One face in the crowd held the shadow of the ghost of the smile of a girl I'd seen on a tram outside Covent Garden years ago, another stranger could have been the long-lost brother of my old headmaster at the Normal School. This series of interplayed mental connections, this bastard combination of paramnesia and nostalgia, would lead me up the primrose path to the crack-up ward.

Passersby on the pavement buffeted me as I crossed in front of Christ Church. Most of the snow had vanished but the Morgan's door openers had availed themselves of the occasion to swaddle in fur greatcoats and hats. To begin with I disdained the entranceway and walked around an entire city block clockwise in order to clear my brain and check dark reflections in store windows for any pursuers. A mangled veteran begged for alms. When I flipped a half-dollar into his cap the wretch raised a metal hook to his eye and wheezed: "Anybody want a duck?"

As an officer and gentleman, second lieutenant in the Seventy-second Highlanders, I gave the victim another dollar to thank my lucky stars. But for the grace of God go you, Mick me lad, or Jack himself, a Duke of Connaught's Own. The entire population was diseased or deformed in some way, within or without, including myself. My ailment needed a name related to its outward symptomology: the futile attempt of placing oneself within a comprehensive whole of variegated, pointless, randomized memory to find significance. I diagnosed myself with a terminal case of Mick's Syndrome. Turning a precise ninety-degree angle onto City Councillors brought no greater clarity. Man had tried to impose a petty order by surveying straight lines, encoding secret equations in dead foundations. Below this system there reigned pure chaos, a blind worm chewing through space. By turning another corner I was satisfied and pushed through a revolving door into the great volume of the store.

Inside I was washed in the soft sea of the female. Perfume poured over me, a rich mixture: attar of rose and lavender, citron and orange and sweet talc powder. I closed my eyes and inspired and for a blessed moment was not cruel and cold and alone. I saw the temporary dream of crystal and chrome glittering as scent bottles and precious things sat ranged before fluttering women.

Shopgirls wore smart navy frocks and waited on furred and feathered doyennes, the whole scene clean and bright, almost alien. Here was a high altar for that sisterhood of wealth, each movement part of a choreographed ritual conducted in discreet undertones. For a moment I smelled myself—sweat and tobacco and fear—and then my heart leapt as I saw Laura select something silver from a shelf. As a clerk passed the woman turned into another rich redhead and I breathed out. By God, this was civilization, why the mills ground fine and forges smelted hot. It was for them, to keep womanhood safe and soft and free from harm. I became covetous and wanted it, this world. I wanted it now.

As I took the staircase to the basement a large clock on the wall read one pip-emma on the dot, time for tiffin. In the toy department painted wooden imps hung smiling on hooks. To one side were train sets and baseball bats, on the other kewpie dolls and tea sets. Beyond a neatly stacked pile of Erector Sets and cowboy rifles Jack chatted up a pretty floorwalker. He touched her face and she flushed, embarrassed. I sent a loose hoop his way, my revolver in my pocket to play its own game in due time. The wooden circle hit Jack and fell spinning on the tiles. Jack turned to me.

"*Adieu, mademoiselle,*" he said.

Jack took the shopgirl's hand, twisted it 'round and bowed to kiss her wrist.

"Valentino taught me that."

He winked at her and she peered over to roll her eyes at me. That was a fine sight and I was secretly delighted. Jack's charm could curdle. It appeared that he'd taken more cocaine as he violently chewed spearmint gum while at the same time smoking a cigaret.

"We're set," he said.

"For what?"

"A little light entertainment."

We went back upstairs and outside and crossed the street to the Princess Theatre. It was closed.

"What's this?" I asked.

"A matinee," Jack said, and smiled.

He turned to the grille of the box office wicket and rapped on the smoked glass. It was impossible to see anyone behind it. A dry voice asked: "Who's calling?"

"Jack London, *San Francisco Chronicle*. I'm here for the interview."

Jack slid a five into the gap. I heard a thumping and a click as a door unlocked. Jack carefully took the gum from his mouth and did a disgusting thing with it. We went into the lobby and found it empty. It was eerie. I fingered my gun and felt anxiety.

"Nice couvert charge," I said.

The dry voice came from a speakerphone above: "Door to the left, dressing rooms backstage."

We followed the directions. The theatre house was silent, empty seats before a half-closed curtain across the stage, a dusty smell of stale tobacco smoke and damp velvet. Reigning backstage we found a confusion of ropes and wires. Enormous padlocked boxes stencilled with Houdini's name sat in the wings. These presumably held the secrets of the Chinese Water Torture Cell and the Milk Can Escape. Until the other night I'd only seen Houdini in a serial at the picture house: *The Man From Beyond*. He'd escaped from a light bulb once, another time from a paper bag.

"He got free from a Russian prison cell stark bollocky naked," Jack said.

Echoing my thoughts again. I turned back on the empty house of crimson chairs. It was haunted. We were spectres. A phantom audience watched me, Ulysses by the pool of blood at World's End as the sightless dead of Hades streamed past. Shakespeare played the ghost in *Hamlet*, fasting in fires. A thin, high, sharp note like the whine of a mosquito rose in my ears and abruptly quit. I turned away and Jack was gone. I noticed a line on the stage floor and bumped face-first like a fool into a large mirror reflecting a room behind me. I went into that and found Jack sitting on a barrel, smiling.

"Pepper's Ghost," he said. "You see how it works."

"I don't and what're we doing here?"

Jack held up a finger and cocked his ear, then very quietly whistled the first bars of "Annie Laurie."

"Bad luck in a theatre," I said.

"Not for me."

We moved 'round the stage machinery and found a corridor leading to the dressing rooms. From behind a closed door came murmuring voices. I made out: "...as the miracle at Cana or walking on the water. Think, lads, what I might have accomplished in those times."

Jack opened the door to a room opposite and motioned me into it. It was a place for showgirls by the scent of powder. In the darkness Jack peered through a crack to see who came and went and consulted his wristwatch, a fine thin Longines. Nothing but the best for himself, my envy thought. I sat down on a wicker chair and was brushed by feathers. As I made to smoke Jack stopped me. He'd taken out his Webley.

"We're going to have a private chat," he said.

"With that?" I motioned towards the revolver.

"We'll see."

He held up his hand at a soft tumult and cry, then the sound of furniture shifting about. I joined Jack at the crack. A tall gaunt man with a long Mackintosh left the room across the way. A light lit his hollow face and left the afterimage of a skull on the back of my eyelids when I blinked. Jack chuckled. Beside me I could feel him set to spring, Jack-from-a-box. Opposite us the door opened again. Two more men exited and I recognized them with some small anger: Smiler and Jacques Price from the night of Houdini's speech. Jack put on his gloves. I saw yellow pinpoints glow in the corner of the dressing room. A cat, I hoped with a sudden chill. We stepped into the corridor.

Inconsequential music ran through my head, bloody "Yes, We Have No Bananas." A neurologist might be able to excise from my cortex the portion responsible for housing such tripe. A selective lobotomy a keen boon for the heartbroken. I took a deep breath to counteract a queasy swelling of excitement. Something unfortunate was about to happen and I felt an elation akin to morphine, ganglia pulsing with an increased cardiac cycle. Jack pushed open the door.

It was surprisingly cold. Houdini was on a chaise longue in the far corner, his eyes closed, for all the world dead. I touched the radiator by the wall and felt its chill. Jack was the first to speak.

"Time is, time was, time's past."

"Who dares?" asked Houdini, opening his eyes.

"Where lies the key?" countered Jack.

Houdini sat mum a moment, then shifted to his elbows and glared fiercely. His eyes were the same cold blue as Jack's.

"You mere man," he said.

"I'm not alone," warned Jack.

"Yes you are."

"There you are in error, *monsieur*."

"What, this?" asked Houdini, looking at me.

"No. You see more clearly, I am sure," said Jack.

There was a pause. Houdini sank back onto his bolster.

"Your masters," he breathed.

"You've pledged to reveal all. This cannot be."

Jack was getting mighty high-flown, in my opinion. Whether this was more than mere catechism I couldn't say. The look on my friend's face was past raillery. This was very serious to him.

"Truth will out," said Houdini.

"Not this one."

"The public must know. It's dangerous for them."

"Moreso for you," said Jack.

Houdini started at this but then winced and pressed a hand to his wide forehead and closed his eyes once more.

"Are you well?" asked Jack.

"Some damn fool struck me. And my ankle was injured in Buffalo."

Jack indicated me.

"My friend here has medical training."

"No doctors," said Houdini from his corner.

"Oh, he's no doctor."

I moved to examine the magician. He waved me off.

"I know why he bends to superstition," Houdini said to Jack.

"Why?"

"I know because the same tragedy has befallen myself. But he cannot listen to that brood. They are jackals, vultures. To fall into their clutches means abandoning reason. I know this."

Houdini looked at his dressing table where rested a gold-framed portrait of an aged lady.

"It is as much for his own sake as that of your people," Houdini continued.

"No good will come of it," Jack said. "Let the foundation rest; the walls are unstable. The key is in the bone box. Leave it there."

"Is that a command?"

"To a greater or lesser degree," said Jack.

"Well. It does not matter. The fire has died in me."

He opened his eyes and looked into mine magnetically. Jack bent over a carafe in the corner. Houdini asked me: "And what is your learnèd opinion?"

The moment extended and I saw the world-famous man weak and alone like the rest of us. He didn't look well. If it was magic he dealt in, magic I'd give him.

"Sacrifice a cock to Asclepius," I said.

Houdini snorted with contempt. Jack handed him a glass. Houdini sipped from it and pulled a sour face. He handed it back to Jack, who ran the faucet in the sink. Houdini sighed and said: "Tell them the secret is safe with me."

"I will."

"Houdini is a man of his word."

We made to leave. I looked back and Houdini's eyes were closed again. The room was a tomb. We threaded our way through the back of the theatre to a door leading out to an alley.

"What's the word?" I asked Jack.

He put a finger to his lips and smiled.

PAST SCRAPS OF dirty snow we made our way over cobbles to the street proper. The sun had come out, warming the steaming pavement; 'twas relief to trade Houdini's mausoleum for the life and colour of the city. The contrast was striking. A pretty girl looked at me through long eyelashes. I was alive, an electric animal singing with power. At the corner a traffic accident had a policeman untangling arguments as vapour hissed from under a green Chrysler's bonnet and people crowded 'round for the free show. We passed an Indian squaw carrying a papoose slung on her back. The baby smiled at me through a horrible cleft palate covered in streaming mucus. My stomach twisted at this, the true face of mankind. Jack walked along blithely and suggested a late luncheon.

He led us west to the Royale for either Oriental or Occidental cuisine. Jack ordered the former, a mess of tapeworm noodles and cat's flesh. My plate sampled the latter cookery, leathery horsemeat with fried crow's eggs. Instead of eating I smoked while Jack forked nourishment into his mouth.

"Not hungry?"

He finished his plate and with my nodding assent started on mine. Replete, he wiped his mouth with a serviette and asked: "Ready for tonight?"

"Yes. How's it look?"

"Swell. Eggs in the coffee. There's something I need to tell you, though. We have a third."

"A third? Who?"

Jack lit a cigaret and raised his eyebrows. No. Not that sharper. Not now.

"We have to," Jack said, reading me.

"Like fun," I said.

"'Fraid so."

"Then you lose me."

"Mick, please."

He reached across our ruined meal and put his hand on my shoulder.

"You can settle your score with him when we're done."

"It's your hand in all this," I said.

Jack leaned back.

"No. Bob met her through the theatre crowd. Laura cottoned on to the circle. Bored, I suppose. When I was at Victoria Hall for that dance she was with him. I didn't know where you were or what'd happened, I swear. None of my business. This is. We need the third arm. Hold your nose and afterwards all bets are off. The trade is at the pier. We're going to hit them before they board ship. The third'll hang back as getaway while we go in for the goods. I've got it all worked out."

"You'd better."

"It will work or it won't. Stakes are high but so's the payoff. To the victor and all that."

"Spare me." I rose and went to the filthy toilet. Over the lavatory I read: "Get ready, the LORD is coming SOON. 'Behold I come quickly and my reward is with me, to give to every man according as his work shall be.'" Below it was written: "If I had a girl and she was mine I'd paint her ass with iodine and on her belly I'd put a sign 'Keep off the grass, the hole is mine.'"

At the basin I washed my hands and looked at the mirror. There was no one in it.

"Oke," I said, back at the table.

"Christ but you're a downy bird, Mick."

He'd paid for our food and was sitting at his ease at the Formica.

"Tell me what was what with your man in the theatre there," I said.

"I will, but later."

"You afraid I'll sing if I'm caught?"

"You can't tell what you don't know. And it's not the cops I'm worried about but the other fellows. They'll clip your ears for fun and games," Jack said.

"That's reassuring."

"I know you're up for it."

"This's all been some sort of challenge, hasn't it? Why're you doing it?"

Jack put his hands together and leaned in.

"What're your plans for the future?"

"Unknown," I said.

"Will you head back?"

"To the Pater's? Not likely. Even with money I don't want him sniffing at me. Without my medical degree I'm a dog."

"Is that so?"

"Whereas you could show up at the door in chains and he'd open his arms."

"Unlikely."

"That's what you think. The Sunday after you ran away and joined the colours he preached the Prodigal Son. He had a scrapbook hidden in his study. The pages were filled with clippings from the 'papers of every action your regiment was in."

"Jesus, Mick, I didn't know."

There was a catch in Jack's voice and I swore I caught a tear quickening in his eye.

"He'd forgive you everything," I said.

"Not everything," Jack muttered.

Now Jack was far away. Brightening, I said, "Well, you could be worse off. In me he sees my mother and hates me for it. Always has. You're different. He chose you. He'd have left me on Skid Road if he'd been able to square it with the book and the kirk and the bloody Battle of the Boyne."

"The Glorious Twelfth," said Jack.

The Pater'd preached the Word to the hard men of the camps past Lillooet, men like the Wolf and Jack's father, who'd disappeared prospecting up the wash one autumn, never to return. When my father'd found Jack he was near feral, shivering and begging for scraps from the Chinese camp cooks and cruel Indians, a cur kicked away from the fire. Indebted for his escape, Jack had played Christian soldier for the Pater, and my upright father prized his wildness and charm, whereas I'd only been a reminder of what my father had lost. I'd killed her by being born.

So I waited and watched as we grew up together down in Vancouver, watched Jack with the prettiest girls and fastest friends, real five-cent sports. My Scripture first was as naught to Jack's second or third. I turned away from John Knox and my father and delved into different patterns of belief. Jack was the golden lad, ace cricketer and scapegrace, romantic and dashing where I was quiet and dark. He led our gang and stole bottles of wine from Italian greengrocers and horses from Siwashes in Chinatown, cursing in Cantonese as I'd learn to, in emulation of my captain. When alone and away from under Jack's flag I'd be waylaid by jealous enemies from rival gangs and be given a good thumping, too small to fight back and too damn proud to run. That was the Irish in me, taking a beating and liking it. From my father there was little save silence when I'd return home bruised and cut. Only the amah cared, swabbing my cuts in iodine while jabbering in Chinook.

My father was born an Ulster Scot but my mother'd been a real dark colleen from down in the south and Catholic to boot. How they'd met and married the Lord only knew. For an amah I had a Carrier Indian, my mother's servant and somehow kinswoman, the Holy Ghost and Old Ones meeting and mingling with Manitou and Raven. When my mother died the amah nursed me. From her I learned the twinned secret mythologies of two broken people. All his life my father's creed had been reason, education, and light. The faith of my mother was tricky and dark. Somehow I'd been made in neither image and was reflected in the quicksilver of Jack: friend, tormentor, blood brother, the man who was going to get me killed one day. I crushed a cigaret out on a greasy plate.

"Better," said Jack, patting his belly.

After the Royale we went to Jack's hotel. He'd moved to the Queen's on Peel and was registered as Jack Greenmantle. Up in his room he excused himself to defecate and I found a bottle of cognac on the sideboard. The alcohol stung and cleaned my teeth as I thought of Laura and Bob, that Yankee bastard. You'll settle his hash tonight. He hadn't seen me as I watched them in that upstairs bedroom. Only Laura, her eye meeting mine in the darkness. There'd been a telling in her gaze, a kind of triumph laced with something I couldn't define. I took another swallow and it came: she'd been expecting someone else. Who? Jack yanked the chain in the jakes and came out buttoning his trousers.

"Yesterday's news," he said.

He sat down and laid out the night's plans. Including Bob, the three of us were going to hit the competition before they ever

set foot on the *Hatteras Abyssal*. The ship was tied up at Queen
Alexandra Pier. Jack and I had one motor and Bob would bring
another. It was Trafalgar Night and the lion's share of the police
force would be marching in the parade or directing traffic. The
plan's virtue, Jack claimed, was in its simplicity.

"That's what you said about the bootlegging and the picture
house. And now look at us," I said.

"It's better this way," said Jack. "I'm not Raffles the Gentleman
Cracksman. Make a meticulous plan and it'll go haywire. I want
to be spontaneous, to improvise."

"Christ, you're like a stick-up poet."

"There you've put it with a nicety," Jack said.

"We were lucky before. This is pushing it."

"Count your money and tell me about pushing it. How'd you
get it, now? Did it come in the mail? You wouldn't have the spon-
dulicks if not for Yours Truly, Esquire."

"I never asked for them. You volunteered me," I said.

"Knowing you as I do. This is bootless, Mick."

"Let's go over the ground at least. Is that too much to be asking after?"

"Lead on."

OUR STEPS TOOK US in the direction of the docks, the streets
still radiating the day's heat. I looked up at a spider's web of tram-
way wires. Underfoot nubs on manhole covers had been worn flat
by countless treads and the metal slipped. My coat hung heavy
on me, steaming with the city. A motorcar nearby backfired and
I flinched, my hand bouncing into my pocket. Jack laughed.
Drunken late-season wasps crawled in the gutter outside a warehouse from whence the sickly reek of rotting fruit seeped forth.
It might've been an alky-cooker distilling cheap fruit brandy.
Minute quantities of wasp venom can trigger anaphylaxis in the
allergic. Put a drop on a needle for the perfect crime. As far as I

knew Jack had no natural nemesis. Mine was the lychee, a lesson learned in Chinatown.

"Wonder how that fellow you shot is doing?" Jack asked.

"The Senator's jobbie? He deserved it. Like Bob."

"Put your animus away for the evening," Jack said.

"I said I would."

"What you do after that's no skin off mine."

"Mighty white of you."

"Ain't it though? Here we are."

We took a dekko along the pier, staying in motion so as not to draw attention. Jack narrated: "We'll park there and wait. You're in the motor and I'll loiter with intent. Bob'll be in another 'car. Four men are coming with the money. They're making the trade onboard. We'll hit them before they pull up to the gangplank."

"What if the set-up's different?" I asked.

"How do you mean?"

"I mean last week we drove trucks to the border. Why're they doing it here now?"

"Boats," Jack said.

"And what'll they have? Tommy guns or pistols or what?"

"That I don't know," said Jack.

"Christ."

"What do you want? These operators have paid for the convenience. This isn't a battleground like Chicago. Montreal's been nice and quiet since Prohibition passed. Last week was an aberration. I was set up and now I've been cut out. Truthfully, I should be on the hook for the shipment lost but there've been no reprimands from Chicago, and do you know why? Because I was to be killed. I was crossed by my own masters for some damned reason and this is my payback. Now I've got the inside dope and aim to clean 'em out."

"Aren't you afraid of the consequences?"

"You'd better believe it," Jack said.

"They pull up, and then what happens?"

"Damn the torpedoes."

"What?"

"Full speed ahead."

"You're crazy. Ram them?"

"That's right."

"Not me," I said.

"Why not?"

"Because the damn things are full of petrol. They'll explode."

"If you're yellow Bob can do it and you drive the getaway."

"He'll blow the works for sure. Fine, I'll do it."

"There's the man."

Jack smiled.

"What happens after I smash them?" I asked.

"I make the grab."

"Then what?"

"You cover me and we hop in Bob's sled."

"Jesus. This is a really beautiful, well-conceived plan."

"Ain't it though?" asked Jack again, grinning that grin.

"Let's get a drink and go over it again."

"If we must," said Jack.

"Believe me, we must."

A long slog in silence took us back to relative civilization and we repaired to another saloon advertising sterilized glasses, ordering two filled up with beer.

"How much do you think this imbroglio'll net us?" I asked.

"The run last week was smaller. This shipment's about five times larger," Jack said. "Say, twenty thousand."

"It's a damned complicated plot you've got us wound up in."

"You don't know the half of it," Jack said.

"Do you really think a bunch of boyos like us can take on this outfit?"

"Why the hell not?" asked Jack. "Who says a pack of lousy Italians are smarter than we? They've got the Black Hand but we've got the Brotherhood."

"The Brotherhood? Are they in on this as well? Whose side are we on?"

"Our own," Jack said.

"That's reassuring."

Jack put down his glass and became very still and serious. He pointed at me.

"Listen to me. What has anyone ever done for you? The King, the Brass Hats, the Archbishop of bloody Canterbury, that lot would've let you be chewed up into hamburger in France without a twinge of remorse, and all for a lie. Believe you me. Now those are the jokers I'd like to take on but they've got a little too much muscle for the moment. We'll just have to wait for the global revolution. Meanwhile I want some elbow room, and that means money. We're stealing from criminals, Mick. Worse comes to worst we get shot for our trouble. Tell me, what's worth living for, eh?"

This was something to consider, but there was more. Jack said: "So we lived through the war. I'm not going to croak an old man in bed. It's this or something else. What difference does it make?"

"That's a damned convincing argument. You should have stood for the bar. A judge'd love that defence," I said.

"To hell with it all," Jack said, and drank.

I looked moodily into my sludgy glass, divining nothing. Perhaps Jack was a blind prophet. In the drinkery a deep burnt-oil smell pervaded and I drank more of the rotten stuff, choking it back.

"We'd better go and wind up that motor," I said.

"Now you're cooking with gas," went my Tiresias.

ON DORCHESTER WE caught a 'cab and took it to the street where the Auburn sat parked. While walking to it I heard hot jazz in my head, as though a record was spinning within, like a movie house pianist accompanying my actions. Someday they'll play recorded music at the cinema like a radio play and make a talking picture, with coloured film for verisimilitude. It'll be closer to real life, like now. Look at the purple grease on the windscreen of the motor, the curled rusty leaves, the indigo sky. The music continued to play in my mind's ear, as it were: "Hot Potato." Jack got behind the wheel.

"Shame they can't shoehorn a wireless into a 'car," I said. "A body could listen to music while driving."

"Distracting," Jack said.

He motioned for the keys and we swung away. The evening sun crept down near the mountain. By taking side streets and quiet lanes we slotted the motor in an unmemorable siding. It was suppertime. Around the block at a dry-goods merchant we each purchased a bottle of medicinal ginger wine, neither Jack nor I in an aquabibulous frame of mind. The bottles held a nerve tonic and stomach settler. The storekeep uncorked one and its contents tasted of Angostura Bitters laced with rancid sugar. We left to tread down empty redolent alleyways leading away from the river, industry winding down at this hour in our obscure corner of the Empire.

What did we talk of? Jack reminisced and we laughed as the tonic made us merry. I put away my shallow resentments and entered the absurd spirit of the thing. The past was ephemeral and faintly ridiculous, a series of harebrained scrapes and foolish amours. As dusk thickened we evoked our lost world of the West: the taste of raw Walla Walla onions big as baseballs, pickled herring, and Indian candy from Ship's Point on Vancouver Island where Cook had anchored near heaps of oyster shells. Finishing the medicine Jack dropped the corked empty bottle in the drink and the river's current pulled it away to join flotsam clinging 'round a rowboat tied up near a small freighter. Ship's rope groaned as Jack discreetly checked his weapon. I did likewise and spun the cylinder of my Mark IV. It was the same sidearm make I'd been issued with my pip. Jack stuck his in his belt under a buttoned jacket and unbelted overcoat. I kept mine safe in an outer pocket. Jack spat in the oily water. There wasn't a soul about, though I heard a faint shouting from some streets behind us. My nine hundred dollars and change was safe upon me so I lit a cigaret and Jack's with the same lucifer.

"Never three to a match," Jack said. "First one the sniper spots, the second he aims, the third he fires."

"Did you see it happen?"

"One of those bits of advice that travelled up and down the line. You heard it all: crucifixions in No Man's Land, ghosts and the Angels of Mons. Dammit, though, it was impossible to tell truth from fiction there, the whole thing was too bloody unreal. Whole world went down the fucking rabbit hole and where it's going now I don't like to think."

Jack looked at his ring awhile and then said: "There'll be another war."

"They'll fight it with Zeppelins and heat-rays," I said.

"Damn me I don't know."

"We'll be gone before it starts anyhow."

"Speak for yourself," Jack said, and spat again.

That was him all over. One minute careless and blithe, then queerly sober. He checked his wristwatch.

"Waiting to go over was the worst of it," he said, "waiting for the whistle."

I yawned, cracking my temporomandibular joint loudly.

"No rest for the wicked," continued Jack.

"Sleep in heaven," I said.

"Or the other place."

We completed a circuit and I looked into the dirty water. Gulls circled and dove. No river is the same river, so sayeth Heraclitus. The St. Lawrence poured towards the sea, thalassa, thalassa. Jack checked the time again.

"He's late, the bastard."

"*Alors,*" I said.

"Wait a minute."

A 'car careened into the crossing near the jetty, the rendezvous between Duke and Nazareth by the train tracks. It was a fawn Oldsmobile that swerved to intersect with us. Jack held up his hand like a traffic cop and Bob braked to a clumsy halt. He rolled down the window and grinned sloppily.

"Goddammit man, you're drunk," Jack said.

"Ain't you?" asked Bob.

"Get out and take some air."

"Oke."

Bob dismounted. To open my bottle of ginger wine I pushed the cork down its neck out of ugly necessity, then took a long swig of the restorative. I handed it to Jack, who pulled and passed the bottle to Bob. Bob looked at me a moment with no expression and I was dead certain he knew nothing of my attachment to Laura. I tamped down a panicky sort of anger. I didn't like him, how he'd touched the love of my life. For the life I couldn't figure why Jack wanted his help. Bob had caused that fracas in the whorehouse. He was unstable. I wanted to smash his pretty face in.

"*Sláinte,*" Bob said, passing the bottle back to me.

"*Guid forder,*" said I, and drank.

Dammitdammitgoddamnationchristinheavensaveus. Breathe. Maintain an outward mien of calm and spit away your corruption. George V is your liege and lord by the Orange Lodge and the Law of this Dominion, so fuck the Pope.

A ragged dog came out from behind a rubbish tip and coughed at us as we waited hidden in deep shadow. I made up my face into a rueful, close-lipped smile as the bottle did another round. When I went to light a fresh cigaret I found one burning in my hand. Time slowed with the universe, entropic. Birds flew southeasterly towards St. Helen's Island. An old lamplighter came our way, the antique figure out of Cruikshank's etchings for Dickens. His toil gave the streets a bluish tint as night fell completely. Jack handed me keys and nodded to Bob. The two drove the Olds to another position. I finished the wine and carefully placed the bottle on a rotten turnbuckle before walking to the Auburn, then made to check my pocketwatch before recalling how I'd failed to redeem it from hock. No matter. There was no music playing in my head now. I felt drained of life. As I sat behind the wheel I listened to my breath and the dull rhythm of my heartbeat. At least the medulla oblongata continued to function. Along my arm came the familiar ache.

Talk about slowness, those days strung out along the opaque dragon's tail, lost in morphia. The endless dreams, the fading to lonely worlds, a glacial death often punctuated by restless strength and creative activity. That was the drug's Janus effect, withering the body and feeding the mind. Nothing on earth had been worse than the panic I'd felt when my supply had been exhausted. Periodic opium raids in Chinatown had pushed me into a corner and the McGill beaks came ever so damned close to catching me out at the Royal Victoria red-handed.

The last visit to the hospital before brokering my departure from the school had been an off-chance of lax security. There were new locks on the door and Smiler was with Jacques Price, the pair dissecting a beggar in the downstairs morgue. Smiler and Price's scalpelwork was no patch on my own, I was pleased to note. Jack and I'd butchered enough deer and moose in our youth to make us old hands at vivisection. Once the Pater had potted a bear out by Yale and brought most of it back to our house in the West End. He'd skinned it for a rug and I remembered finding a tin rubbish bin in the yard with its lid held down by a brick. Inside had been the animal's head, alive with writhing white maggots stripping the flesh off the trophy. Later the amah'd boiled the skull clean and the Pater'd mounted it on a wall near my bedroom.

My childhood home had been a sort of emporium, the attic filled with books, charts, photoengravings, and testaments. In a trunk were my mother's few surviving effects, her communion papers and a golden shamrock of the Apparition at Knock. My amah had died while I was in Victoria getting a baccalaureate, the house now another museum of a broken colonist family, near empty save for the Pater in his rocking chair.

Returning to the present and the automobile I found myself thirsty and yenned for a cup of tea. The old streetlamps cast an arctic glow. What'll newspaper headlines read like tomorrow? This was a very serious crime we were on the verge of committing, a chancy undertaking. Illogically I trusted in Jack's star. I'd play my part, was all, and do what was necessary. It'd been a long day already, the longest one yet. I closed my eyes.

And opened them again as a long white saloon car pulled in. From Jack's sketchy form in the darkness came the Scout whistle. I started the Auburn and shifted into gear, the headlamps off, accelerating over the short distance to ramming speed. I saw startled clean-shaven faces staring my way as the machines collided. There was a crunch of tearing metal and I was thrown onto the wheel as I caved the saloon's passenger side in. My chest burned as I pulled out the Webley and opened the door to step down onto the road. A neat job, Mick, I thought, as I pointed the barrel through the rear glass at a surprised middle-aged man in the back seat. Jack was shouting. There he was in front with his gun on the driver. The front passenger lay slumped over where the Auburn's grille had met the wheelwell. A radiator hissed steam. Jack shouted something across the bonnet at the driver, who reached down. Jack fired. The man I was covering hunched and I pulled the trigger. Glass cracked and shattered and his head bucked forward. Jack came by the driver's side while the last man put up his hands. Jack shot again and the cabin filled with black gore. He pulled the handle and a bloodied body with a ruined face fell out clutching a black leather case. Jack grabbed the satchel, his revolver smoking in his left fist. He turned to me and yelled: "Ankle!"

I looked up at the moored ship; the men on the deck were just starting to stir. It had been quick. We ran, hotfooting from the slaughter. Maybe half a minute had passed. Suddenly I was lucid, my body heaving as I followed after as fast as I could. We made it over slippery cobblestones to the idling Olds. Jack hauled open the rear left passenger door behind Bob.

"Go!" shouted Jack as we clambered in.

He threw the bag onto the front passenger seat. Bob engaged the gear and we were off, my heart screaming and ears roaring from the gunshots and the crash. My hand tingled as Bob veered crazily, fear making him stupider. He got the 'car under control as we turned up McGill.

"Shit," he said.

A procession of torches and mounted policemen holding Union Jack banners blocked our way ahead, the Sons of England.

"Trafalgar Night," shouted Jack. "Turn right!"

Bob swerved at the Customs House and now we were caught in the crooked warren of the Old Town, passing the firehouse and a small square with a thin rough obelisk at its centre. It was a rat run with the risk of getting trapped in an old byway behind a horse and wagon or running into an outriding constable from the parade. Bob was driving too fast.

"Slow down," I said.

He turned to me with a vacant stare. The man was more than drunk, he was on dope. I could tell if anyone could.

"Slow down!" I said again.

Bob focused and came back to his senses. Jack was clenching his teeth and muttering, his gun still gripped in his hand. We rolled left through Place d'Armes and around the statue of Maisonneuve and an Iroquois brave covered in gullshit, tomahawk at the ready. From Notre-Dame bells rang the changes. What time was it? An arc onto St. Lawrence Main heading northerly and slowing when Bob's arm suddenly swung around at me with a gun at its end. Before he could fire Jack's right wrist came up in time. Bob shot through the roof and I was deafened. The Olds skidded and slewed as I clawed at the door latch and fell out, out of a moving Goddamned 'car. I landed hard on my side, rolling and losing my grip on the Webley. The machine pitched Jack out after me, turning an awkward somersault to hit his head on the pavement. My ears were screeching from the report as I watched Bob get away, the rear door flapping as he straightened the Olds's route out and powered off. And with him, the money. I looked for pedestrians or bystanders or police but we were lucky, lost on a rough corner with only a scavenging rag-and-bone man lurking in a dark storefront with his pushcart, near Craig and a long way from cover as my mind scrambled for what to do.

Jack waved and shouted as he rose. He staggered to pick up his hat and trotted off blindly. I scooped up my weapon and followed, pain coursing through every fibre and furious, ready to kill again. Jack turned up an alley and I knew where we were, able now to make out what Jack's mouth was shouting: "Chinatown."

MY REFLECTION IN A PANE of glass amethyst from the glow
of a neon sign. I was a lean monkey with a gun in his hand.
For a moment I could picture myself many-armed and fierce as
a Hindoo idol, wielding knives dripping blood. I ran through
the little *quartier chinois* and in another window saw a hetero-
geneous collection of objects: a wooden Confucius painted
vermilion, shadow puppets from the Dutch East Indies, a Mos-
lem screen of a white-veiled man before a dazzling blue pea-
cock, a green copper bust of Emperor Augustus, *dominus et
primus inter pares.* I kept burning shoe leather trying to catch up
with Jack and wondered how much the Celestials were charging
for Caesar.

Ahead of me Jack stopped, looked back, and hustled down
a grimy stone staircase to a subterranean entryway. He rapped
a sequence. The door opened and Jack pushed in past a small
Chinaman in his pajamas. Bitter opium smoke and sweat drifted
as I followed. My sense of smell was strangely acute, perhaps
compensating for my deafness. I also tasted cordite and petrol.
Sounds came faintly to me as the ringing in my ears lessened
in intensity. I heard Jack bark in his rough honking Cantonese:
"*Hem ga san puk gai.*" Out of my way.

He grabbed a skinny fellow by the neck and barked: "Kwan!"

Jack pushed the Chinaman down a flight of wooden steps
leading deeper underground. I roughed my way in and shouldered the door closed behind me. My vision adjusted to make out
cat-eyes glittering in the light of burning spills for the pipes. We
were a fearsome sight for drugged Orientals: a pair of armed *gwai
lo* barbarians with big noses sniffing at the stink. In the gloom
I thought I saw a white woman being ministered to. This sewer
was a crypt and I wanted a better way out but had to follow Jack
down. The scene was something out of a pulp journal, the dread
den of the dragon. Its inhabitants didn't put up much fight and I
pushed them away like yellow scarecrows.

A flickering electric bulb in the next room had the effect of turning everything into a staccato Zoetrope reel. Brass pots bubbled with a hellish brew while a wet Norway rat cowered by a sewer grating. Noise beyond led me out of the foul kitchen into a chamber with a stove and a table surrounded by fan tan players. A serene picture of Dr. Sun Yat-Sen faced me. Jack still held the skinny beggar by the scruff, then shouted loud enough for me to hear: "Police."

I came in and backed his play, growling: "Nobody breathe."

Jack shoved his captive to the ground and turned to me. There was a wildness to him, effect of shock and the blow to his head. He cocked his revolver and the gamblers sat still as hypnotized chickens. What was his intent?

"I want Kwan," he said, as though to answer.

In the table's centre was the black numbered square surrounded by money. The croupier had a downturned bowl in front of him. Jack stood still but seemed unbalanced: blood on his forehead, collar undone, coat torn. The gamblers let their cigarets burn. Six players sat 'round the table and the wretched coolie sprawled on the floor made seven. Jack reached over and lifted up the bowl. The croupier looked a dry stick with a thin beard. He betrayed nothing as the buttons spilled on the tabletop. Jack put the bowl on the man's head, a terrible affront.

"Kwan," Jack said, almost politely.

Still nothing. I was becoming nervous. We were trapped down here in an underground dead-end. The upstairs servants might've signalled for help and we'd be boxed in neatly. I held my gun at my side and was having trouble concentrating. The heavy odours and the stolid Chinese, with their blank faces and dark slitted eyes, unsettled me. One was holding a clay cup of tea. I felt like fainting. Jack hit the croupier a sickening blow to the head with his Webley. He shoved the counters off the table and gathered up the money.

"Kwan," he repeated.

Jack stuck the barrel in the mug of a little shrimp wearing a collarless shirt. Clockwise he went from face to face. Jack's mouth was open and spittle slavered off his jaw. He settled on a Fu Manchu type by me who lifted a bony hand. I saw light through long transparent fingernails and jabbed my gun in the gambler's back. He twitched, then very slowly the victim moved a finger and pointed at the stove. Jack went to touch it and laughed. With a straining heave he pulled the stove away from the wall to reveal a gap with yet more stairs leading down.

"Get that," Jack said, pointing at a light. "I'm going in. Stay here and cover me."

I handed him the oil lamp. He crouched and went into the hole. I kept up a forbidding façade for the Chinamen but was outmatched by their studied impassivity. They were damned lucky to be here in Montreal. An act was passed by government a few years back against all Oriental immigration. No more Gold Mountain. In Vancouver I'd been a child when the Asiatic Exclusion League had smashed windows throughout Chinatown. Had they half a chance these characters would make me into chop suey as recompense.

Jack's voice came from somewhere far away and I shuffled to the hole.

"Mick. Mick," he said.

"What?"

"Come down. Watch your head."

I took the stairs backward with the circle of motionless watchers staring at me, statues in a tomb. I turned and another dozen steps brought me to a narrow way filled with rotting burlap. A light flickered ahead as I came to a room lined with shelves stacked with old fowling pieces, rusty pikes and swords, a set of measuring weights, pots of opium, and boxes labelled in Chinese. Jack stood in the middle with a laughing man wearing a real pig-tail.

"Kwan here thinks it's funny I took their money," Jack said.

"Very funny, very funny," Kwan said.

"Some joke," I said.

My eyes roamed this Aladdin's cave and my heart stopped when I saw a familiar rectangle of black metal. Jack and Kwan bantered and Kwan handed Jack an automatic pistol, a Browning. While they were occupied haggling I sidled over to the object of interest and opened it up. My nerves thrilled and pain receded. I closed the box and turned back to the pair. Jack gave Kwan some money and they shook hands curiously. When I pocketed the black box I tipped over Jack's oil lamp. It smashed to the ground and I jumped back as the oil spilled over sacks and wicker pots. Jack and Kwan turned as flames spread to the shelves. In the enclosed space the smoke started choking and the fire blocked the way back upstairs. Kwan swore and hopped over to a corner where he began scrabbling at the wall. Jack staggered in the poisonous smoke and I pulled him over to the Chinaman. Kwan found what he was looking for and the wall crumbled away. We shoved into a recess and to a ladder leading up. Jack yanked Kwan down from it and started pulling himself up. I followed suit and kicked at Kwan as he clawed at me. Jack pounded on a trapdoor above through the thickening smoke and finally cracked it open in a shower of rust and dirt. He pushed up and out and I came after into an alley crowded with rubbish bins and restaurant waste. Smoke poured from the secret shaft and we could hear a rising wail around the corner. Kwan's head poked out the ground as we dragged ourselves to the alley mouth.

"*Du nu loh moa!*" he screamed at me, then in English: "You son of bitch."

"Shut up," I said.

He came at me but I pulled out my gun and pointed it at him. It was too much and I was exhausted.

"Bugger off," I said.

He spat and stamped and slouched away, shaking his fist at me. Jack was laughing broadly, tears streaming down his face.

"You're a wonder, Mick, really you are. You truly have a gift."

I was now lightheaded from the dope smoke but had enough presence of mind to straighten up and help Jack walk away as machine guns started clattering.

"Firecrackers," Jack said.

Jabbering Chinese ran about and one had already wrenched open a fire hydrant as others began a bucket brigade. More limped and scattered away from what would soon be a welter of firemen and police. Jack and I went along St. Urbain and turned left. In a few minutes we were on a quiet street behind St. Patrick's, where D'Arcy McGee had lain in state after he'd been assassinated in Ottawa. And where was Louis Riel? Buried facedown with a stake through his heart for treason. Old Tomorrow had said, as I did now: "He shall hang though every dog in Quebec bark in his favour."

From the neighbourhood came a rising howl of wolves roused by the fire engine and ruckus. My hearing had improved. The St. Patrick's bell rang eight times. Only eight o'clock. It felt much later, the witching hour. Jack sat on the grass near an old wall. I stamped my feet to keep the blood moving. It was cold and I remembered I had nowhere to stay.

"That was bloody marvellous, Mick," said Jack, shaking his head.

"It was an accident."

"Of course it was. You've a rare talent. The perfect capper to a hell of a night."

"I agree."

"Now then, have you any money?" asked Jack.

"Don't tell me you're skint again," I said.

"'Fraid so."

"Well then."

That son of a bitch Bob. It was the least I could do to give Jack two hundred dollars without asking where or how he'd lost his own stake. It meant I was down below seven hundred, but I held a hole card that'd make money irrelevant.

"What're you thinking?" I asked.

"I was thinking how I've been nursing a viper at my breast this whole while. Dammit but I was napping."

"Bob?"

"Aye. Now that Kwan's buggered I've lost a line. What a balls-up. It's going to take some time to straighten this mess out."

"I could use some rest myself," I said disingenuously.

"All right. We'll split up for the time being. Were I you I'd change hotels."

"Easy enough."

"It's Friday night. Check in a few days at the Hotel X for a message, name of Conrad."

"You want any help?" I asked.

"Not just now. The money's enough."

"What're you going to do?" I asked.

"*Tace* is Latin for candle, old man," Jack said.

"Well I won't whisper. We've done it now. Murder."

Jack sized me up a moment.

"There is that. The wheel spins."

He got to his feet.

"Remember, the Hotel X," he said.

"Oke."

Jack shook his head and reeled off into the darkness. I walked until I came back to Bonaventure. In the station I read an advertisement on a board for the Hotel Boniface so I telephoned in advance for a room, then walked over to Windsor Station and picked up my bag. In the grill I ate a hasty sandwich, drank a coffee, and pocketed a spoon. The hotel was on Dorchester and en route I stopped at a night-owl chemist for an apparatus. At the Boniface I signed the book Thomas Scott, paid three days in advance and asked for a candle. Upstairs behind a locked door I cleaned my hands and face in hot water with soap. I lit the candle, took out the vial from the black metal box I'd stolen, and began. Carefully I tipped salts into a spoon. The colour of the grains told me it was indeed morphine, not heroin, a relief. I fitted together a new hypodermic needle from the drugstore and bound my arm tightly with a towel. The salt and water solution I heated in the spoon and when it was ready I filled the device, drew the mixture, and injected myself. Slowly I blew out the candle, felt pain withdraw, and soon was gone to another place far away.

INTERREGNUM NARCOTICUM

THERE WAS ENOUGH morphine in the vial to keep me from pressing concerns for a considerable length of time. My injuries receded, and I fell into a deep lassitude born from physical exhaustion. Betimes I slept behind a locked door, loaded revolver by my side. When I woke I made another injection and watched the sun move across the arch of the sky. Inward flooded a bliss, and later, fear.

Through a blunted consciousness arrived concerns for my fate. Besides the transgressions I'd committed and the failure of my life, now the fatal substance had returned and clutched me in its grip. Soon all other considerations would dwindle and it'd be the drug alone that I'd seek, its peace. I looked at my wounds from the automobile collision and a purple bruise on my chest that described part of the wheel's arc.

Later the hotel room took on the dimensions of a prison cell. Unsettling fancies: a warrant out for my arrest, everything known to the world. Footsteps in the hallway were the police come to take me away. The wide-open brown eyes of the man in the saloon 'car stared at me as I pulled the trigger and plunged the hypodermic syringe home. A warm itch turned to a settled coolness and calm.

I was a slave to Venus, a scorned acolyte. Babe Ruth beat Celeste the good-time girl from the whorehouse with his baseball bat. Laura melted into shadows in a palace on a mountain with a knave. Queen of Diamonds, Queen of Hearts, and I a deuce or trey or Fool. The lovers in the garden beneath the sun. Jack and the magician Houdini building the Tower. Laura my love, priestess of desire, a whore like all the rest. I should've forgiven her but I couldn't. The devil in womankind's cunning. Satan wasn't a fallen angel lording it in heaven but a small voice whispering in a dirty alleyway: "Would you like to experience the ultimate pleasure?"

Pain crept back and a forewarning of this stage lead me to the bathroom where I heaved, nauseated. I'd taken too much in haste. It was dawn or evening by the light; a chambermaid or sin-eater worked in the hallway. My instructions to the clerk: Do not disturb Room 34. When I opened the window I smelled pollen, as though spring had returned. The air was cold. From the far end of the world sounded the long low moan of a train's whistle, the heartbreaking sound of remotest melancholy, a soul in the far country. You'll join it, for you've killed a man.

THE SABBATH. Saturday had vanished and a fickle rain fell. Now I rested cocooned from the world, a deadly chrysalis. What would I become? Nothing better, certainly. When was the last time you did a turn for your fellow man? Never a nickel to a beggar or a kind word for the stranger on the street. Instead you harboured fantasies of revenge. With the money you have it'd be better to end this; take a suite at the Ritz and cut your throat in the bath. Instead, I switched to my right arm for the next injection, then took especial care dressing. Freshly attired I went onto the street and into a swarming plague of gnats.

I set a pace on Stanley and felt a new bloom of strength as I walked uphill. In need of retreat I followed the street into the park. Rain accompanied me up through the thinning cover of small trees, the mountain's aroma deep and heavy, dead brown maple leaves heaped and mouldering in odd fastnesses. My eye picked out a reward in the gloaming, a straggling low creeper with small wild strawberries. Their taste was a quintessence, pure ruby sweetness that filled my mouth as I huffed and puffed up worn stone stairways to the gravel promenade road. Clopping downhill past me came a fine glistening sorrel steaming in the cold. Astride the beast rode a girl in a plum riding habit, an equestrienne who looked sidelong at me as she goaded her charge lightly with a little leather crop down the slope. As I continued up, bearing southwest, I felt the dim luminescence of the dusky city to my left and saw the spread of Notre-Dame-de-Grâce through the trees, the church spires of Charlevoix and St. Henri stretching to the Lachine Canal and beyond, almost to the rapids. The road to China. It was grand to feel the drug's warmth and be alone above the coalsmoke and mire.

Despite the cool night air and rain I perspired through my hatband as I turned north to Beaver Lake. The bowl of the hill was filled with a Scotch mist and a pair of lingering swans floated on the water, mingling with late season ducks. Above me a small solitary river gull circled, crying piteously. Beneath the bird sat a woman on a bench. We were the only two on the mountain and I abandoned my route up to the lookout. There was an old Anglo-Saxon riddle I remembered from a book in my father's study and I said it, softly, to myself: *"Ic ane geseah idese sittan."*

My boot scuffed a stone on the path and the woman turned. She was pretty and dark, obviously French, with a severe part in her hair showing a white line of scalp. When she saw me her look turned from one of pleasure to disappointment, as though she'd been expecting someone else. I'd seen that expression before. Laura. The penny dropped and I felt incredibly cold of a sudden.

"*Bonsoir, mademoiselle,*" I said.

She looked at me and shook her head. Without breaking stride and with the feeling of being punched in the chest I turned towards the gates of the Protestant cemetery to walk amongst the obelisks, decapitated angels, and draped urns.

Last winter I'd climbed to the top of the mountain in the dead of December and had been on the high rise as a burning orange sun dropped over the white wasteland. Land stretched north forever over Quebec province to Hudson Bay and the Northwest Territories. Then I'd been battered by the wind in my wool Navy jacket and stared into the orb as it sank. Soon the fierce cold would return and freeze the ground to an iron-hard tundra once again. In anticipation the gravediggers had already excavated a few expectant holes at the corner of the cemetery by the road. I walked down and out through the Hebrew boneyard to the other side past Park, over the field to St. Urbain where trams jerked along. The hike had stimulated a thirst and I sought a beer parlour open on St. Lawrence Main in defiance of the Sabbath law. At a corner grocery store I bought an envelope, a leaf of paper, and a red penny stamp with the Prince of Wales's face on it. This was dangerous territory, the frontier between English and French. Dark-eyed families in their Sunday best walked solemnly along the street to evening mass. I saw a priest, two nuns, and an elegant gentleman with the carriage of a sei- gneur of Nouvelle France pass by. These were Charlie Trudeau and the Senator's tribesmen. For safety I ducked into a watering hole on the west side of the boulevard. While I wrote an Irish- man in the corner sang: "Let Bacchus's sons be not dismayed but join with me, each jovial blade. Come drink and sing and lend your aid to help me with the chorus..."

I sealed the envelope flap and ducked out to put the note in a nearby mailbox. It'd be picked up in the morning and delivered with the afternoon post. When I got back the whole bar was in full throat, an Englishman, a pair of bohunks, the landlord, and finally myself joining with: "We'll beat the bailiffs out of fun, we'll make the mayor and sheriffs run, we are the boys no man dare dun if he regards a whole skin. Instead of spa we'll drink brown ale and pay the reck'ning on the nail, no man for debt shall go to gaol from Garryowen in glory."

By the end and despite myself my eyes were teared up by this camaraderie. I thought of chums scattered across the country or dead, places I'd never see again or ever visit. The Englishman shyly bought me an ale and suggested we have a bit of fun, with a nervous wink. When he went to relieve himself I paid and slipped out.

On the cold street I turned into myself again, an enemy of humanity. On a hidden piano someone practised a phrase from Mendelssohn over and over. Here on the sidewalk sprawled a poor young Hebress blowing soap bubbles that floated and disappeared over the tenements as a hard wind came gusting down from the north. People huddled into their overcoats against the gale. I skirted overflowing rubbish bins and the music prompted a memory of the recent past, the cathouse on Mountain with that bastard Bob plunking out "Darktown Strutters' Ball" by Willie Eckstein and the Melody Kings on His Master's Voice. The little dog sticking his face into the gramophone funnel, the Senator's bitch Rex licking at itself, Celeste my whore and Lilyan Tashman with her stockings off and Laura, always Laura. Happiness in stolen moments with her and now I was apart and alone, anonymous, forgotten. Write your emergency testament on a clean white piece of foolscap and affix your signature, a holograph will. Leave Jack the Webley and case of shells.

The gun weighed my pocket down as I neared Chinatown. Would have to find what Jack had called the Hotel X. I under-

stood that it was in the old quarter but couldn't bear to see what
I might've wrought at the gamblers' hell so made a right instead,
west on St. Catherine, away from any Oriental. In the darkness
neon-lit storefronts painted me wild colours and I was a corpus-
cle in the metropolis's bloodstream again, feeling the thrum of
life as I shouldered through the crowd, my hat down and collar
up, a figure modern and dangerous.

Nowhere like Montreal, the city a raw and freezing compromise between enemies, a manqué Paris fused with a poor man's
New York. Often it felt Russian, a tsar's whimsy like St. Peters-
burg, or Petrograd they called it now. The difference was we'd
never storm the Hôtel de Ville and burn the Golden Book as
the Bolsheviks had invaded the Winter Palace. No, our King
wouldn't allow it. We were the fair-haired child of Empire, run
for profit by the Scotch, fingernails pared, shoes well-tied, clean
behind the ears. What Kipling called "Our Lady of the Snows":
still, empty, cold. A worse wind whipped down St. Catherine
slashing at my face, bringing with it the smell of scorched toast
and engine oil. I was driven into the Turf and the moment I
entered felt a delicious frisson as warmth melted me down, a
pure moment of welcome.

When the girl appeared I ordered a Western and coffee, suddenly famished. After eating, a postprandial cigaret burned as
I stared through a liquid window at the world outside. Painted
on the brick wall of the Bercy building up to the cornice were
advertisements inciting citizens to purchase Darkie toothpaste,
ivory hairbrushes, surgical trusses, ginger ale. The Dupuis Frères
department store down the street offered a ruinous line of credit
to the natives; between the company and vulture-priests in black
soutanes the French-Canadians were picked clean to their last
sou. For poor English the Eatons did the same. O Ogilvy's, o
mores!

Time waited on my leisure. The waitress ripped off a bill, making me forty-five cents poorer with a dime to the girl for her pains. A dollar would yield four German marks and that would take you a good long way, with the Krauts paying reparations in gold and having the devil of a time of it. I could live like a king in Berlin these days for nothing at all. I tied my serviette in a knot and left it in the centre of the dirty plate as I went out. The faintest tinnitus from Bob's pistol shot continued to ring in my left ear. My hands began to shake and I recognized that another hunger needed satiation. The city sent me cues that I translated from an obscure code: tattoo drumbeat of a boiler on a roof conspiring with the traffic standards' syncopation, green, yellow, red. On the street figures watched me, signalling covertly to undercover police agents. I began to lose my sea legs and staggered, wanting more than anything another injection of morphine. Teeth chattered, sweat dripped along my spine. I'd left it too long and they'd never let me back in the hotel. The gods had been angered. I was jostled, pedestrians tripping me up and stepping on my toes, crowded here with greasy pavement underfoot. An antique figure in long grey beard and ragged buckskins lay sprawled in front of the Union Tobacconist at Phillips Square, a ratty fur cap on the ground in front of him. Seized with superstition and wanting to propitiate the Fates I peeled off a hundred dollars and dropped the notes in amongst the few tarnished coins. His eye caught mine: a silver flash, a sigil of knowing. The man was Isaac Laquedem come over on the boat with John Cabot to the end of the earth or Hy-Brasil. He'd planted the banner of St. Mark and been left behind, fated forever to wander the earth.

Thoughts thus abstracted and with my hands stuffed in my pockets I stepped badly on the pediment of the statue in the square and went down. At the last instant I pulled them out in time to save my face and pearly whites. It happened too quickly.

Now my hands were scraped and bloody. Like any idiot I looked around for a witness to my tumble. Out of the gloom a woman materialized and handed me a white mouchoir, a demimondaine alone away from the busy traffic, an angel, speaking very rapidly in a French I couldn't quite catch. I embarrassedly thanked her and slunk off, staunching my wounds with the cotton cloth. She'd done something human, graceful, and selfless and I'd been too damned shamefaced to stop even a moment. The white light from a marquee lit the squalid scene and I saw the show's title: *So This Is Paris.*

Behind the glass I read part of a review aloud to myself: "Monte Blue displays his virile mannerisms as the suave but willing Dr. Girard who leaves his wife and braves a gaol sentence to follow a will-of-the-wisp flapper in the person of Madame Lalle, played by Lilyan Tashman as a complete little vixen with a bag of cosmopolitan wiles and constant verve."

Back in the hotel at last I wasted away, a knife blade on a whetstone, as I pushed the needle in. Next door a drunk sang psalms in a broken key.

WHEN I RETURNED to life the first thing I did was reach for the dwindling vial of morphine powder. The needle entered me dully, blunted by overuse. I put pressure on and dressed the puncture with styptic. A black line had burned across the bedsheets where I'd passed out with a lit cigaret. I imagined waking on fire and realized that I had, burning for the drug. My head sank back into the dense, mossy pillow and I closed my eyes.

Later there was the hullabaloo of a working day: shouts of men, grinding axles, the klaxon of an ambulance. Likely it was taking a poor beggar to a ward in the Royal Victoria and I diagnosed him from afar with hypoxia leading to coma and death, what Houdini braved upside-down in the Chinese Water Torture

Cell. Could picture myself stretched out on the starched rough linen of a hospital bed listening to the din of the world, of milk carts clattering past and newspaper hawkers shouting headlines: "Queen of Rumania to arrive at Bonaventure Station Wednesday!" "Hurricanes in Cuba!" "End of the World Nigh!"

Very soon I'd have to visit the selfsame dispensary should my present pattern of consumption be continued, to join specimens in the morgue and be flensed by the coroner. It was getting there that'd be the trouble. Danger lurked all about, Turks disguised as Ruskies in the pay of the Kuomintang wanting vengeance for the fire I'd started in Chinatown. You will need to tread warily, boyo. Remember the post and that you must find Jack's hotel at some point. Prepare.

With a tube of Ipana and a brush I scraped away whatever covered my teeth and tongue, the dentifrice stinging at my tender gums. I raggedly shaved my face. The hotel room seemed to have constricted even closer during the course of the night and now felt no larger than a coffin. The largest item in the space was the black metal box of morphine and next to it my Webley. I aligned my spinal column and dressed. Suddenly irresolute and fearful, I sat again and leafed through the magazines to read a thriller about a fat detective working for the Pinkertons. Jack and his game: it explained those missing years and the postcards we'd received from far outposts of America. Why had he joined them? What larger design did he pursue? So much was beyond me now that my concerns were restricted to the necessities of life: morphine, morphine, and money. I lit a cigaret and let my thoughts drift.

Recently as this last summer I'd fancied I'd broken the habit, sitting on a dock with my feet in Lake 'Magog, watching the idle rich at play on their boats. At night light and music from dances at the Hermitage Club would carry across the water to my shack, where I plotted an abstract revenge on their class and its chief exemplar, Mademoiselle Laura Dunphy, her very lovely self. The sins of the one visited upon the many, wishing to string them all up on gibbets.

Our last painful meeting had been on a day in April, near end of term. The weather'd been raw, windy, unpleasant. She'd smelled bourbon on my breath and recoiled from a kiss. How little she knew, thinking me a mere drunkard. I was already far, far worse.

"Michael," she'd said.

"Yes?"

"I must go now."

So cold. The thaw'd just broken the river proper, bringing seabirds inland above the melting ice. It was twilight and we stood in a crowd of people on Sherbrooke close to the university gates. We'd met for tea but she'd taken no more than half a cup and then the mob had hurried around us as she rested her gaze on me. It felt like scientific appraisal of what I was, no trace of feeling or passion. I hadn't been able to meet her green eyes until the very end, catching a flicker of her distaste. What do you do when the woman you love doesn't love you in return? Laura put her gloved hands in an ermine muff as some idiot jostled me from behind and by the time I turned back she'd joined the crowd and was gone. I stayed rooted to the spot sick and dead, a hollow tree waiting to be blown over. The cigaret burned my hand and brought me back to the hotel.

I flicked the stub out the window onto Aqueduc. The fading evening glow, timorous grey snow patches in doorways, motorcar horns blaring and horse hooves striking stone and the fading pressure of her hand on my forearm where she'd touched me for the last time. I unbuttoned my shirtsleeve and slapped my forearm to raise a vein. It didn't hurt. Nothing did.

A euphoria grew and with it the most marvellous sensation, a play of association linking Venice with Vinland. I laughed weakly and began to sing a childish song as I sank underwater: *"Il était un petit navire, il était un petit navire, qui n'avait ja-ja-jamais navigué, qui n'avait ja-ja-jamais navigué."*

Don't get seasick. Put something in your stomach, beans on toast or sardines and catsup. The thought alone caused my gorge to rise. I stood, shakily, and at the window watched an old lady in a blond wig fishing for treasure from a bin with a piece of hooked wire. She reminded me of the poor bloody panners of Williams Creek, still scratching away for gold forty years after the rush. The Pater'd succoured them with little more than the Good Book and a square meal now and again. My father wasn't a fire-and-brimstone man like Billy Sunday. On the wireless I'd hear gospel charlatans from down South and the Foursquare Gospel of Aimee McPherson, who talked in tongues, built a temple in Los Angeles, and had been kidnapped last spring. The woman outside pulled up a piece of scrap and danced a jig. Shining iron pyrite, fool's gold.

Sparrows darted by on their way to hibernate. I turned to the mirror and saw Mr. Hyde—not as played by John Barrymore in the pictures but as a kind of ogre, dark and difficult to please. Bury me facedown with a stake in my heart, never to see the winter sunlight.

I held a volume of anatomy in my grip and turned pages to the circulatory system, tracing the morphine's route. Radiators in the room felt cool to the touch and I had no need of their heat as my own *calidum innatum* burned just fine. I ran a hand over my face and marvelled at my organism's subtle construction, then chewed at a thumbnail. An itch along my leg prompted me to pull up a trouser cuff to reveal a line of insect bites, bedbugs, what you got when you lay down with dogs.

I went downstairs, where a clerk knotted his brow at my question, then snapped his fingers, saying: "The Hotel X? But of course! The Exceptionale."

I thanked him and telephoned the hotel from a booth to learn that Mr. Conrad was not in fact in, but did I care to leave a message? I did not.

Evening broadsheets gave me the latest on the queen of Rumania, a burlesque similar to when the Prince of Wales had visited the States. They'd fallen all over him and started sporting thickly knotted neckties and drinking brandy sodas. Amazing how Yankees tumbled for a blueblood in the Republic. Snobs in their own way, worse than the Imperial Court of the Japanese. Canadians were little better, a fault of the Empire. From Hong Kong to Salisbury, Calgary to Singapore we'd kowtow to our nobility. Wait until the Commonwealth falls to new masters, the Communists or Martians. They were coming, according to the 'paper. The red planet was closer than ever, in one way or another.

It was strangely hot out, or perhaps my blood boiled. Sunshine fell on the north side of the street while high above a 'plane buzzed lazy circles over the city towards the aerodrome in St. Hubert. An organ grinder tortured a scabrous monkey, a Siwash begged for alms, and a pretty flower girl ignored me. There was a triple feature on at His Majesty's: *Greed, The Gigolo,* and *Suicide Sonata.* An elegant French-Canadian couple, what the Parisians would call chic, walked a small Pekinese. Morphine tailed away and I thought of Jack. He'd better be dogging down that four-flushing double-crosser Bob. I didn't want him doing anything else. Look him up in the morning. One of the wicked grey prison streetcars cut me off as I crossed the street; a mournful criminal looked at me on his way east.

This time I took McTavish up and the stairs near Ravenscrag. It was near five when I broke through the elms and birches to an Indian path by a still cool pond, a mountain tarn. Here the maples trembled autumn golden and a zephyr dried my sweat. It was near the gloaming and I followed a track to the top. From the highest point I watched the river cringe away from my majesty and the city huddle up against me for warmth. I was the beacon on high, not that skeleton cross of Christ. At five o'clock as the sun set I stood still as a brazen statue, lodestone of the true north, and there was no one else on the face of the earth.

WEDNESDAY

TWO DAYS LATER I ran out of morphine. My hands quaked and blood sang in my ears, worse than any conceivable hangover. Pressure mounted alongside the craving. When I ran out of cigarets I'd be forced into the open. Abandon yourself to fever and the black horses of nightmare; you'll never wake. The prognosis is inescapable, boyo. Check yourself into a sanatorium under an assumed name.

Shaking and bloody were my hands, covered in filth and microscopic vermin. I'd accidentally injected a pathogen through the needle's point, *Pasteurella pestis* hidden resident on pollen spores from high Afghanistan or Burma, bacterial refugees of the Black Death. From the poppies it came though rendered opium to morphine and was now inside me. Check lymph nodes for buboes and watch for bloody sputum after coughing. Feel the creatures multiplying inside, a riot of animalcules. All sexual desire was now absent and in its place aching low pain and hunger. I'd been a fool, using up the last of the Chinaman's deck. I should kill him. How? Blink. Every time I did, someone died. Next it would be me at the end of a rope. I needed to rediscover an instinct for self-preservation and accomplish something. Leave this room.

Outside the birds watched me from bare trees. People got in my way, stepped on my heels, grimaced in my direction. A beggar with a goiter and crutches eyed me suspiciously as I walked past. A streetcar's trolley pole jumped off the overhead wire and lost its electrical connection. The operator got out to replace the pole and, hauling at the dead cable, spat at me in blame.

It'd been raining for some time, perhaps days. The wind was from the northwest with the first bite of real winter in it and found a way through my clothes to my skin where it nipped at the husbanded warmth therein. I shivered violently and thought how fitting that I was headed for the hospital. At this odd hour in the afternoon classes would be completed if the schedule hadn't changed. I might be in luck, and made a blasphemous prayer to that effect.

If I knew my man he'd be just where he always was. "Smiler" Smilovich. A pushy striving bastard, all side, his the first hand raised for every question, volunteering for every study. Vice-president of the Medical Students' Union. I trusted he'd pulled extra duty at the hospital liaison office, where I hoped to find him. He'd either be there or ostentatiously walking the wards with a stethoscope and thermometer. Smiler was the source of Jack's cocaine, it seemed. That being the case it was no stretch to determine Smiler could also supply my chosen nostrum. He had access to the dispensary and if the man wouldn't accept my money I was prepared to use other measures.

It was only last spring that I'd surrendered those keys myself. I remembered the faces of my reviewing board as I handed them over, with Dr. Meakins grave as Moses. Laughing at them when they threatened to expel me and turn my carcass over to the Sûreté du Québec. I'd made my play, alluding in no uncertain terms to the tale I might spin should I be prosecuted. A pretty piece of blackmail, and one that produced a stalemate, my freedom, and a franked transcript. Now I returned to the scene.

I hurried under bare black elms through the campus's gloomy Scotch ambience, indifferent grey limestone buildings flanking the quadrangle. On a small field to my left three Redmen ran football patterns in the mud. Lights were on at the Redpath Library and through the windows I saw students hunched over books. Laughing varsity-sweatered types passed by and two serious-looking Jews were deep in conversation about Trotsky. From Macdonald a clatter of engineering students in royal purple gave throat: "We are, we are, we are, we are, we are the engineers..."

During orientation week medical students had their own ritual of hazing, a program that culminated in formaldehyde-and-seltzer cocktails down the throat whilst blindfolded in the morgue. The morning after my apprenticeship I'd woken on a gurney with a splitting head and both legs in drying plaster casts. *Grandescunt aucta labore.* By work all things increase and grow, my alma mater's creed, my century's religion.

At University I crossed Pine to the Vic. Smiler'd been in the dressing room backstage at the Princess before Jack and I'd spoken with the Handcuff King. What had he and Price been up to? I skirted around to the private entrance and thence into a back hallway. Inside it was noxious with camphor, carbolic soap, and disinfectant. Underlying all was the sweetness of disease. The eastern wing was still and silent and I trod the scrubbed tiles with feigned confidence. A young nurse pushed a man in a wheelchair. The wet wool of my clothes gave off the odour of dog.

The next corridor was deserted. Turn right, turn right again, and right you are. A light burned behind the pebbled glass of a door that read "Resident Warden." An interesting position to occupy, as I had, and unique to McGill and the Royal Victoria, as far as I knew. One's duties were varied—assisting in the wards, a little human husbandry, liaison work with the faculty, and so forth. In reality the job had one specific, obscured function. My knowledge of what went on would be the lever to pry morphine from a cabinet.

Gingerly I turned a well-oiled knob and opened the door to a familiar figure behind a desk. Smiler wore a white laboratory coat and was furiously raking his hands through tonsured hair. He didn't notice me and my first impression was of the room's unusual disarray. Smiler was a prim, tidy bastard. He muttered to himself in an agitated fashion. As my presence made itself manifest Smiler's wide eyes turned my way.

"Mick," he whispered.

He was pale and frightened. Of me? Perhaps. So he should be.

"How, how'd you know? Who told you? Who *else* knows?"

"Knows what? Look at yourself in the mirror, man. You're a wreck."

"Oh God, what'm I going, what're *we* going to do?" he moaned.

"Calm down, for one."

Something was very wrong. At his best Smiler was no lion of courage, for all his bluff. He loosened his necktie and rubbed his face. Whatever had happened here presented me with the ideal opportunity. If Smiler was compromised my duty was to exploit the situation. Here was one apple he couldn't polish away.

"It's all over. My God, I'm ruined."

He ground the heels of his hands into his eyes.

"It's not as bad as all that," I said. "We'll work it out. Tell me what happened."

"Don't you know? Why're you here? Who sent you?"

"Listen, man. I know what goes on. Tell me. I can help."

"Help," Smiler said, in a faraway voice.

"Yes, help."

I moved into his field of vision.

"What is it? Cops? What'd they find out?"

"No, no, no. No police, not yet, but they'll be here. They'll know. I knew it was bound to happen sometime but why'd it have to happen to me? Why me?"

Slowly and soothingly I spoke: "Smiler, tell me what it is and I'll see what I can do. It's me, Mick. Did I grass when I was kicked out? No. I know what goes on here but I never breathed a word. What happened? Did someone do something?"

The last query I barked sharply and Smiler started. His stammer jumped with fear. "It's, it's bad."

"How bad?"

"Nothing can save me."

"Maybe, maybe not."

"I wasn't even, I wasn't even supposed to be here today. I've got a pharmacology paper due. Jacques couldn't come in. I'm co-, co-, covering for him. He was supposed to be here for the, for the, for the . . ."

"Delivery?" I asked.

"Yes," whispered Smiler.

So that was it. Several things could rattle a resident student: one was to inadvertently provide the cause of death. Opportunities for error were rife: in my second year a poor fellow had somehow managed to inject a large quantity of air into a hoyden's vein and prompted a fatal embolism. Mistakes often happened. and for all its rigours the discipline of medicine was as prey as any others to pure bad luck. Second to that was being caught out with a stolen dead body. Worst was finding dead a person you knew. "Show me," I said.

"No, Mick, I can't," protested Smiler weakly.

"Why not? I know what this's about. Let's have a look."

"I can't. My God, the police. The police. They'll tell my parents, they'll put me in gaol."

"No one's going to gaol."

I put iron in my voice. The need for morphine made me strong and guileful. Here was a different kind of luck and my advantage must be pressed. Do what Jack would. Turn this to your advantage. Get what you want. All that was required of me was to apply correct pressure to his flaw, his cowardice. Before me he snivelled and wiped his nose.

"They came in early this morning with her," he said.

"Her?" Fear tingled through me. "Who is she?"

"I was here to pick up some notes. I to-, I to-, I took delivery but I didn't have time to check. I had class, biochemistry. I told Jacques about it but he couldn't make it this afternoon so I came in to cover for him. I should've known, should've known something was wrong right away."

Involuntarily electricity ran up my spine and I felt my *arrectores pilorum* muscles tauten, forcing my hair to stand on end. Smiler's tone was genuine and there was a quality about what he said.

"Show me," I commanded.

Smiler rose and moved automatically. The word that came to mind was: robot. He went around a dividing wall to the closet in the corner and touched the hidden latch. The secret door slid open to a staircase. My knowledge of where that staircase led had been the trump I'd played to the reviewing board. It was a time-honoured practice. Subjects were always needed, by hook or by crook. Every medical faculty in Christendom and beyond had a similar facility. Here the resident warden's true role was as chamberlain to the world below. I followed Smiler underground.

Twenty-one paces down. My initiation had been with a resident named Jones. He'd played it up as an experience out of Poe and had been onto something there. At the far wall of the subterranean chamber was a heavy door bolted shut that led through to a concealed alley with space for horse and cart to turn around.

There was the smell of meat and chemicals, dampness and earth, with unclean instruments on a table by the sink. The weird scene was lit by a lambent green radiance, phosphorus in the stones. Smiler spoke in the dark.

"I should've known something was wrong. We weren't expecting a, a delivery, and they didn't ask the usual amount. They wanted less."

Smiler turned to me guiltily. I understood. He'd been planning to pocket the difference. Typical Hebrew. He'd changed his mind, however. It was becoming difficult to stand this anticipatory tension.

"I only just unwrapped it, her. Ten minutes before you arrived. I, I thought you knew somehow."

I couldn't take this at all.

"Who, Goddammit?"

"Mick, I, I can't."

"Turn on the light."

Smiler went to the switch and flicked on the current, then shrank away. My eyes adjusted and at first I didn't understand what I was seeing. The shape gained discernible form and I felt a terror. Every fear had been realized, here, before me now.

No.

No.

No.

Laura was on a slab in the middle of the room, her eyes closed.

"GET OUT."

"Mick?"

"Get out!"

"What're you going to do?"

"Go and strip a bed. Bring back sheets."

"Sheets?"

"A shroud, man."

Smiler stood up, his laboratory coat dirtied by the abattoir walls. My eyes had been blinded, seemingly. He came to me.

"Bring half an ounce of morphine powder from the dispensary," I said.

"What? What for?"

I grabbed Smiler's necktie.

"I'm going to get you out of this scrape so don't ask stupid questions. Understand?"

"I'll do it. I'll do it."

"Sheets, clean ones. Find a bag, a large one, for hockey equipment or a duffel for the laundry. Clean ones, get it? Don't talk to anyone. And make sure they're clean. It'll be dark soon and we have to move. When did the body snatchers bring her in?"

"Around six this morning."

"And she's been here all alone since then?"

"Yes. The office's been locked."

"Keep it locked. Get going."

The last order jolted Smiler to life, now Dr. Frankenstein's assistant. I couldn't do what the German had, the new Prometheus. I couldn't bring her back. My sight restored with tears, hot and stinging with salt. I blinked them away and heard the door close above.

I turned to Laura. She was resting on the oilskin tarp the resurrection men had brought her in. I wondered how many bodies had been rolled up in it before today. They probably hosed it down and hung the damn thing to dry on a clothesline in a backyard. Common understanding had the profession passing down the generations of a local French-Canadian family since the Patriot rebellion of 1838. Grandfather, father, and son, a caste of untouchables. With shovels and picks they sold the fruits of their labours to the *tête carrée* doctors and students at McGill, an arrangement out of Hogarth or engraved by Doré, a waking nightmare.

I could see livid bruises corresponding to fingers and thumbs around her throat. Her face was very slightly blue and the smallest tip of a tongue protruded. She'd been strangled. I touched her skin. Cold. Her hyoid bone was broken. There was dirt in the folds of her clothes, in her ears, her hair. She'd been in the earth. Someone had wiped her face. She wore a dark brown velvet riding coat, silk chemise, woolen skirt, and leather boots. Nothing indicated that she'd been violated. Her hands were gloved and a strand of pearls was looped around her neck. That was incredible. The grave robbers usually stripped valuables from bodies, a privilege of the profession. I'd seen corpses with jaws that'd been broken open so teeth with gold fillings could be yanked from the bone by pliers. Fingers with rings would be snipped by strong shears. I touched the pearls and didn't need to rub them against the enamel of my teeth to know the pale orbs were real, not paste. The only element missing was a reticule or purse.

Her auburn hair was pinned up, more or less how she wore it in life. In life. I touched my own face, and felt my mouth tighten. She was gone, forever, and yet here she was again, one last time. It was such an incredible sequence of events leading me to this infernal place at such an instant, scarcely credible, and yet here I was. The man who loved her more than anyone in all the world stood over her lifeless body. I needed a cigaret.

In the close atmosphere was a deep, evil savour I didn't overmuch like. So many things had happened that I'd already begun to forget or couldn't tell myself the truth about. I wanted brandy, opium, a needle to numb me. With impious hands I lit a vesta and with it a Forest and Stream. A pretty picture in the crypt. Smoke cleaned out my lungs and the fag end was on the ground by the time Smiler returned. He was quiet and ghostly. I took a large sheet from him and wrapped Laura as tenderly as I could, breathing over her and smelling the faintest hint of her toilet water and powder, of herself mingled with earth. I made her up as an Egyptian mummy, a pharaohess, Tut-Ankh-Amon's queen. Smiler'd found a bag and helped me hoist Laura into it. Once upon a time and on the open sea she'd be sewn into her shroud but in this age it was a sack of rubber closed with lightning fasteners. Suddenly I was incredibly tired.

"Did you bring the rest?" I asked.

Smiler flinched.

"Yes, yes I did, but what do you need it for?"

"Hand it over."

My eyes burned into his and he saw how serious I was. Smiler took two stoppered vials from his coat and handed them to me warily. I took them to the table and opened my deck next to the rusty blood-spattered lancets, saws, probes, clamps, and broken Erlenmeyer flasks. It was an unprofessional mess. Regardless of the fact that this was not a room for careful work the instruments should have been washed and dipped in disinfectant, for the sake of those of us still living.

I dripped water in a spoon and put powder in, then boiled with a match. A new hypodermic would've been fitting considering the surroundings but there was no time for such niceties, not with the elixir so close. I removed my coats and rolled up a sleeve, bound the cord over a bicep, and held it taut with my teeth. Smiler watched me and I watched him as I made the injection, pushing the plunger to its resting place. Loosening the cord my body went slack; I floated backward to a wall, Smiler's mouth agape.

The black magic worked its charm and in a very few minutes I was back on my toes, ready to move. I re-dressed and tested my strength at the slab, placing my hands under the clammy rubber.

I lifted. She was light as a bird, hollow-boned even at dead weight. With the amount of morphine I'd taken I felt flushed with fresh power.

A jerk of my neck had Smiler scuttling to unshoot the bolt of the vault door. He swung it open on creaking hinges and fresh air came in.

"Follow me," I said.

"What, now? Where to?"

"We're going to put her back in the ground, and then alert the authorities. This way you're safe."

Smiler goggled and followed as I shuffled down the passageway. There was an angled trap above my head. It was difficult to climb up the slanted scuttle; bags of waste were normally dragged out to incinerators by another route. This was typically a one-way channel. Smiler and I came out into a quiet yard with no overlooking portals, another precaution of the planners. Above us on all sides were shuttered, barred windows. In the mean, grassy square we heard the scurry of rats.

"What time is it?"

Smiler consulted a pocketwatch.

"Half-four."

Tricky dusking light had fooled my eyes. We wanted no witnesses to our departure. Between this wing of the hospital and a freestanding block crept a narrow passageway. I hoisted the heavy bag over my shoulder and walked between the dripping brick walls. By following a little-used path edging a football field I came out through a broken wooden fence. The grade led upward to the covering thickness of trees. Judging that our movements had been unobserved I stopped and set my load against a trunk. Smiler wheezed behind me. I unbuttoned my collar and fanned myself with my hat.

"Where're we going?"

"'The burying ground. They're gravediggers, so they must have found her in the cemetery."

"Which one?"

"The Protestant, naturally. We'll see if we can find out what happened. Perhaps something was left behind, a clue. Then we can get them."

"Do you know who did this?"

I cast my mind over the preceding days. "I believe so."

"Then... then, what?"

"We'll put her back. You can telephone the police. Use a call-box and disguise your voice. The body snatchers won't breathe a word; they're probably drinking to forget it as we speak. This way the dons won't find out, your parents neither."

Lame as it sounded to my own ears, Smiler seemed to find this plan plausible enough. I wondered about him. He wasn't a bad fellow, really. Recent adventures with Jack had toughened me to whipcord. I now took activity such as this in my stride. At this rate I wouldn't be surprised if I ended up flying an airplane onto a dirigible accompanied by a drunken Eskimo quoting F. Scott Fitzgerald. Poor Smiler, though, was gobsmacked with shock. In his experience transporting a body up a mountainside in the gloom was a perilous challenge. To me this fatal course felt pre-ordained.

It was cold enough to keep good people by the hearth in their homes. No such luck for yours truly. The sky now a dark purple and the terrain ideal for camouflage, concealment. I might be making a mistake, but it didn't feel like one, instead as though it was my destiny to walk this trail. Who other than I understood the significance of these surroundings, this landmark to my frustrations and disappointments? None now breathing. Near here I'd found strawberries, on the side of the mountain once an old Huron boneyard. Their palisade stood hereabouts, rotted away and ruined by succeeding ages. Everything fades to dust and tonight would be lost for all time. Only the rock would stand, the royal mountain, and even it would one day erode in the rain and snow.

Tangled roots underfoot on the steepness. Smiler forged ahead now, visible in his white coat. What was he thinking? Frightened of me, of the evidence of crime I carried, of losing his place in the world through implication and accessory after the fact. They were all reasonable fears. I kept an ear out for any disturbance. In these parts burrowed red foxes that hunted at this sneaking hour. Smiler's breathing had regularized but my heart hammered under the strain. Laura was ninety-five pounds, no more, her hair fine and red, her features delicate and precise. My God. This is what I'd come to, carrying the corpse of the woman I loved through the night in my drug-bolstered arms. I slowed. Smiler rounded a curve. Beyond the slope, past the breaking clouds, I saw a smear of deep maroon where the sun had set and, low on the horizon, a sharp pinpoint of scarlet: Mars. We'd covered a mile on an ellipse up the northwest flank of the mountain and were nearing the edge of the park proper. In a ragged stand of pine I stopped to catch my breath and gently placed Laura on a declivity. The second and final rigor mortis had not yet set. Smiler jogged back to where I rested. He squatted and huffed.

"So," I said. "What'd you talk about with Houdini at the Princess?"

This startled him. He hopped up, eyes darting nervously to Laura, mute witness to this macabre scene.

"I saw you with Jacques Price and another fellow. What happened?"

"We, we went to see him."

Smiler sat again and it poured from him. He spoke rapidly, the sound of his own voice reassuring himself. I kept a careful eye on his panic. He was on my leash yet and needed to stay tied to me for the time being.

"Jacques and I went to, we went to talk to Houdini. Jacques was going to sketch him for the school 'paper. There was a knock at the door and someone showed up."

"Who?"

"Whitehead."

"Who?"

Smiler told me. It was a character named Whitehead. Apparently, he was a divinity student and a Christian. He'd begun asking Houdini screwy questions about the Bible.

"What kind?" I asked.

"Did Houdini believe in it? Had Jesus performed the miracles or were they put-ups?" said Smiler.

Whitehead asked Houdini if Jesus had walked on water and healed the sick. Houdini demurred but replied that if he'd been alive back then he could've done the same stunts and the world would now be praying to Harry Houdini. After that statement Whitehead punched him.

"Pardon?" I asked.

"Whitehead had heard that Houdini could withstand any blow, and Houdini nodded. So Whitehead punched Houdini in the stomach."

"What'd you do?" I asked Smiler.

"Nothing. It came right out of left field. Whitehead stuck around a bit and then left. Houdini didn't look too good and asked us to go. He had a show that night."

"That's it?" I asked.

"That's it."

Smiler's tale was fishy as haddock and had Jack's fingerprints all over it. We'd waited in the dressing room while Jack consulted his 'watch, that I recalled. This Whitehead character was probably Jack's cat's-paw. To what end?

Near half an hour had passed and my sweat had cooled on
me. Neither beast nor fowl could be seen or heard in the stillness
fallen over the woods. I'd taken the precaution of leaving a half-
dose in my syringe and injected it now. In the near dark I saw the
expression on Smiler's face, contempt crossed with fear.

"Let's go."

Again I lifted the unwieldy sack onto my shoulder. We
resumed the climb along a devious path that, after several minutes, opened to a wide area bordered by a wire fence. Through
a ragged opening we climbed up onto a bluff overlooking the
graveyard. Here we stood on the tomb of the Molsons, their
crypt a tall lighthouse with the clan's crest carved on the stone.
The ground from here sloped down to the south, studded
with headstones, draped urns, and obelisks leaning off-true. A
light peacefulness reigned as a wind stirred scattered autumn
leaves. Enough light remained to lead us up a rise to a far and
quiet corner. Then the sky went black and through frazzled
clouds I saw the first stars come out. Smiler followed me, not
smiling now.

There it was, just over there, a neat hole in the ground. We
stopped. Three open graves waited, with pyramids of dirt piled
by each. Two were untouched since their original excavation.
The third site had been disturbed.

"Here," I said.

I set down the bag and sat, drained and sweating. Smiler said
nothing and rubbed his hands to keep them warm. I summoned
a little strength and with as much care as I could muster went
down into the first hole and gently settled Laura into it. I said no
prayer but climbed out of the pit and told Smiler: "Bury her."

He looked around for a spade and then at me.

"Fill it," I said.

"How?"

"Get your hands dirty."

Smiler began to protest, then sighed and started pushing dirt into the hole. He kicked with his feet then got on his knees to shovel and scrape. In twenty minutes the earth was level again. I lit a cigaret and stepped back.

"How's that?" he asked.

"Not bad."

He turned to me.

"Now you," I said.

"What?"

"Get in the next one."

"What? Why me?"

Smiler noticed the gun in my hand.

"Mick?"

"Get into that hole, you lousy son of a bitch."

I pointed the Webley at him. For reasons of his own, Smiler raised his hands. His mouth opened.

"Mick, please, please no."

"Do it or by God I'll shoot you down like the fucking dog you are. You did it."

"I did?"

"You killed her."

"Mick, you're, you're mad! Why would I kill her?"

"I caught you."

"No! Mick, I, I swear!"

I cocked the hammer. Smiler moved crabwise to the middle grave and slowly inched his way into it. He stood, his hands still held high, white lab coat dirtied.

"Mick, it wasn't me."

"Yup, that's true," I said.

"Then, why this?"

"'Who will help the widow's son?'" I teased.

Smiler's voice filled with relief. It was as black as the ace of spades now. Only the faintness of his coat was visible.

"I'm on the level," Smiler said.

I looked down at him in his hole. "You sure are."

"The square." Smiler then said something that was probably the Mason Word and put down his arms. Houdini, Jack, Sir Lionel Dunphy, they were all the same. I was outside looking in.

"Mick, Mick, you know! You know I didn't do this. I didn't kill her. Laura."

"Yes, I do," I said.

"Then who did?" asked Smiler.

"Me."

There was a moment of silence. Smiler broke it by blurting in terror: "I come from the East!"

"Well, I'm from out West," I said, and shot him in the chest.

He fell back into the pit and I fired again, a brief flash illuminating the red on his coat. His body twitched with the third shot and I stopped. My ears were ringing again with the noise and my nose was filled with the stink of gunpowder residue. My right hand was tensed, the flesh throbbing with the phantom echo of the Webley's action. Smiler was still and dead. I breathed in and out and felt a black, almost Satanic holiness well up within me. The next half an hour saw me grimed burying the man. I walked up and away through the darkness, invisible and free.

IN THE GLOAMING near to night was when she came to me. A victoria pulled by geldings brought her to the mountaintop. I waited as she stepped down and paid the driver, who took her paper money and tipped his hat. The letter I'd mailed her Sunday had hit home, though if I'd signed it with my own name I would've waited in vain. As it was, a forged request for a rendezvous proved my point: she'd acquiesced and had appeared right place, right time. This was my favourite hour, the dying day.

On the lookout side lingered a few sightseers and one or two folks strolled by Beaver Lake, but for the most part the park was empty with night falling fast. I stood on a stone in a thicket with a view all directions and watched the horses guide the 'cab back down the promenade road. Soon the sound of hooves on gravel faded and a deep stillness fell. Laura waited composedly by a weathered plinth and gazed out over the city, a faint shimmer on the indigo river and a low fluttering pulse of electric lights coming to life on the part-finished harbour bridge to the east. Soon Laura was alone, and then I went to her, chilled. She turned and saw me smiling.

"Michael," she said.

"Expecting somebody else?"

"Frankly yes."

"Well, he couldn't make it. He sends his regrets and asked me to take his place."

"I see."

"How are you?"

"I'm well."

"Beautiful night, ain't it?"

"Michael."

"Seen any good movies lately?"

"No."

"Shame."

"Michael, I really haven't the time for this."

"Is that so? Well then, the least I can do is walk you over to the road. You'll never get a taxi up here, not at this hour. Not safe for you to be alone in the dark."

Laura had no answer to that, wrapped in her still reserve. I made careful not to get too close. It was like coaxing a wild animal out of the woods.

"Just over there," I gestured vaguely.

She looked back and forth. I was right. The park was empty. At last she said: "Very well."

We walked down the path.

"You look fine, Laura."

"Michael."

"I mean it. Really."

She was silent, strange to me.

"See the swans?"

We were on the height above the lake and we were walking to the macadam road. The tram stopped running at four-thirty, I was certain. A sole motorcar chugged along, too far away for use.

"In England swans are property of the Crown," I said. "It must be the same here, with the same King. That's a royal prerogative, to know what swan tastes like."

Laura remained mute.

"Beautiful colour of the leaves this autumn. At this time of year out west you hear firecrackers and fireworks, for Hallowe'en. Love the smell of the smoke from a Roman candle. Of course you set them off around here for Victoria Day. *Fête de la Reine.* It's not the same, somehow."

I continued in this vein as we went to the road and came upon the open gates of the cemetery, talking to her of St. Jean Baptiste and Dollard des Ormeaux. We waited in the cold for some minutes to flag down another motorcar.

"Don't see anything," I said.

Laura started at my voice. I kept a healthy measure of humour and good cheer in my tone and tried not to seem possessed of a jealous, delicate madness. Perhaps she sensed a disquietude and had a small idea of what she'd walked into.

"I think that I should go," she said.

"All alone? I won't hear of it. Who knows what's lurking in these trees. Tell you what, there's a better chance of finding someone out on Park. We can take this shortcut here and the

path out to the avenue. There's bound to be lots of taxis there or
you can snag the tram."

Laura shivered and looked away. The gates were open. I
sauntered away from her down the path. It's what you do with
ponies: they become curious and follow, an ingrained instinct.
Laura seemed weaker than I remembered. How had she twisted
me around her finger? I almost laughed aloud to think on it. Of
course, in the meanwhile much had changed. I'd killed. I slowed
my pace, hands in pockets, whistling Jack's tune, "The Man
Who Broke the Bank at Monte Carlo." I turned. Laura was coming. I let her fall in beside me.

"It was you who sent me the letter," she said.

"Who, me?"

"Yes."

"All I can tell you is that he asked me to meet you," I said.

"I don't believe you."

"You should."

"No. You're lying. I should have known."

"That I'm a liar? Pot and kettle, my dear."

"I should have known that you'd stoop to this baseness."

"Baseness is it?"

I stopped.

"What was that you were doing with that joker then? Who did
you really want to see you two on that bed?"

"Certainly not you."

"As I thought."

Laura walked away downhill between upright markers.

"You play your pretty games and torture me," I cried.

"I want nothing to do with you!" she screamed.

It was a pleasing landscape with nary a soul: no old widows
tending graves, no mustachioed gents perambulating past fallen
comrades. Laura was increasing her pace, slipping away. I came
up quickly after her.

"You didn't want me at all, did you? You wanted him. All this time you wanted him. Do you realize that we're going to kill your pretty boy Bob? What do you think of that?"

Laura stopped. She put her hand on a tombstone. I saw where we were. Now I was hot.

"You didn't know that, did you sweetheart? That fucker's going to get it, with this."

I showed Laura my gun. She stumbled backward, eyes widening. I moved forward and felt her shrink before me.

"Oh, but you've got nothing to worry about," I said. "Not from this toy. Bob tried to kill us, not that you'd care if he had. He tried to blow my brains out."

"Please, Michael. Stop."

"We kill now, didn't you know? Your three musketeers. And who made me do it? You did, Laura. What did I ever do to you? I loved you and you let me believe you felt the same way. Then I saw you rutting like a sow with that son-of-a-bitch. What can I do? Tell me! No, wait, I'll tell you. I'm going to kill that Yankee bastard Bob. And then I'm going to shoot the love of your life. I'm going to kill Jack."

"Michael, no."

I closed with her and grabbed her shoulders. We were next to the empty graves I'd seen the day before. She reached up with her gloved hands and tried to break my hold. I crushed the velvet of her coat and pulled her closer. She struggled. I drank in her powder and scent: lemon and sugar. Her cloche hat fell off and she kicked at me with her booted feet so I pushed her onto a nearby cairn. Laura stumbled and her skirt rode above her knee. I went at her now in a blind rage, choking, unable to breathe. I put my hands through the white silk of her blouse and gripped the pearls around her porcelain doll's throat. By God she was beautiful. She gasped and fought as I tightened my grip and started squeezing.

My hands tangled in the pearls and thumbs dug into her trachea. I felt her weaken and a bloody mist clouded my vision. Her arms came up and I pushed and pulled her roughly about. Coming in close I saw the green in her eyes and wide staring pupils. Laura gazed at me and her pink tongue came out. Her light sparrow's body clenched, spasmed, and pulsed and her head rolled back as I strangled her. My teeth were bared, penis erect, heart dynamiting in my ears, a torrid heat raged though my blood. I tasted her warmth and her last gasp. She stopped moving and went still. I let her fall to the grass by the heaped mound of earth, then dropped down beside her and cradled her in my arms, eyes pouring tears. Poor Laura. Poor all of us.

For a long, lost time I lay watching the stars come out, taking in clean cool air, feeling my pulse return to normal. At last I set to work. I picked up her hat. Digging in her purse I took the note with Jack's name on it and burned it with a vesta. Her money I kept, twenty-odd dollars. Now was the moment for a ceremony. I was not in my body, but became an actor performing a dark rite. I lifted Laura and placed her in the hole. I arranged her hair as she'd always liked it, considered her face, her eyes, but there was nothing there. So I closed them forever and placed a coin in her mouth, for Charon. I climbed out of the grave and started to push dirt in, faster and faster, kicking and scraping, filling the empty space, consigning her to the earth's indifferent care.

I rubbed my hands, chucked soil out of my trouser cuffs, and leaned back against a stone, then lit a cigaret and with the lucifer's glow surveyed the scene of my crime. I started laughing, quietly at first, then louder and wilder. Strange thoughts filled my head, demonical notions. Grateful spirits whispered, congratulating me on my ascent. I walked away from the boneyard a king among the damned. The world belonged to me.

THURSDAY

O N WAKING I resolved to quit the filthy habit of smoking, substituting cinnamon chewing gum in tobacco's stead. There was, however, no alternative to sweet morphine. Putting away every notion of restraint I prepared the drug again and relaxed. I'd bought the bulldog edition of Wednesday night's *Star* and now read the transcript of a speaker at the Kiwanis Club. The Dominion of Canada would possess a population of one hundred and thirty-five millions in nineteen eighty-six. That was sixty years from now, a time too far in the future to contemplate. I was no longer interested in any possibilities; life was merely the here and now.

It was time to raise Cain and find Jack. I wanted to get even with Bob and take another scalp, add to the three thus far. I had the taste for it now, and I liked it. Time to count coup over a fallen enemy and take back what he'd stolen from us, a satchel full of money.

For luncheon I knocked back a schooner in a tavern on Stanley and began to lose my sense of the in-between. Automatic footsteps guided me to any port of call, a beautiful day to be in a bar amidst the unwashed sans-culottes swarming 'round the free lunch. I lit a cigaret to mask the stench of cabbage, corned beef, wet Stanfields, and rotten breath. Hunched in the corner I shivered with my hat down and collar up, unaccountably cold in an oven of close-packed humanity.

Concentration became difficult. There weren't any women and I needed one to prove I could still love. A living carcass at the bawdy-house on Mountain would suffice, or a two-dollar tumble on Bullion. Lilyan Tashman would do anything for me in return for my wealth of morphine and money. We could finish what she'd started. Two workers next to me grouched about the price of steak as they hacked into hanks of coarse beef. Meat. Hole and a heartbeat was the cry of the barracks, man's view of the weaker sex. I was a beast. We were all beasts.

Above the din rose a voice, a woman's, lusty and loud. Conversations retreated as a path cleared for a big, brassy creature. She worked over the chorus of a number from last year: "A cup of coffee, a sandwich and you, a cozy corner, a table for two, a chance to whisper and cuddle and coo with lots of hugging and kissing in view."

Between the tables she weaved, carrying a bouquet of cheap crepe-paper roses, her tits nearly spilling out her dress, a ratty fox fur ringing her neck. The singer seemed drunk, crimson lipstick slashed across her face. Old grey duffers dropped nickels and dimes into a shawl wrapped around her waist. I was trapped. She came directly towards me, trilling: "I don't need music, or lobster or wine whenever your eyes look back into mine. The things I long for are simple and few: a cup of coffee, a sandwich and you."

The creature stopped and curtseyed before me and looked at my face with infinitely deep black eyes. Who was she? Madwoman, priestess, avenging Fury? I took out a quarter dollar and handed it over. She winked at me and men began hitting their hands together so she began the tune again from the beginning but was not permitted a drink in this house, the law of Quebec. It must've been a racket: an ex-opera songstress fallen on hard times wiggling her rump for pocket change. Nevertheless it was unnerving the way she'd beelined to me, dark eyes into mine.

Did I wear a brazen mark on my forehead? The experience belike a crow flying at your head on a lonely country road. I paid up and left behind the muttering gaffers.

On the street I grew wary. It seemed incredible that the police weren't already on my heels. My suit was wrinkled and soiled, soft collar grimy and necktie askew. The impression I left seemed not to matter. What I'd done on the mountain remained a secret. The gravediggers couldn't have uncovered the two bodies on the hill yet. Rain spattered at me as I passed the pawnshop where I'd traded in my father's hunter back at the beginning of the month. I had no more need of the time. In the window I saw arranged an odd collection: a framed portrait of Georges Clemenceau wearing gloves, a tuba and guitar, a samovar. There were several desperate, frightening objects: spectacles, crutches, false teeth, a wooden leg in harness. What straits would drive you to pawn your choppers, and who on earth would be interested in buying them? I put the question to myself and watched my lips move in the glass, hearing no sound.

At the hotel I paid my outstanding bill and booked two more nights. The clerk confirmed that the Exceptionale was near the stock exchange. It was time to find Jack. I went to my room and fingered through the Gladstone, uncovering the tintype of Laura, which I put in my wallet amongst my Army papers.

I slept. For how long I wasn't sure, but it was evening when I came to. I took more morphine and went out into the pouring rain. The clerk gave me directions but I quickly became lost in a strange corner of town. Streets lacked lamps and caged doors were locked; it became increasingly grim. I started to curse. Here you are bootless in a desolate city, an outcast and pariah, murderer, Raskolnikov and Count Dracula rolled into one. Near to abandoning my hunt I turned up a side street and saw the dimly rendered sign for the hotel. A meagre hope quickened and I pushed at the door.

By contrast with the nondescript façade, the interior was quiet and vast with muted lighting and a roaring fire in the grate. In the lobby were comfortable empty Chesterfields scattered here and there and folded newspapers on the sideboard. I walked in as though I owned the place. This had to be it.

"Any message for Conrad?" I asked a sleek blade behind the counter.

"A moment, if you please."

He turned to the cubbyholes and picked out a folded piece of paper, which he handed over. I opened it to read: "News. Bar here nine nightly."

"The time," I asked the sharp.

The clerk irritably gestured at a clock. Quarter past. I noticed a door marked "Lobby Saloon," stepped over, and was met by applause as I entered. A gent started playing the piano, "Rosy Cheeks." Well-attired women and tuxedoed men buzzed in this hidden place. I'd never heard of it before. Jack drank at the bar, talking to the 'tender about South America. He was in a gay mood. I tapped his shoulder and he swivelled to me.

"Mick, me lad! Grand seeing you. Pull up a pew."

Jack turned to the 'keep. "My man, do me the kindness of pouring this poor sinner whatever he wants on the good green earth."

"Whiskey," I said.

"Make it a triple, neat and Irish," said Jack, "or this spudeater'll turn savage before your very eyes. So boyo, how're tricks? Long time no look-see."

"I'm ducky," I said.

The storm outside justified my ruined appearance. I looked over the toffs with their bespoke eveningwear and pink cocktails and bottled my rising wrath at their moneyed ease.

"What's up?" I asked, and drank.

"This and that," Jack said. "Tied up a few loose ends. Remember Martin?"

"Who?"

"The third driver, Charlie's man. The one who got away."

"Oke."

"I dug him up and got his story. Had to push his teeth around a bit. He's sound, as far as it goes."

"So that donnybrook with Charlie and the Senator was for nothing."

"Somewhat. The whole affair a mistake, as it happens."

"Shocking."

"Don't give me that. If you knew half."

"Try me," I said.

"Bob. He's the one sold out the shipment. That family of his got in bed with a Chicago mob that wants the whole market here. I'll confess that I don't know all the workings higher up. We'll get it straight from the cheat's lips when we track him down, that and the dough he stole from us."

"Us."

"Right-o. I'll be after your help with this one."

"Swell."

Jack explained that in the last few days he'd been working on a meet-up to square things with the Senator and that Brown the Customs agent had feelers out at all the border crossings for anyone matching Bob's description. As best as Jack could determine Bob had signed a hotel register last night at the Internationale, and therefore hadn't left the country yet. Something was keeping him in Montreal. Our aim was to track him down and get back the satchel we'd hijacked on Friday.

"We're back in the game," Jack said. "You ready to play?"

"Alki," I said.

"Skookum," replied Jack, and winked.

We passed a few more hours getting drunk and fell in with a group of rich college kids up from New York for hooch and jazz. At one point I excused myself from the merry stupid crowd to use the gentlemen's convenience. My intention was to make an injection but upon reflection and due to a state of utter inebriation the notion faced rejection. Perhaps my salvation lay in constant drunkenness. Ha, you joker you. Back at the bar people shouted. A long-legged girl in a short skirt danced on the piano with her eyes closed and I buttonholed Jack.

"Let's take the vapours."

Jack settled up and kissed one of the American beauties, starting a scuffle with her chaperone. Before it escalated the skirt fell off the piano and caused an uproar so Jack and I sloshed into the lobby, tight as owls.

"We're up against it, lad, and no fooling," Jack said. "We might need a 'car. Going to get a line on that Judas. It's no laughing matter."

"So you say."

"What, you milky?"

"Never touch the stuff," I said.

"Then let's get cracking."

Jack yanked me out onto the Rue Télégraphe. We were on our way. I wanted more than anything a pretty redhead with pale skin asleep in my bed next to me. We neared a hateful neighbourhood. Nearby were smelters and machine works where they fabricated locomotives. I tried to imagine what the area had looked like eighty years ago and what it would eighty hence but couldn't. Tomorrow beckoned with malevolence, more electricity, dynamite, barbed wire.

On the sidewalk stood humans, shift workers at the plant and conspiring labour agitators, the hoi polloi. Were they my kinfolk? No more. I was now a breed apart with blood on my knife. Every single thing was under my control, Jack for once drunker than I. There was nothing to do but continue.

Jazz was in the air, coming from a bar. We stumbled to it and from an apartment above us I heard the machine-gun clatter of a typewriter, typewronger, a news-hawk burning the midnight oil, grinding out a story for the afternoon 'paper. Jack and I were the perpetrators of a string of crimes that had shocked Montreal, starting with a bootlegging run that'd ended in the death of two, armed robbery of a cinema, beatings and shootings on the Plateau, a deadly fire in Chinatown, and other, private crimes. The Lord alone knew what Jack had been up to and how many heads he'd cracked. Ahead of us a corner boy with fresh pulp and ink under his arm cried: "G'zette!"

We entered the saloon, a Negro club for Pullman porters and their ladies out for a night on the town. Eye whites glittered in the gloom and black faces glistened with sweat. It was hot as the jungle and onstage a fat darkie played piano. He pounded away, some crazy roll. We made it to the bar and held it up. Space was left us, the only whites in the house. Jack looked every inch the Pinkerton op, I an informer. He ordered whiskey and they refused payment so Jack let coins spill sloppily along the counter. It was good jazz and bad liquor. Presently a high yellow dame singer came out to join a tall bass player and squat drummer. She went to the front of the stage and the combo started in like a thunderstorm, the gal belting: "I just saw a maniac, maniac, maniac, wild and tearing his hair, jumping like a jumping jack, jumping jack, jumping jack, child you should've been there."

"Nice tune," grinned Jack.

The house started reeling and the Negroes got up to dance. I willed myself still. The booze tasted of petrol and burned going down. Jack bobbed his head and rapped his knuckles to the beat of the drums. We had a wide berth, an island of empty space around us. I caught stray suspicious glances.

The band really hopped and I downed more fuel. My uneasiness grew. If the cops raided the joint we'd be up to our necks. I also felt a gnawing, a craving. The drug.

"Let's get out of this hole," I said.

"Oke."

Back in the night my sense of direction fled. A nasty wind had picked up and Jack was quiet now.

"This way," I said.

He followed me down an alley in a direction. With a swede I lit a cigaret and passed it over. The hot tongue of my addiction licked at nerve endings and ran up my spinal column. I needed to fix that. Where? Our rambling took us past a factory and an office building covered in fire escapes. I could swear I saw a raccoon on a rubbish tip. At last we came onto a well-lighted square and with confusion I saw it was Place d'Armes. How'd we ended up here? Before us was the Bank of Montreal, a classical temple surmounted by Indians.

"Let's go set a spell in the portico," I said.

"Agreed."

Jack reclined on the hard steps and I hid in a spot screened by wide columns. Jack looked at me and shook his head as I made up a shot. It went in, ice and heat, another withdrawal from the banking account of my life. What was my balance now? Probably overdrawn, paying negative interest. Jack hummed a tune. Something was not right, a numbness, an inability to feel my hands or feet. No. Bad sign. Very cold now.

"Jack."

"What?"

"Help."

"What?"

He turned to me.

"I'm sorry, I . . ."

"Jesus, Mick. What is it?"

"I took too much," I said. "Help."

SATURDAY

COBWEBS HANGING FROM the ceiling of an unknown room. I regarded them for some minutes, then managed to turn my head to look at my body. I lay in my combinations, with a cloth bound around my right foot. An ugly pain coursed up the leg and a terrible black dryness parched me. Jack came into the room, carrying a bottle of hydrogen peroxide.

"You kicked the mirror over there somehow," he said.

"Bad luck."

He undressed the wound and poured alcohol on my foot. I winced. Jack laughed. The bastard took pleasure in my pain, repayment for playing nursemaid.

"Where are we?" I asked.

"Somewhere else."

"What time is it?"

"Ten," he said. "Saturday morning."

"Saturday?"

I'd been out for a full day.

"Thought you might go west on me," Jack said. "I had to call in Jacques Price to look at you."

"How's he?"

"Scared. The school's up in arms. Smiler's disappeared."

Jack re-tied the dressing.

"The police are looking for him. They dragged the river near to where the bridge is being built. Jacques said folks think he's offed himself."

"Did he?"

"No one knows. It could be suicide. He had a paper due and never turned it in."

Jack looked at me queerly. I sat up.

"What is it?" I asked.

"There's something else."

"What?"

"Laura's gone."

He studied me.

"Where?"

"Another mystery. She's been gone for days."

"Same time as Smiler?"

"The day before."

"Together?"

"That's the question."

"What do you think?" I asked.

"You know what I think."

I didn't really. Had I revealed my guilt in my delirium? I was lucid enough right now and felt much improved, actually. If Jack suspected me he never let on. At last he said: "I think she's run off with that Judas Bob."

I almost laughed in his face. He went and sat in a chair by the broken mirror, looking exhausted. It occurred to me that he might be concerned for my well-being, or at the very least, his own hide.

"Jacques showed me how to fix you up a dose," Jack said. "It's no time to wean you off. I need you. How long've you been back on the spike?"

"Since Chinatown," I said.

"Mick, Mick, Mick."

"You don't have to tell me, I know. But what'd you expect? Place temptation before me and I fall. Thus endeth the lesson."

"Very well."

Jack sighed and rubbed his eyes. He yawned.

"Price told me to get a little food in you. I took the liberty of having your suit sponged and pressed."

My mind turned to my overcoat and the wad of cash sewn into its lining until my eyes spotted it hanging from a hook.

"What for?" I asked.

"We've an appointment," he said.

"We do? Who with?"

"You'll see."

I sat up and felt the world turn several revolutions My brow felt heated, my body clammy.

"What happened the other night?" I asked.

Jack informed me he'd manhandled my corpse into a 'cab after I'd collapsed and told the driver I was dead drunk. In this apartment he tipped me into a tub of cold water and first thing in the morning called Smiler at the Royal Victoria, then Jacques Price at the school. Price came and determined that my overdose wasn't a serious one. On the table had been left a stopgap Jacques brought to help lower my needed dosage, a bottle of Browne's Chlorodyne. I thanked Jack for his forbearance. It was a part of his nature I rarely recognized. On the other hand, none of this would've happened without his impetus. *Prima causa* Jack. At the back of my mind I wondered, though. Had I done this on purpose?

"You're a downy one, you know that," Jack said to me, smiling.

"The downiest."

For a few more hours I lay prone and helpless, drinking my medicine to relieve fatigue. I experienced a slight lacrimation, tears for myself and my state. Jack went for a flask of soup and arrowroot biscuits. From outside came a droning airplane. After eating I tried my pins and was surprised to find strength. I took a Scotch bath, shaved, looked at the tender holes in my arm, then climbed into my suit and tie and was ready to go. Jack came and with a mock formality handed me back my Webley. I followed him out of the room and away from this, another run-down bolt-hole in another bad part of town, Charlevoix by the canal this time. We took a taxi to a café on St. Catherine. Jack ordered java, I a Sal Hepatica. Morphine had made me constipated and I needed a blow.

"What's on the menu?" I asked.

"It's the peace pipe," Jack said. "Word from on high."

"Sounds peachy."

"Keep your eyes open and on me. I'm afraid it may be a trap," he warned.

"Where?"

"Avalon."

I buttoned myself up as we walked the last few blocks to Jack's rendezvous. At Sherbrooke I watched men working atop an enormous apartment building, a great Caledonian chateau of limestone and shining copper like a CPR hotel. As it happened I was glad my suit'd been cleaned. We climbed steps to where a blackcoated ape stood with his hands over his groin. With a nod at Jack massive oaken doors opened to let my friend and myself into the Mount Royal Club.

The receiving room was quiet and august, all dark wood and polished tiles. We were in one of the Empire's redoubts, all of a pattern wherever nabobs ruled: Cairo, Cape Town, Bombay, Rangoon, Shanghai, Vancouver, Dublin, London, Montreal. Each club was cut from a cloth, with portraits of racehorses on the walls, bound copies of *Punch* in the reading room, wog waiters in waistcoats ironing weeks-old copies of the *Times*. Ci-devant colonial administrators, remittance men, and third sons in old school ties sponged drinks at the bar and damned the natives. A muted grandfather clock sat ticking, set to Greenwich Mean Time. Over the fireplace hung a framed visage of the sovereign, Queen Mary an inch lower. A stern man in a hard white collar, silk tie, grey vest, black swallowtail, and gold-pinstriped trousers met us at reception, his shoes polished to a glossy jet. He resembled a sergeant promoted officer in the field. Jack appeared damned natty and I wasn't shabby enough to be booted out. Standards, don't you know. I resisted a fierce urge to pick my nose.

We signed the book and I noticed that Jack had given in at last and written Richard Hannay, his beau ideal. I amused myself by putting down Patrick Murphy, a true Mick's handle amongst these long-nosed Saxons. Jack moved in stride as we were escorted by the chamberlain past a massive globe of exotic wood, turning right down a corridor to a private room where a gross figure awaited us, a fat man spilling out of a leather chair. The Senator.

He was alone, neither of his thugs in sight. The club had stretched a point letting one Frenchman in; accommodating two roughnecks to boot wouldn't be cricket. The Senator toyed with his fob chain. At its end was a gold triangle. He reached his hand to a burled wood box filled with cigars and selected one. I saw his ring and finally, finally I understood who was in charge. Some Brotherhood.

"Here we are," Jack said.

"*Alors*, Mutt and Jeff, yes," said the Senator.

He was alone until the terrier bitch popped onto his lap.

"How's Rex?" asked Jack.

"As you see, she is well."

"That's not who I'm talking about."

"Ah, *oui*."

A mischievous spark burned in the Senator's black eyes as he sucked wetly at the cigar. Jack walked over to the box, took a cylinder for himself, and sat down.

"He is, we will say, aware of your service," said the Senator. "It is accomplished?"

"Last Friday," said Jack.

"Very admirable. When do you expect it complete?"

"*Bientôt.* Keep your hair on. It takes a little time to work. No traces."

I studied a marble Mercury on a table. Pieces fitted together.

"Then the threat, it is eliminated," the Senator said.

"Yes," said Jack, lighting up.

"*Bien.*"

"As for the other business, I apologize," Jack said. "It was an error of judgment."

"Mistakes, they happen."

"Keep your eye on the 'papers," Jack said.

"I will," said the Senator. "Yes, I will."

My morphine hunger returned as I drank in the rich cigar smoke filling the room. The Senator hadn't lit his. A panel in the wall slid open to our left and the club's majordomo appeared.

"You are wanted," he sniffed.

Jack stood and looked at me, then imperceptibly shook his head. Through the opening I saw a sitting room with a tall striking man standing with his back to the fire. He wore a toothbrush moustache. With a shock I saw it was Laura's father, Sir Dunphy.

"Then we're square," Jack said to the Senator.

The Senator smiled and closed his eyes. I didn't like his crafty look at all. Jack turned to me and said: "*Siu sam.*" Look out.

The Senator stroked Rex. He spoke to me.

"Your friend, how well do you know him?"

"*Depuis longtemps,*" I said.

"He has done the world a service, I think."

"*Comment?*"

"There are, how do you say, a people who wish to destroy this world. Cosmopolitans who want impurity."

"*Vraiment?*"

"Here, there. You have seen them in Russia. Now they work in Quebec."

"Cosmopolitans?"

"*Oui.*"

The Senator twirled the cigar, pushed it into his *gueule*, and rubbed his hands together in a grasping manner. Rex turned to look as the door slid back open. I was disgusted by the Senator's words. Christ, the higher up the tree the more rotten the fruit. Jack re-entered. Sir Dunphy now faced the fire, his hands behind his back. The panel closed. Jack nodded at me.

"We're finished here," he said.

The Senator took out his pocketwatch and opened it to look at the time.

"*Oui. Vous êtes finis.*"

Rex tried to follow us as we were ushered out. The Senator gripped her close.

NEAR DORCHESTER I glimpsed the grey Sisters of St. Ann at their devotions in a formal garden protected from the street by an iron grille. My foot pained me and I felt weak, monomaniacally obsessed once again with the drug.

"The left hand doesn't know what the right's doing," said Jack.

"How's that?"

"He wants me to find her," Jack said.

"Who?"

"Laura."

I halted and almost broke character, then found myself.

"Well, if anyone can it's you. Pinkertons and all that."

"It's nice and neat," said Jack.

"Are you sure she's with Bob?" I asked.

"Where else? You saw them at the party."

In Jack's voice quavered a tremor of uncertainty. Such a sensation must be rare for him, rare as his apology to the Senator. For a crushing moment I almost felt sorry for the man. He'd killed her, without even knowing it. But emotions such as these were indulgences. My consciousness had no time for them.

"Jack," I said, "I need it."

He looked me up and down.

"You most certainly do. Let's go."

Back in Charlevoix I made my injection.

"What's it like? Cocaine?" asked Jack.

"Much better," I said.

"Can you sniff it?"

"Not a wise idea. Why?"

"I'm out of salt," Jack said. "Smiler's gone."

"Right."

"Thought I might try yours. How'd you feel now?" he asked.

"Archie. I could administer it epicutaneously, through your skin. You don't need a needle. Or there's intravitreally."

"What's that?"

"Put some on your eyes," I said.

"Christ, no thanks."

I wanted to frighten Jack off. My needs were severe enough that I didn't wish to share a single grain. Soon the pain retreated. I was borne aloft in bliss. I looked at myself in the shattered mirror. Jack sat down and said: "There you are, you rascal." He pulled from under the chair his sharkspine stick, then lit a cigaret and began twirling the vertebral column around and around.

"Who's your master?" I asked him.

"I am."

"What happened last Friday? You told the Senator you'd done him some service last Friday. What was it?"

"That was the left hand."

"And finding Laura's the right," I said.

Jack began to talk. Sir Dunphy had been the one who'd orchestrated the Royal Commission when the Customs scandal began to break. In the House of Commons Rex King stood up and said: "A detective has been sent to Montreal."

"That's me. I'm in Hansard. Look it up."

"How'd you get picked?" I asked.

"Pinkertons recommened me to Sir Dunphy. Helped that I was a true fellow and brother, naturally."

Jack worked the docks and traced the smuggling pipeline back to the Senator, then the Minister of Customs. Jack and he forged an understanding and combined forces, gamekeepers turned poachers. That was last fall, before a new group of Italians moved in from New York under a boss named Lucania. A fight started: New York Sicilians versus Chicago Neapolitans, with Montreal in the middle.

"Bob's family waited on the fence until I was given the black spot. After Bob double-crossed us he went off the reservation. Shadow in the wind. Wants all the money for himself, I reckon. Man's moved from cocaine to heroin lately. Spent all week twisting arms and busting doors. Pretty boy's still in town."

"What's our plan?" I asked.

"Hunt him down. He's been seen with a woman. That'll be Laura."

I controlled myself.

"Have a feeling he's going to skip town today or tomorrow. Montreal's too hot for him," Jack said.

"Welcome to the oven," I said.

The whole world could go hang fire. I prepared another syringe and rode it home.

JACK ROUSED ME.

"Come along. It's close to five. You need to eat."

We caught a 'cab and this time went east. I could smell burning. The 'cabbie's St. Christopher medal swung like a censer as he sped and braked to a stop at Place d'Youville.

"There," said Jack, pointing with his white stick.

Exiting a small cod-classical building was our man Brown. He stood in the doorway for a moment under a weathered stone Britannia fixed on the architrave. There was a vignette of Empire for you, if you liked: a petty Scotch official in a provincial backwater below the faded shield and trident of old Albion. With the setting sun turning the square and stones a mandarin orange the tableau had a certain shabby nobility to it, a minor, mournful grandeur. The 'cab pulled alongside the wee man and Jack shouted: "Hop in."

Startled, Brown spun and fixed his eyes on Jack's crooked finger, the digit beckoning through an open window. Jack got out and waved Brown in with a jesting courtesy, back to his old tricks again. The Customs man sat between us, smelling of cheese. His cheek bore a faded mark where Jack had struck him. Jack ordered the taxi east to just beside the construction site beneath the bare pilings of the harbour bridge.

We got out by the lee of a wall before a brick barracks. I could now almost taste the atmosphere; instead of smoke, it was the sour, thick odour of barley and hops, effluvia from the redbrick Molson Brewery nearby. In the wall was an olive-coloured door and a smaller inset door within it. Jack motioned Brown through and I followed them to an empty courtyard. In its centre stood a plinth supporting the statue of a green man bearing a flag. The barracks house appeared deserted.

"Recognize these, Brown?"

Jack held up several yellow slips of paper.

"Aye."

"Your markers from the barbotte house on Cypress. Canny investment, wouldn't you say?"

Brown stayed shtum. He shivered in his cheap snuff-coloured tweed.

"You know what I want," Jack said. "Hand me the 'gen on our Yankee friend and you can start digging a new grave for yourself at the tables. Fair trade, eh?"

Brown nodded weakly. It occurred to me that the pair were both gamblers. Jack had probably already burned through every dime in his pockets, hence his desperation now. For all his control Jack was grasping at straws. The Scotchman was a last resort, a long shot.

"Cross me on this and I'll feed you to the fucking wolves," said Jack. "On your knees."

Brown shook off his inertia and stiffened with the auld resolve of Carlisle.

"There's no need."

"Kneel," Jack insisted.

For a moment I thought Jack would kill him. We were alone. The courtyard was abandoned. No navvies swung from the partly built river span overhead, bearing witness. My senses sharpened. I handled my Webley. Jack was being needlessly cruel, I thought. Brown was broken; there was no need to kick the cur. The Scotsman creakily lowered himself, the brief flare of rebellion doused. I saw him for what he was, a small, frightened functionary in over his head. For a brief moment I had a fellow feeling that I quickly banished. I'd gone too far the other way and we could quarter the man for all the difference it'd make.

"Do you know this place?" asked Jack.

"No."

"It's where they hanged the French Patriots, the ones who burned down the Assembly. They were traitors. You won't be given the length of a rope, Brown. I promise you that."

Jack moved in, grasping the handle of his white stick. Brown flinched, waiting for a slash or blow. With an animal smile Jack slowly pulled a steel blade from within the sharkspine.

"*Dieu et mon droit.*"

He tapped Brown's shoulders lightly with the sword, left, right, the burlesque of a knighting.

"Arise."

It was dangerous to humiliate a man thus. Jack had refined his cruelty to the weak. He'd changed, and so had I. I was dead to pleasure, outrage, pain. I was a killer. Wind gusted off the water. There was no morality, only exigencies. My ethos: morphine and money. She was gone, at my hands, and I had nothing else to tie me to life. Brown would now pass along his shame to one weaker than he, the back of his hand to the wife, his belt to a child, the boot for a dog. The world spun ever thus.

"*Homo homini lupus est,*" I said.

Jack looked at me.

"On your bike, Brown," he said.

The man got to his feet and shuffled off. Jack came over and lit a cigaret.

"'Man is wolf to man,'" he said.

"Alpha plus."

"Thank your old man. Not much Latin in the camps."

He replaced the sword in its scabbard. We walked away together in another direction. I spotted a copper on the street and reached down to pinch it. It was an Indian Head from the United States.

"Find a penny, pick it up," I said.

"Put it in your shoe for luck," said Jack.

"Not how it goes. Here."

I flipped it over to him and he called heads, caught it and laughed, then put it in his pocket.

On Viger we hailed another 'cab and stopped at the Victoria Tavern on William. Inside the bar a skeleton played a wheezy concertina: "Nearer My God to Thee."

"Like last call on the *Titanic* here," said Jack. "Let's go elsewhere."

We settled at the Victory and I sprang for all-dressed steamed Frankfurters on white bread with mustard and Kiri spruce beer to wash them down. We chewed and swallowed.

"Do you know what?" I asked.

"I don't."

"We're not the sterling heroes in this tale."

Jack ate.

"What d'you mean?"

"I mean you're no Hannay and I'm not Tom Brown."

"Who are we then?"

"The Black Stone."

It gave Jack pause. I lit a cigaret and continued.

"We're the ones you never read about, the ones who lean on weaklings and hand out beatings. Look at you, taking orders. We're not racing to save the crowned heads of Europe or stop the next war. We're the ones that the hero worries about when there's a knock on the door. All our troubles come from that. No honour in it."

Jack swallowed and cleaned his mouth.

"Honour means nothing. *Amor fati:* love your fate. Accept it. We're here and others aren't. I know damned good men who're six feet under while fat bastards feed on ortolan drowned in Armagnac. We do what we have to, and that's all I have to say. Grab your things."

In Griffintown jack o'lanterns lit up windowsills. Children wearing ghoul masks carried bags door to door. Shrill voices from ghosts and goblins piped a strange phrase: "Trick or treat!"

Tomorrow was Hallowe'en and a church Sunday so tonight was the night for fun and games. All Hallows' Eve. Side by side we marched to Duke, intending to pass the night at Jack's haunt. Before heading up we went into the tavern across the way for one more. The bar was packed and thick with smoke from wavering oil lamps. As we came in from the cold I sensed pairs of eyes on us. I bought two bottles of Black Horse and took them to a flimsy bench by the far wall. Jack was as uneasy as I and he started to grate on me, a result of our enforced companionship and relative lack of success. It was the same with any company reaching the end of the line.

He whispered the plan: if anyone resembling Bob crossed the border from Quebec Brown would be telephoned or wired here in Montreal. Jack aimed to get on Bob's trail from that point. Meanwhile we waited, killing time. Jack had ten dollars left and I promised him half my leavings. It was only just. I'd been wrong earlier; sometimes there was a fraction of honour, even amongst thieves and killers.

We were being watched, I was certain. I scanned a room filled with Neanderthals, dark pitiless morlocks. Was that an averted gaze from the two fellows in the corner? Who were those yeggs by the window? Slanted mirrors embossed with the names of the great whiskey houses allowed me a fractured reflection of the chamber. I saw Jack's hair shining amber in the low gloom. Around us groaned a murmuring, persistent chorus. It was late. The 'tender rang a bell.

"Time, gentlemen."

A boy dragged a black curtain across the windowpane and a great galumph locked the front door. By staying put Jack and I joined the blind pig after closing hours. I bought two more stouts and drank mine mechanically, hand on gun.

"Got a feeling," said Jack out the side of his mouth.

In a Jameson's mirror I saw two vaguely familiar men in flat caps at a table looking at a grey square of paper. One peered over his compatriot's shoulder and accidentally caught my eye. The paper was a photograph. In a burst of light my mind recognized them: the Senator's goons.

"We've been shopped," I whispered.

"Where?"

"Corner. Flats. They've got our picture."

"Right," Jack said.

My eyes flitted over the crowd.

"Two more," Jack said. "Black homburgs, ten o'clock."

He was right. We were boxed in.

"Choice of enemies," I said.

"After you," he said.

"No, you," I insisted.

Jack got up. I watched him walk to the back door. One of the big fellows in homburgs shook his head. Sweat pricked my scalp and my hand clenched the Webley tighter. Jack moved past the bar. Another fellow was posted there. A collective ripple like wind on a wheat field seemed to flutter through the remaining drinkers. Out the corner of my eye the wizened bartender started to crouch. Suddenly there was a shrill whistle, the electric lights went up and someone yelled: "Police!"

The pair at the window jumped and the homburgs did the same. I leapt to my feet with the Webley's hammer cocked. Jack grabbed a short bastard and held the naked blade from his cane to the man's neck. I pointed the Webley at the mirror and pulled the trigger. There was a boom and Bushmills Irish Whiskey shattered, glittering to the floor. Topers hid under tables. I swung the gun to point at the cops, to the lummox at the front door, then back to the Senator's goons. I was a piece of stone, frozen with fury and fear. The broken looking glass coursed down in silver shards.

"Move and I'll burn your brains!" I roared.

"This one gets a knife!" shouted Jack.

The four cops were nearly identical in black coats and hats. One muttered to another.

"*Ta gueule!*" I yelled and took aim at his yap.

"On the ground, all of you, or this one's dead!" shouted Jack.

Silence. The cops reluctantly bent. I kicked my way through prone bodies; innocent bystanders, one might call them, except everyone's guilty and I'd kill them all to get out. Eyes down, eyes up, over to Jack.

"Open it," he commanded his prisoner.

Jack reached into his coat and took out his Browning, jabbing it into his hostage's lumbar. My arm trembled and I submitted to total tachycardia, my body bursting with searing blood, my skin ice, hair on end. We were in for it now and no mistake.

"You won't go far!" one of the plainclothesmen shouted.

"In a pig's eye!" yelled Jack.

He pushed our bartering chip through the door into the dark. Nothing happened. Jack darted out and I covered. I took one last look around the tavern. I'd never forget it. Came Jack's voice: "Ankle!"

I stepped into the night blind. Jack's hand grabbed me.

"This way," he hissed.

He kicked the hostage in the arse and took off down the alley. I peeled after him, fast as I could. Nightmare, nightmare. I wasn't fast enough. My body was heavy, no air to breathe. Run. Run. Goddammit, the police at last. It was dark, too dark, I couldn't see a Goddamned thing. My eyes strained wide for light, trying to follow Jack as he ran. Dogs? Were those dogs chasing us? I turned and tripped and dropped my gun, scrambled to my feet. No time to find it. Run.

I broke out of the alley into a lit street and saw Jack sprinting down a narrow *ruelle* between two high buildings. There was the screech of tires and a pair of yellow headlamps rushed at me. Hanging, it would be hanging for me if I was caught. I charged into the darkness with my legs burning, soaking wet, running. Faster, faster. They won't hang you; they'll shoot you down like a fucking dog in the street. Go, Goddammit. Go.

Jack dashed to the left and I caught him turn, then turn again. Footsteps pounded like slamming doors after me and there were echoes and gunshots. I heard shouts, police whistles, dogs barking. No. I slowed for a moment, gasping, chest heaving. I grabbed at my necktie and pulled open the noose. No, there was no one, the noises were in me. I picked up the pace again but Jack was gone. Shit. My head spun wildly looking for a way out, an escape hatch. I turned another corner and hands grabbed the front of my coat. Cardiac arrest.

"Quiet. Breathe through your mouth. Don't move."

Jack pushed me down. He had a gun in each hand and we were hiding behind rubbish bins in a loading bay. A rotten stench filled my nostrils. I brushed a waxy brick wall and smelled my fingers: fat. We were behind a butcher shop or slaughter-house amongst waste meat and filth. I could hear a slithering movement and a squeaking. Rats. My teeth were bared, my eyes staring insanely. My stomach roiled and turned. Don't. Don't spew, you'll give us away. Jack cocked his head and froze. I didn't dare move. For an agonizing lifetime we waited as the vermin scratched and scratched.

"Lost my gun," I said at last.

"Here."

Jack handed over his Webley. We waited for anything. I was parched and screaming for water. We waited for our pursuers, for whistles and shouts, motorcars, footsteps, horse hooves, dog howls. Nothing.

"It gets better and better," Jack said to himself.

"We've got to keep moving," I said hoarsely.

"They know where to find us."

"The Senator sold us. Why?"

"Damned if I know. Town's too hot now," said Jack.

"Took them long enough."

"They've got us. They'll cordon off the area and set up patrols. There'll be a uniform at every callbox and a flying squad ready in a trice. We've got to get off the island."

"How? They'll call the stations and blockade the bridges. Even if we grab a motor—"

"We've got to get off," repeated Jack.

"No, let's go to ground," I whimpered.

Jack rounded on me.

"Where? If they knew we'd be at that dump they'll have the jump on us wherever we bolt. Use your head."

His venom put my back up. I tamped down my rage for the moment. "Follow me," I said.

"Where? Gaol?"

"No. Never that."

We crept to the alley mouth and argued over our bearings. I told Jack my notion. He thought it over a minute and shrugged.

"Could be worse. Not by much."

It was touch and go. The most dangerous moment was crossing the wide, well-lit expanse of McGill Street from Griffintown into old Ville Marie. We passed the Customs House and prowled along to the river. Jack stuck by me as I worried our way along, stopping at every noise. We wouldn't last a night plus the light of day on the run in this city, no friends and the police after us. It would end in a bloody fusillade. By pussyfooting it we came to our goal and fortune smiled on failure. It was there.

"Luck of the bloody Irish," Jack said.

MY OLD COMRADE managed a tight grin as we stepped out from our concealed position to the deserted promenade between Alexandra and King Edward quays. I looked down at the rowboat I'd seen tied up by a freighter on Friday when we'd killed the moneymen.

"What was the boat called?" I asked.

"The *Hatteras Abyssal.*"

"Gone now," I said.

"Back to Holland," said Jack.

For the nonce there were no other large freighters moored nearby. Either chance or design, it didn't matter. We coasted to the rusty ladder and Jack climbed down. I spied a nightwatchman or harbour patrolman walking towards us.

"Hurry," I breathed.

I shoved the Webley in my belt and followed Jack onto the skiff. I wobbled into the stern.

"You row," Jack said.

I untied us and pushed away. We were in a dark canyon between piers. With the oars I pivoted us around and out of the slack through an eddy of detritus and buoyant trash. We moved into the river proper and I pulled to place us beyond pistol range. I could see the watchman's head but he never broke stride. My gun barrel bit into my crotch so I passed the gun to Jack. He lay low at the bow with his wrists steady on the rim, ready to fire. In five minutes we were well past the end of the pier and soon entered the wide, strong current of the St. Lawrence. Jack turned and I rested at the oars, letting the flow push us downriver. We gazed back at the dirty maroon incandescence of Montreal.

Headlamps blazed along the wharves. I heard police sirens, far away. We'd slipped the net. Black silhouettes of church spires and the mountain framed the night against the burning luminous city, stars high beyond, Orion rising. The shore retreated, diminishing as we were swept along. A massive steamship at Jacques Cartier Quay boomed its whistle and was echoed by a train pulling along the shore. We had a way to go to make our escape and Christ knew what was on the other side, wherever we ended up. Our skiff passed into the fast current in line with the clock tower at Victoria Quay. It was now past midnight.

"Meet me under the clock," I said.

A reckless hilarity welled up in me. I saw Jack grin at the Vancouver expression, the timepiece at Birks under which everyone met. I sang: "Merrily, merrily, merrily, merrily, life is but a dream."

Past St. Helen's Island and the looming foundations of the harbour bridge we struck land at the southern shore and ground up on the rocky shingle at Longueil. Jack jumped out and tugged the lead rope. I leapt after. We took heavy stones and staved in the rowboat, Cortés at Vera Cruz. Jack sat and took off his hat, then held his wristwatch to his ear.

"Stopped," he said.

We climbed through the thin trees lining the riverbank to higher ground. I looked back at the city. Jack kept walking. I met him at a ditch angled away from the wind. We lay down in an empty field back to back for warmth, coats tightly buttoned. Orion hunted above us, our companion through the long watch.

HALLOWE'EN

THE GREY FIGURE stirred with the morning light. Frost had formed on the dying blades of grass and the ground was hard and cold.

"Dreamed I was ironing the carpet," Jack said, rolling and levering himself upright. He swiped smut from the corners of his eyes, then dirt and leaves from coat and trousers. We were near a wire property fence and I sat with my back to a post studded with rusty nails. Earlier I'd taken breakfast: a shot of morphine.

"I dreamt I couldn't sleep," I said.

Jack laughed and stood to take account of himself, his billfold and lost cane, then pissed a steaming stream of urine in the growing sunshine. He buttoned, tucked in his shirt, smoothed his hair, replaced his hat, and jumped up and down to come alive, then checked the Browning and the Webley. Done, he walked to me and handed me my weapon.

"What now?" I asked.

"How much money do you have?"

"Six hundred or so," I said.

"It'll do. Want to tie up a few loose ends. Then we hit the road."

"Oke."

Jack put the pistol in his belt at the small of his back. He sorted through a sheaf of papers: stray banknotes, Brown's gambling markers, lucky playing cards. I stood and shook like a dog before the day's ramble. Jack vaulted the fence and I followed; our boots started crunching over field stubble. A bell for early mass slowly tolled in the bright, cold air. We walked towards its source.

At a crossroad east of the church stood a garish Crucifixion, the blood a startling red against the blue sky. Jesus was snow-white; his peeling paint lent the martyr a leprous cast. At the foot of the execution device someone had planted coloured cellophane flowers. We continued past Golgotha to Rome.

"Saint-Zotique," Jack said, eyeing the clapboard. "Wonder who he is when he's at home."

Old women in black and bearded men congregated at the open doors. Atop a wagon hitched to a sad dray sat a dour moustached man and his enshawled wife with their seven silent children. Horses stood next to farming lorries and a collection of old Fords and Frontenacs. Abutting the church was a straggling orchard. Jack pulled tough little apples from tree boughs and we walked west, the sun warming our backs.

By degrees the sky lightened. Clouds thickened into pleasing discrete masses serene and indifferent to us in the sparkling blue. There was the play of sun warming the earth and from bare branch to rose trellis before a tidy square house flitted a pair of tardy, ragged robins. Jack bit into an apple and spat.

"Sour as hell."

We walked along the verge as the day came to life, touching our hats to ladies and nodding at men.

Half an hour more and we reached Longueil proper, a *quartier* of low buildings. I was exhausted, dampened by the drug and a fatal indifference. Minor traffic moved afoot on the macadamized roads past a closed bank, shuttered barbershop, the Knights of Columbus, a general store open for business despite the Sabbath. Jack pointed and said: "The Bell."

The sign read "The Bell Telephone Company of Canada, Local and Long-Distance Calls." We entered the store. To clean my teeth I bought a spruce beer off the lackadaisical shop proprietor and eavesdropped on Jack in the booth.

"Trunk call to Montreal," he shouted into the tube. "Hotel Montmartre."

He winced as the connection clicked and screeched. Cross the river south and you were in another city, another world, French Canada.

"*Bonjour, monsieur.* Name's Marlow, room something. Can't remember. I checked in a few days ago. Marlow without an 'e.' By chance are there any messages for me?"

Jack closed his eyes and seemed to will himself still. I'd seen him like this at the races when his horse broke from the pack near the post. That gambler's lust within him. Here was his long shot and he wanted it. I sipped the gentle beer and watched. A minute passed. He opened his eyes, that fierce blue.

"*Parfait. Merci, monsieur.*"

Jack rang off and grinned wickedly at me.

"Our bird's in flight. We'll bag him yet. Let's go."

"Where?" I asked.

"For a ride."

Outside on the porch Jack oriented himself and then continued south to a cluster of irregular shacks between the highway and the freight tracks. He turned down an alleyway and we surprised brown rats skittering over a smoking mound of trash. Jack and I stepped over burnt vegetable waste, greasy crushed cans, and broken Coca-Cola bottles then through the slats of a fence bordering a decrepit house. Behind it sat a lorry with a jerrycan in its paybed. Jack touched the truck's bonnet for warmth and shook his head. We went 'round an outhouse to the back porch and a screen door. Jack took out his Browning. All was still.

The door swung open creakily at his touch and we entered a dark, cluttered kitchen. Bedroom to the right, to the left a sitting room with a cold Quebec heater. Jack and I did a circuit. He found nothing in a wardrobe or under the stained mattress of the unmade bed. I spilled a glass jar of green-blue rusted pennies and Indian quarter-anna pieces on a table covered in scorch marks from forgotten cigarets. The icebox was bare and smelled of mould. The whole place was dirty, depressing. Jack pushed swollen copies of the *Journal de Montréal* off a seat in the living room and settled in.

"What're we looking for?" I asked.

"Keys to that truck."

"Whose is this dump?"

"Martin's," he said.

The third driver from our convoy all those eons ago. If, as it appeared, the Senator'd crossed us and sicced the police on Jack and myself, it seemed the least we could do was return the favour to his creature.

"We'll settle his hash," Jack said, crossing a leg and lighting a cigarette. My yen for the tobacco awoke flickerings of another, more substantial need. I swallowed and swallowed again.

"And your telephone call?"

"Brown came through. Bob and a woman crossed the border at one this morning. If I know my man they're holed up in a hotel."

"Where?"

"Plattsburgh."

Jack smiled. I chewed my gum metronomically. Time passed. After awhile came the sound of heavy feet. Jack opened his eyes, yawned, and picked up his Browning. The front door opened inward and a burly man entered. He wore a stiff black wool suit and round hat. Jack waited. The man lumbered into the room, sniffed, and stopped at the sight of us.

"They seek him here, they seek him there, those Frenchies seek him everywhere. Is he in heaven or is he in hell? *Comment ça va, Martin? J'espère que tu as pris ta confession avec le curé ce matin, connard. Assieds-toi.* Now."

The imperative was given with a vigorous flick of the pistol. Martin's knees buckled at the anger in Jack's voice. He put a hand to his mouth and I remembered that Jack'd beaten the teeth out of his skull only a week before. In this frame of mind my friend was ruthless. If he ever learned about Laura I could expect the same. Sensibly, Martin sat.

I picked up a pack of cards near my chair and flipped through them, an unusual antique deck with gilt edges. The queens were uncanny: clubs held a red flower, diamonds a mirror, hearts a bird, and spades a feathered fan. The ace of spades was worse, with a jester bearing a large spade on his back and beside him a puppy in a hat and a gnome holding a flail. Above all smiled a nasty sun surrounded by black stars. I shivered. That was my hunger. I went to the kitchen to prepare another syringe.

When I returned to the sitting room, Jack was speaking: "There's no point. *Donne-moi tes clefs.*"

Martin pulled out a ring.

"*Lentement,*" Jack said. "There, on the table."

Martin put the keys down.

"*As-tu faim?*" asked Jack.

"*Non,*" Martin said.

With the aid of my drug I could smell the driver, a sharp pungent note of fear. I kept my distance, alerted by Jack's posture.

"No, I insist. You must be hungry. *Le petit déjeuner,*" Jack said. "*Comme le serpent.*"

He tossed Martin one of the sour little apples from beside the church. Martin reflexively grabbed at the fruit and there was a thunderclap. The driver dropped to the ground holding his stomach. I nearly leapt out of my clothes, notwithstanding my presentiment. Jack's pistol smoked. He said: "If he lives Charlie Trudeau and the Senator can pay the doctor. If not, the gravedigger. Either way, it's a message, COD."

I looked at the body of the man, at Jack, back at the body, then down into my own hands. I felt a perfect accretion of nothing.

"Fitting," I said, and flicked the card that was on top of the deck down onto Martin.

"What's that?" asked Jack.

"It's your card. Jack of diamonds. The laughing boy."

We left Martin to his fate and climbed into the lorry. Jack punched the ignition and we drove through Chambly to the southeast. I lowered my window and breathed in the crisp air as the miles passed, small towns and telegraph poles one after another casting hard black shadows on the flat earth.

I slept, and when I woke Jack was singing: "I patronized the tables at the Monte Carlo hell 'til they hadn't got a sou for a Christian or a Jew, so I quickly went to Paris for the charms of mademoiselle, who's the lodestone of my heart. What can I do, when with twenty tongues she swears that she'll be true?"

He saw me alert and said: "They crossed in a Graham-Paige roadster, Bob and Laura, I'm sure. Damn him: the money and the girl."

"Sir Dunphy'll be pleased," I said, laughing inwardly.

"Well, he is hyas muckamuck."

"Very hyas. Is he the one ordered you to shut up the magician?"

"That came from him through the tyee," Jack said.

"What, the chief?"

"You bet."

The prime minister. I'll be damned. When he threatened one last astonishing revelation, Harry Houdini made the wrong enemy.

"How?" I asked. "How did you shut him up?"

Jack looked at me slantwise and smiled, raising one eyebrow. We rolled on in silence for a stretch.

"The glass of water, I suppose."

"You're a wonder, Mick. Alpha plus."

"And what was it?"

"Biological agent. The Germans cooked it up in the war. One of their subtler killers."

"Jesus Christ."

"No, William Lyon Mackenzie King."

BY EARLY AFTERNOON we'd passed through St-Paul-de-l'Île-aux-Noix and Notre-Dame-du-Mont-Carmel. I was hungry.

"Bob crossed at Champlain. Rousses-Point coming up," said Jack.

"What do we say?"

"We're going over for a load of potatoes. Odds are we're waved through. If not, the devil take us."

Our concerns were mooted by the border. Both sets of guards had abandoned their posts for an early supper. We drove through unchallenged. Thus it was on the medicine line between the United States of America and the Dominion of Canada this day. Jack made a right at a building where the Stars and Stripes flew. The country felt different, as it always did, in myriad small ways: street signs and mailboxes, the Piggly Wiggly, billboards for Burma-Shave. Another hour of driving down lonely roads brought us to the outskirts of Plattsburgh.

"All these one-horse towns," I said.

Jack pulled over beside the tracks of the Rutland line behind an Episcopal church. The afternoon sky had grown overcast; rain was coming. We got out of the truck and Jack hoisted the jerrycan. He splashed petrol on the lorry and the near side of God's house, stepped back, selected a Turk from his cigaret case, and scratched a Redbird vesta. I offered him a playing card from the shack in Longueil to light. He handed me his cigaret and threw the burning ace of hearts on the fluid. A wave of flame swept across the ground and with it warmth; Jack and I moved away from the mounting conflagration and headed for town. Jack's cigaret tasted delicious.

Along our route hollowed jack o'. lanterns sat on porch steps. Three children carrying sacks passed, a ghost, a witch, a skeleton. From them that weird shrill cry: "Trick or treat!"

"Trick," Jack said, gravely.

That stopped them. I didn't understand the custom. Jack reached into his pocket and pulled out coins. He gave each ghoul a Canadian nickel and let fall sundry pennies. The children ran off. We continued on and came to the town square. My fatigue allowed only a forward momentum. This was how it felt on march. Whatever would happen would. Jack sang: "As I walk along the Bois Boulogne with an independent air, you can hear the girls declare: 'He must be a millionaire.' You can hear them sigh and wish to die, you can see them wink the other eye at the man who broke the bank at Monte Carlo."

The town square. A golden eagle above the courthouse shimmered as electric streetlamps flickered to life. Their buzz of electricity was overwhelmed by a bell ringing: warning, danger. Jack appeared familiar with the town and so I shadowed him.

The bell rang with a greater urgency. Townsfolk came out onto the street and milled 'round. One reported the news: fire at the Presbyterian, another contradicted, no, the Baptist. I smiled up my sleeve. Jack spread the confusion by telling a portly chap in braces that a small girl was trapped in a burning house. This rumour spread and whipped up a panic. From afar came the faintest aroma of smoke mixed with the excitement of chaos. A lone patrolling beat policeman was pelted with questions.

In this air of delicious calamity automobiles were cranked up and roared along the streets. The crowning moment finally came: a red fire engine crowded with volunteers in shining golden helmets screamed past, lights spinning, siren wailing. Everyone was delighted. Children and their parents chased the disaster and soon the square stood empty once more. Jack and I stepped out from where we waited on a stoop. He seemed pleased with his work.

"What I suffer for my art," he said.

Dim orange firelight from our arson competed with an early moon in the east. Jack put on his gloves and we stepped across Main to State and pushed through an ostentatious and unnecessary revolving door into the Republic Hotel. The lobby was vacant save for an anxious clerk who buttonholed Jack for news of the fire. Jack told him several half-truths and asked for the time. The clerk turned to the clock and Jack bashed him in the back of the head with the butt of his pistol. He placed the gun on the countertop and vaulted the wood. The clerk groaned as Jack kicked him quiet. He spun the register to me. I ran my finger down the line of guests.

"Mr. and Mrs. R. Fitzgerald," I said. "Two nights. They're in 201."

Jack picked a spare key from a pigeonhole and jumped the counter again. He crossed the lobby and shot the bolt, locking the revolving door. We climbed the stairs and approached their door. With his right hand Jack slid the key into the lock and as the gears tumbled said: "Room service."

Nothing sounded as we entered. Room 201 was lit only by a crooked bed lamp, the air stale and humid. I saw two unmoving figures on the rank bed, a man in trousers and unbuttoned shirt and a nude woman. The man's shirt cuff was rolled past his elbow and the pair stirred as our presence was felt. My gaze fell on the dresser, which showed hypodermics, a quantity of powder, the usual paraphernalia. A bottle of rye and two tooth glasses sat next to a woman's purse. Jack pulled the blankets away from the woman.

"Tashman," he exclaimed.

It was Lilyan Tashman, the actress. I bit back a grin.

Jack rushed around the bed to Bob and grabbed him by the throat. Lilyan came alive and pulled the sheet up. Bob gagged, groggy and weak.

"What've you done with her?" Jack shouted. He cocked his Browning and held it to Bob's blond head.

"Who? Who?" asked Lilyan, now aware and frightened.

Even dishevelled she possessed a languid erotic charm. Jack ducked down, saw something he liked, and changed. No thought of Laura anymore. I began to regret what was sure to come next.

"Mick, the money," Jack ordered.

With the Webley in one hand I pulled a familiar satchel out from under the bed, undid the clasp, and whistled. Like the playing cards these were gilt-edged. I ran my thumb across the stacked sheaf, an inch or two thick.

"Negotiable securities," I said, "denomination of two hundred fifty each, American. Must be forty, fifty thousand here."

"Happy Hallowe'en," Jack said to Bob.

"Lilyan, sweetheart, this calls for a wet. Pour Mick and myself a drink."

Carefully she drew the sheet up around her and went to the dresser. I looked up from the satchel to Jack.

"And now for the coup de grâce," he said.

He grabbed Bob's neck and Bob's pretty features turned terrified.

"No! No!"

"Oh yes," Jack said.

Lilyan stood frozen, the bottle in her hand. Jack pushed Bob through the bathroom door. Lilyan fumbled at her purse and said to me: "Have to make my face."

I heard two loud cracks from within and turned to the door. There was a moment of silence, then Jack came back into the room. An expression of beatitude lit his face.

"*Exeunt omnes,*" he said.

He motioned to Lilyan Tashman and reached out his hand. Trembling, she handed him a glass. I stood and took the second. She was beautiful in this light, her chestnut hair loose. I thought of Laura. A train whistle moaned. Lilyan inhaled sharply. She stood proud before us, looking from Jack to me and back again. Jack raised his glass.

"If you were born to be shot you will not be hanged," he said.

"Here's to us what's like us," I replied. The time seemed nearly at hand.

Jack and I drank. The rye tasted odd going down and I felt my lips and tongue go numb. My throat started to close. Lilyan lifted her hand from her purse, in her grasp her little black vial. She pointed it first at Jack, then at me. She said:

"'Trick or treat.'"

HOUDINI TAKES SECRETS WITH HIM TO THE GRAVE

. . . .

HARRY HOUDINI'S mysterious feats of escape, which thrilled spectators throughout the world in his life, today were locked in the mystery of death. The magician hailed by his fellow workers as the greatest of them all, died in Detroit last night, taking with him the secrets of how he escaped from manacles, chains, coffins, straight jackets, and other contrivances, performances which no man has ever duplicated.

Montreal *Herald*, November 1, 1926

COMING ATTRACTIONS

. . . .

GOTHAM PRODUCTIONS
Spring 1927

LILYAN TASHMAN

— Is —

The Woman Who Did Not Care

. . . .